Praise for The Country Club Murders

"A sparkling comedy of errors tucked inside a clever mystery. I loved it!"

– Susan M. Boyer,
USA Today Bestselling Author of *Lowcountry Book Club*

"Set in Kansas City, Missouri, in 1974, this cozy mystery effectively recreates the era through the details of down-to-earth Ellison's everyday life."

– *Booklist*

"Readers who enjoy the novels of Susan Isaacs will love this series that blends a strong mystery with the demands of living in an exclusive society."

– *Kings River Life Magazine*

"From the first page to the last, Julie's mysteries grab the reader and don't let up."

– Sally Berneathy,
USA Today Bestselling Author of *The Ex Who Saw a Ghost*

"This book is fun! F-U-N Fun!...A delightful pleasure to read. I didn't want to put it down...Highly recommend."

– *Mysteries, etc.*

"Mulhern's lively, witty sequel to *The Deep End* finds Kansas City, Mo. socialite Ellison Russell reluctantly attending a high school football game...Cozy fans will eagerly await Ellison's further adventures."

– *Publishers Weekly*

"There's no way a lover of suspense could turn this book down because it's that much fun."

– *Suspense Magazine*

"Cleverly written with sharp wit and all the twists and turns of the best '70s primetime drama, Mulhern nails the fierce fraught mother-daughter relationship, fearlessly tackles what hides behind the Country Club façade, and serves up justice in bombshell fashion. A truly satisfying slightly twisted cozy."

– Gretchen Archer,
USA Today Bestselling Author of *Double Knot*

"Part mystery, part women's fiction, part poetry, Mulhern's debut, *The Deep End*, will draw you in with the first sentence and entrance you until the last. An engaging whodunit that kept me guessing until the end!"

– Tracy Weber,
Author of the Downward Dog Mysteries

"An impossible-to-put-down Harvey Wallbanger of a mystery. With a smart, funny protagonist who's learning to own her power as a woman, *Send in the Clowns* is one boss read."

– Ellen Byron,
Agatha Award-Nominated Author of *Plantation Shudders*

"The plot is well-structured and the characters drawn with a deft hand. Setting the story in the mid-1970s is an inspired touch...A fine start to this mystery series, one that is highly recommended."

– *Mysterious Reviews*

"What a fun read! Murder in the days before cell phones, the internet, DNA and AFIS."

– *Books for Avid Readers*

"If you liked *Gilmore Girls*, you'll love *Watching the Detectives*. It has the same sarcastic humor and wit, with a loving, but dysfunctional multi-generational family of strong women. You'll have all the feels following the adventures of life, love, and murder with the Russell women."

– *A Cozy Experience*

TELEPHONE LINE

The Country Club Murders
by Julie Mulhern

Novels

THE DEEP END (#1)
GUARANTEED TO BLEED (#2)
CLOUDS IN MY COFFEE (#3)
SEND IN THE CLOWNS (#4)
WATCHING THE DETECTIVES (#5)
COLD AS ICE (#6)
SHADOW DANCING (#7)
BACK STABBERS (#8)
TELEPHONE LINE (#9)

Short Stories

DIAMOND GIRL
A Country Club Murder Short

TELEPHONE LINE

THE COUNTRY CLUB MURDERS

HENERY PRESS

Copyright

TELEPHONE LINE
The Country Club Murders
Part of the Henery Press Mystery Collection

First Edition | June 2019

Henery Press
www.henerypress.com

Trade Paperback ISBN-13: 978-1-63511-547-5
Digital epub ISBN-13: 978-1-63511-548-2
Kindle ISBN-13: 978-1-63511-549-9
Hardcover ISBN-13: 978-1-63511-550-5

Printed in the United States of America

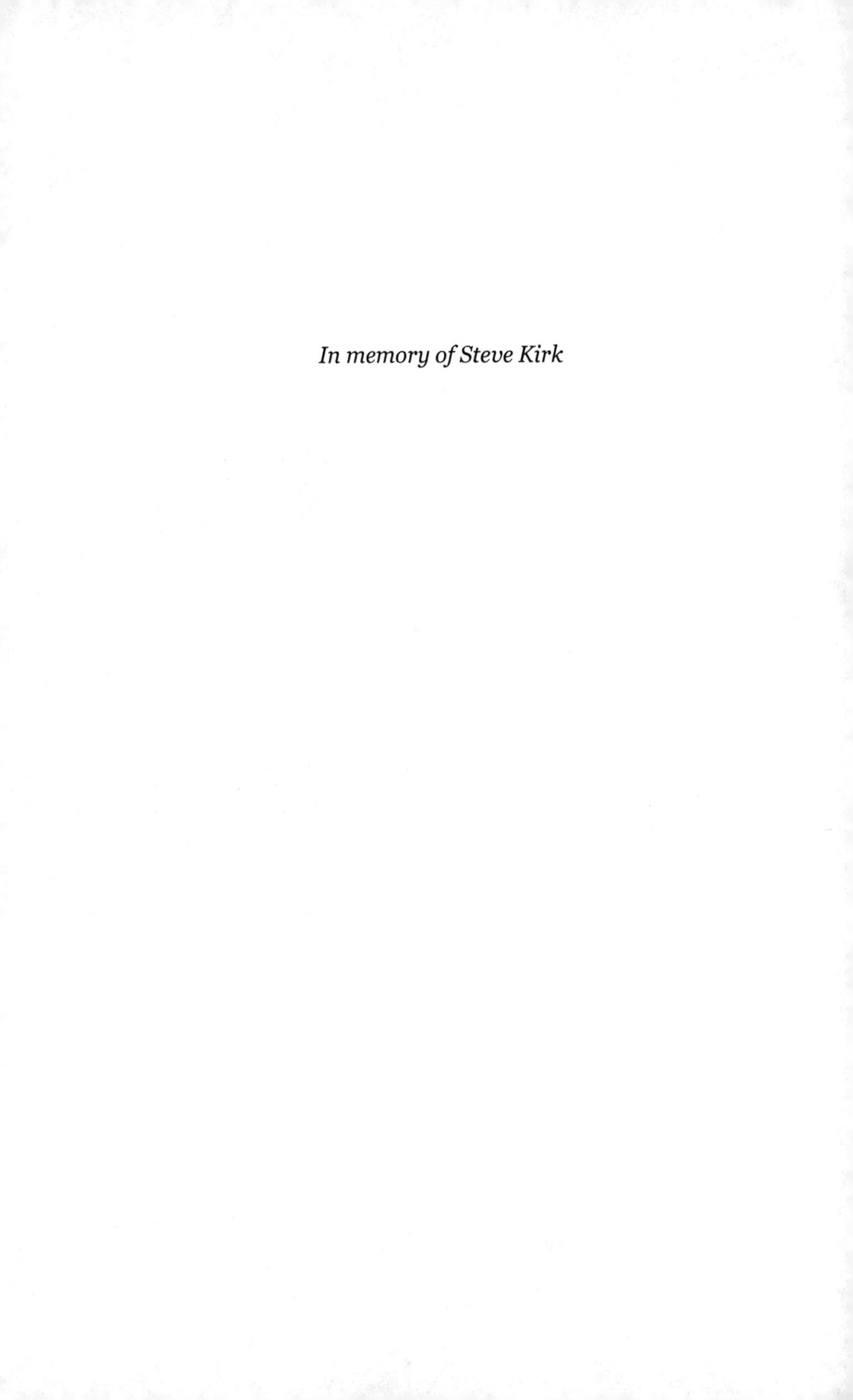

In memory of Steve Kirk

ACKNOWLEDGMENTS

Thank you to Katie who puts up with boring dinners, to Matt who eats boring dinners without complaint, and to Mer who gave me an idea.

Thank you to Margaret Bail for finding Ellison a home.

Thank you to eagle-eyed Edie Peterson.

As always, my thanks to Gretchen Archer who talks me off ledges.

Finally, my thanks to the staff at Henery Press.

ONE

April 1975
Kansas City, Missouri

The heels of my hands and the balls of my feet pressed into the yoga mat. My hips stretched for the ceiling.

"Deep breaths," the instructor intoned. "Breathe through your body, all the way to your toes."

I wasn't Zen enough to breathe to my toes. Breathing through my lungs was all I could handle.

"Reach," said Marigold, the woman at the front of what had once been Winnie Flournoy's third-floor ballroom—now the enormous room served as a yoga-studio. "Breathe."

Next to me, Libba muttered. Apparently, today's yoga class wasn't living up to her expectations. Instead of the gentle, easy exercise Winnie promised us, we'd sweat. Sweat hard enough for dampness to stain my leotards. I would ache tomorrow.

"Sink into a child's pose," Marigold told us.

We sank.

"Let's move to our backs."

We moved to our backs.

"And breathe."

We breathed.

"Close your eyes."

My eyes closed to half-mast.

"And find your center."

What?

"Breathe. In through your nose, out through your mouth."

That I could do. So could Sharon Michaels. She stretched out on the mat next to mine and followed directions. Loudly.

I concentrated on the music—something with a sitar and a violin. Normally, such noises would annoy me, but the pitch and tone suited the moment.

The room was dim, the mat was comfortable, and I'd had little sleep.

"Relax and breathe."

I closed my eyes.

"Drift on a cloud."

I drifted.

"Melt into your mats."

I melted.

I drifted and melted and dozed until the record skipped.

My lids fluttered open.

Around me, women remained melted on their mats.

Sharon Michaels snored softly.

Marigold was nowhere to be seen.

I pushed up from the mat, went to the record player, lifted the needle, and dropped it at the beginning of the album. The music began again.

Someone sighed.

I tiptoed to the bench running the length of the windowless wall and collected my shoes and handbag.

No one moved.

The door was just to my right. I turned the handle and pulled. The door didn't budge.

I pulled again. Harder.

Nothing.

I pushed. The door still didn't move.

"Winnie," my voice was low but every woman in the room

except Sharon opened her eyes.

"Does the door stick?" I asked.

"Of course not."

I pulled again. Hard. "How well do you know Marigold?"

Winnie sat up on her mat. "Why?"

"Because she locked us in."

Winnie pushed herself to standing. "Don't be silly."

I stepped aside and let Winnie try the handle.

The door remained immovable.

"I'm sure there's a mistake."

Marigold was probably downstairs cleaning out Winnie's jewelry drawer. "Do you have a phone up here?"

"A phone? Up here?" She glanced around her private studio. "Why would I have a phone up here?"

In case her yoga instructor locked her in.

"Are any of your neighbors at home?"

"How would I know?" Winnie wrung her hands and looked back at Libba, Kate, Sarah, Betsy, and the still-sleeping Sharon.

Leaving her at the door, I picked my way through the yoga mats and peered out the front window. The street was quiet. The neighboring houses were far away. We might yell for hours before anyone heard us. "What time is your mail delivered?"

"Three o'clock."

I glanced at my watch. The time read a quarter past ten. Spending five hours locked in Winnie's ballroom wasn't on my agenda for the day. There had to be another way out. Besides, in that five hours, Marigold could steal Winnie blind. "Is there a towel up here?"

"A towel?"

"Yes. A towel."

"Why?"

"Because I have a new tube of paint in my purse." I'd picked up the tube from the artists' supply store on Saturday and hadn't yet put it in my studio. As long as Winnie's towel wasn't cobalt blue, we were set. "We can write a message and hang the towel out the window."

"What kind of message?"

"I'm thinking SOS."

Winnie shook her head. "I don't know, Ellison."

Libba joined me at the window. She scowled down at the line of cars parked next to the curb on the quiet street. "Your yoga teacher is probably downstairs helping herself to your grandmother's pearls."

Winnie turned a sickly shade of green and disappeared into the half-bath muttering something about how Marigold would never steal from her. She returned quickly and thrust a hand towel at me. "Will this work?"

"Do you have anything bigger? Or two more?"

"I'll look," she snapped. Any semblance of calm or Zen Winnie possessed had disappeared.

Neither Kate, nor Sarah, nor Betsy retained any Zen either. Their arms were crossed across their chests and their eyes were narrowed.

"What a disaster," declared Kate.

"I'm just glad our purses are here and not downstairs," said Sarah.

Betsy merely shook her head. "Do you need help painting the towels?"

"She's an artist," said Libba. "She can manage an SOS."

Sharon snorted in her sleep.

Winnie reappeared with an additional two towels.

I spread them on the floor, and finger-painted an "S," an "O," and another "S." The letters were as large as I could make them and brilliant blue against the white of Winnie's towels.

We hung one towel per window and sat down to wait.

If I hung SOS towels out the window at my house, my nosy neighbor, Marian Dixon, would call the police within a half-second then step out onto her lawn for a better view of the action.

Too bad Marian wasn't across the street now.

"Winnie, would you turn that infernal racket off? Please?"

Betsy pointed to the record player.

"I'll do it." Libba lifted the needle off the album.

The absence of sitar was a gift.

"How well do you know this woman?" Sarah demanded. "Did you get references?"

"I'm sure she didn't mean to lock us in." Winnie was lying to herself. And us.

"I have a tennis game at one," said Kate.

"I have a dress fitting. I can't be late." Betsy's sweet voice fooled no one—if she missed her appointment, there would be hell to pay.

I leaned against the window and stared at the street. Libba's Mercedes convertible was parked between Sarah's BMW and Betsy's Oldsmobile station wagon. Then came Kate's Cadillac and Sharon's Volvo. Behind the Volvo was a blue car. I turned back to the studio. "Winnie, when I pulled up, I saw a plum-colored Gremlin in the drive. Is that Marigold's car?"

"Yes. Why do you ask?"

"Because there's a blue car I don't recognize parked on the street." I tapped my fingernail against the glass.

"People park on the street all the time." Winnie dismissed my observation with ease.

Outside, a figure appeared next to the blue car. I pounded on the glass, then raised the sash. "Help!"

The person next to the car looked up at the house, at me, at the SOS towels, and covered his forehead with his hand as if a glare impeded his view—that or he was hiding his face.

Libba hurried to my side in time to see the man toss a large duffel bag into the front seat, slide into the car, and drive away. "Didn't he hear you? Didn't he see your sign?"

"He heard. He saw."

"And he drove away?"

"He did." My stomach knotted into an impossible yoga pose. Something was very wrong.

Behind us, conversation continued.

"Just where did you find this Marigold?" Kate sounded deeply annoyed.

"She came highly recommended—" Winnie's voice had a how-dare-you-question-me tone that wouldn't win her much support among the women locked in her attic "—and you've been to dozens of classes here. There's never been a problem. Not until today. I'm sure this is a misunderstanding."

"Dream on," Libba whispered.

"No kidding," I whispered back.

"Look!" Libba pointed out the window.

An older woman and her dog had rounded the corner. They strolled toward Winnie's house.

I wiggled my upper body out the window and yelled, "Help!"

The woman on the sidewalk stopped. She glanced over her shoulder. She looked across the street. She even stared down at her little dog.

The dog barked.

"Up here! Up here!"

The woman shifted her gaze to the attic and her jaw dropped. Surprise was a reasonable response. How often did one see grown women leaning out an attic window?

"We're locked in," I explained. "Would you please call for help?"

The area near the window was suddenly crowded.

"That's Gertie Kleinman. She lives three doors down. Ask if she'll come in and unlock the door."

"Mrs. Kleinman, will you please come in and open the door?"

The woman nodded, and she and her dog hurried up Winnie's front walk.

We waited. Was the front door locked? Gertie Kleinman was taking forever.

"What's taking so long?" wondered Betsy. She still sounded sweet as pie, but the expression in her eyes was scary.

Winnie squeezed her eyes shut and tapped her forehead. "I can't remember if the door is locked."

Gertie Kleinman reappeared on the sidewalk. Running. Away. She dragged her little dog behind her.

"What's she doing?" Acid etched the sweetness in Betsy's voice.

"Gertie!" Winnie nearly took out my eardrum.

Gertie didn't stop. She didn't even slow down. Gertie ran.

"What's that all about?" Kate demanded. "Is she unbalanced?"

"The door must be locked. She's in a hurry to call for help. She'll send someone." Winnie's voice was full of bravado.

"But why didn't she stop and tell us that?" insisted Kate. "She just ran."

My stomach twisted into that upside-down yoga pose where feet crossed like pretzels. Gertie, who was no spring chicken, hadn't just run—she'd run like a fox pursued by a pack of hounds.

The tight crowd of women near the window made breathing difficult. Or maybe the difficulty came from the sudden dread pressing against my chest.

After a moment or two of watching the empty street, Kate and Sharon and Betsy faded away. Winnie watched a bit longer, then she too stepped back from the window.

That left me with Libba and Sarah.

I breathed deep.

"Why did Gertie run like that?" asked Sarah.

Why couldn't my stomach take a nice *savasana* pose—easy, relaxing, serene? But, no—my intestines contorted into something impossible, a *visvamitrasana* (I'd seen it done once and still didn't understand how it was physically possible). "I have no idea."

Sarah stood with us for another moment before she too drifted back toward the mats still spread across the floor.

I wasn't surprised by the first siren's claxon blare. Nor was I surprised when three police cars parked in front of Winnie's house. I might—might—have blinked once or twice when Anarchy and his partner, Detective Peters, arrived. "We're locked in the attic," I called down to them.

The two men looked up at me.

Anarchy rubbed his palms across his face.

Detective Peters, who, despite the sunshine, was wrapped in a rumpled overcoat, merely scowled.

"Who's that?" Sarah rejoined Libba and me at the window. She pointed at Anarchy.

"Ellison's boyfriend," Libba replied.

Her eyes widened. "I thought he was a homicide detective."

I swallowed a sigh. "He is."

A few moments later, a uniformed officer ushered us down Winnie's service stairs and into the backyard. All of us were happy to be out of the attic—all of us but Winnie. She expected to stay in her house.

Anarchy, with his cop-face firmly in place, stepped outside and approached us. Detective Peters followed him.

"Who's the homeowner?" Anarchy asked.

"I am. I'm Winnie Flournoy. What's going on?"

Anarchy ignored her question. "I take it you all were having some sort of exercise class?"

"The instructor locked us in the attic," said Sarah.

Betsy glanced at her watch. "I have an appointment in less than an hour. May I leave? Please?"

Sharon merely yawned.

Anarchy waved over a uniformed policeman. "Officer Carson will take your statements. Ellison, Mrs. Flournoy, will you please come with me?"

We followed him to the far reaches of the patio. Libba trailed after us.

"What was your yoga instructor's name, Mrs. Flournoy?" Anarchy asked.

"Marigold."

"Do you have her last name?"

"Applebottom."

Seriously? I glanced at Winnie. "Marigold Applebottom?"

Winnie didn't look as if she were joking. She looked exhausted—as if answering Anarchy's question had drained the last of her reserves. “That’s right.”

“How long has she worked for you, Mrs. Flournoy?”

“Since January. It was my New Year’s resolution to practice yoga six days a week. It started out with just me then some of my friends joined the class.”

“Do the same people come every day?”

“Heavens, no. They have bridge games and now that the weather is better, they have golf and tennis games. Sharon has a book club every other Wednesday. Libba is a spotty attendee—” Winnie glanced at Libba and shrugged “—I’m sorry but it’s the truth, dear. We never know when you’ll show up.” She shifted her gaze to me. “This is Ellison’s first time.”

Marigold Applebottom had been coming to Winnie’s house for more than three months but today—the one time I’d come (under duress)—was the day something happened. Lucky, lucky me. “Libba and I saw someone.”

“You what?” Anarchy’s coffee brown eyes widened.

“While we were locked upstairs, someone carrying a duffle bag climbed into a blue car and drove away.”

“What’s the big deal about that?” Detective Peters had snuck up on us. Maybe he couldn’t help his snide tone.

He could. He liked treating me like the village idiot.

“Whoever it was heard us yelling, saw us waving, and drove away.”

Peters snorted. “Maybe they didn’t want to get involved.”

I glanced up at Winnie’s Georgian home. “With towels hanging out the front window, you’d think he or she’d at least call for help.”

“What did he look like?” asked Anarchy.

“Average height. Tan windbreaker with a hood. I was too far away to see features.”

“What about the car?”

“American made and blue.”

Anarchy nodded. Slowly. As if he wished I’d been more observant.

“I’m sorry I’m not more help.”

"That's okay." He turned to Winnie and a sympathetic expression settled on his face. "Miss Applebottom is dead. We need someone to identify the body."

Winnie paled. "Dead?" She swayed as if the spring breeze might knock her down.

"I'll do it." One of these days, I'd think before I spoke.

"You're sure?" Winnie clutched my hand. "You don't mind?"

Yes, I minded, but I'd seen enough bodies over the past months that one more wouldn't give me nightmares. "I don't mind."

"Thank you, Ellison. You're a good friend."

I followed Anarchy into the foyer and stumbled to a halt.

Marigold Applebottom hung from a rope tied to the second-floor bannister.

"She killed herself?" That's what it looked like. But that couldn't be right. "What about the person in the street?"

"We were meant to think it was a suicide," said Anarchy.

"But it was a murder?"

Peters snorted. He didn't appreciate my stating the obvious.

I looked up at the woman. "That's definitely Marigold."

Anarchy nodded at a large man in a KCPD jacket. The man set a ladder under Marigold and lifted her body until the rope hung slack. Another man on the landing untied her.

The first man descended the ladder and gently placed Marigold's body on the floor.

"Has Winnie been robbed?"

"Nothing seems to be disturbed."

"When I discovered we were locked in the attic, I thought Marigold was a thief..." I couldn't look at her another second. I shifted my gaze to one of the paintings hanging in Winnie's front hall. "I bet she was helping the person with the duffle. She let him in. He stole whatever they were after. Then he killed her."

Peters rubbed his chin. For the first time ever, he regarded me with something like respect. Then he remembered who I was, and he sneered, his upper lip brushing against his bushy mustache.

"You're probably right." Anarchy sounded tired. "Is there someplace Mrs. Flournoy can go?"

"Go?"

"It will take us hours to process this crime scene."

"She can come to my house."

We stepped onto the patio where Winnie and Libba waited.

"Is it her? Is she—" Winnie held a shaking hand against her mouth "—dead?"

I nodded. "You should come home with me."

Winnie covered her eyes with her palms. "I need to call Lark."

Detective Peters shook his head. "I'm sorry, ma'am, we can't allow you inside until the scene is processed."

Winnie was tall and thin, with a shingled haircut and good bones. Imposing. And, right now, she looked like the Angel of Death. If I'd been on the receiving end of the look she gave Detective Peters, I'd have retreated a few paces.

The only sign Peters even noticed was his mustache bristling.

"Come with me, Winnie. We'll have coffee—" the ultimate enticement "—and I'll loan you some clothes."

"You've done enough, Ellison. If someone will bring me a jacket, I'll wait here until I can get into my house." She coupled this pronouncement with another Angel of Death glare at Detective Peters.

He shrugged. "Where do you keep the coats?"

"You're sure you don't want to come home with me?" It felt wrong leaving her alone in her leotard, with a passel of policemen. "I can stay."

She shook her head. "If you'll call Lark's office and ask him to come home, that's all I need."

"Detective?" I added a heaping teaspoon of sugar to my voice and called after Peters' retreating back. "Has anyone called Mr. Flournoy?"

He paused, stiffened, and walked on without replying.

"I'll call Lark as soon as I get home."

"Thanks, Ellison. For everything. If you hadn't kept watch,

we'd all still be locked in the attic."

Our time in the attic—halcyon moments before I'd somehow become embroiled in another murder. Mother would be apoplectic.

TWO

Libba tightened her hands around the steering wheel and stared straight out the windshield. "I'm sorry."

"Sorry?"

She cut her gaze my way. "This morning wasn't exactly the stress-reducer you were hoping for."

"No. But that's not your fault."

Libba sighed and pulled into my circle drive, stopping the car near the front door. "Still, yoga was my idea."

"It's okay. Really. Do you want to come in? For coffee?"

"No, thanks. I'd rather go home and shower."

Hot water wouldn't wash away the stains left by murder. Being locked in a room while a woman was hanged to death downstairs made an indelible mark—one impervious to soap and hot water. I'd brushed against death often enough to know first-hand. Then I remembered Libba hadn't seen Marigold hanging from the bannister. I sighed, opened the car door, and put my feet on the pavement.

"Call me—" she grabbed my hand and gave it a squeeze "—if you need to talk."

"I will."

I watched her drive away then opened the front door.

Max greeted me with a grin and take-me-running nudge of his head.

"You'll have to wait," I told him.

His ears drooped, and the dejected expression on his face

would have broken a softer woman's heart.

"I'm sorry, but I need to sit down for a few minutes."

He followed me to the kitchen where he flopped onto his bed with a put-upon snort.

Aggie, my housekeeper, stood at the counter checking a list. She wore a daffodil-hued kaftan and had the glow of a woman who'd spent the whole weekend with a man who adored her. She smiled and a golden aura settled on her shoulders.

"Good weekend?" The answer was obvious.

She blushed and stuffed the list into her handbag (brown leather painted with smiley faces).

"How's Mac?" Mac was the new man in Aggie's life. He had the easy-going, eager-to-please disposition of a Labrador puppy. He sent Aggie flowers just because. He owned a deli that stocked my favorite Finocchiona salami. He made Aggie smile. I liked him.

Aggie's blush deepened, and she hooked the handbag over her shoulder. "He's fine." She took in my current state and her dreamy smile faded away. "What happened?"

"I went to yoga with Libba, and the teacher was murdered."

Aggie dropped her purse on the counter. "Sit down. I'll make coffee."

Aggie was good people.

I collapsed onto a stool, told her everything, and drank some of Mr. Coffee's magic elixir.

"What can I do?" She topped off our mugs then rinsed the near empty pot.

I shrugged. "Nothing."

"I was on my way to the market when you came home. I can pick up the ingredients for a Bundt cake—"

"Who would we take it to?"

She ceded my point with a quick nod of her chin.

"Go do your errands," I told her. "I know you have things to accomplish today."

She picked up her handbag. "I won't be gone long."

Max and I stood at the door as she drove away.

I scratched behind his ears.

He rubbed his head against my leg and looked up at me with liquid can-we-go-running-now eyes.

"Later. I promise."

Brnng, brnng.

I let the phone ring three times—was tempted to let the answering machine pick up. But some masochistic streak deep within me had me reaching for the receiver. "Hello."

"Tell me it isn't true." No *hello*. No *how are you*. Mother was deeply outraged.

I should have let the machine pick up. "Tell you what isn't true?"

Mother huffed as if she didn't have time for my foolishness. "Tell me you did not find a body at Winnie Flournoy's."

"I did not find a body at Winnie Flournoy's." I hadn't found the body. Gertie Kleinman found the body.

"But you were there?"

"Yes."

"And someone was murdered?"

"Yes. The yoga instructor."

Mother's answering silence spoke volumes.

I wrapped the phone cord around my fingers and waited.

"You were taking her class?"

"I was. She locked us in the attic."

A moment of silence ensued.

"Maybe this is a good thing."

I blinked in surprise. A good thing? Being locked in the attic or the murder? I was pretty sure Marigold Applebottom's loved ones would consider her death a bad thing. "What do you mean?"

"You've found your body for the month. You won't have to worry about someone being murdered at the gala."

The gala. Against my better judgment, I'd agreed to be the chairman for the museum's gala unveiling the Chinese exhibit. The exhibit would appear in only four cities—San Francisco, New York, Washington, D.C., and Kansas City—and the opening gala was a big deal. The committee and I had been planning and meeting and discussing flowers and food and table linens for months. Months. Now, the countdown was on. Only a few weeks remained to iron out the final details. The evening promised to be the social happening of the season. Mother lived in fear a murder would spoil the event. Given my track record, her worry was justified.

"I didn't find Marigold's body."

"Marigold?" I could *hear* the curl of Mother's lip.

"Yes."

"What a name."

I didn't argue. Nor did I tell her about the Applebottom part of Marigold's name.

"I didn't mean that her murder was a good thing. It's just that—" Mother thought my proximity to Marigold's murder should count for something with the deity who regularly put dead bodies in my path.

If only I was that lucky.

"There's been enough upheaval this month already." Mother was absolutely right. And we'd barely dipped our toes into April. "You should be concentrating on the gala." She was singing to the choir. "Promise me, Ellison, you won't go looking for trouble."

"I never do."

Mother's silence was louder than a jackhammer.

"I don't." Then, because I sensed she had more to say about my finding bodies, I added, "Listen, Mother, I'm a sweaty mess. I'm going to jump in the shower. May I please call you later?"

"I'm on my way out for bridge." She exhaled loud enough for me to hear the depth of her worry. "Go. Take your shower. And try, Ellison, to stay out of trouble."

"I will. Bye." I hung up the phone.

Max lifted his head from his paws. A run? Now?

"Sorry, buddy. I promise I'll take you. Later." I had things to do.

He huffed his displeasure and lowered his head.

Ding, dong.

Seriously? What now?

Max leapt to his feet and took off down the hallway.

I followed at a more sedate pace. I didn't want people on the front stoop, I wanted a shower. And there was something I needed to do before I stepped into a stream of hot water. Something I needed to check. Something important.

I opened the door.

Marsha Clayton stood on the other side. She took one look at my messy hair and sweat-stained leotard and said, "I'm sorry. I should have called first."

I might look awful, but Marsha looked worse—like something the cat dragged in. Her face was pinched and pale. Her honey-blonde hair was a fright. Her lipstick had bled into the tiny lines around her mouth.

"What's wrong?" I asked.

"You don't know?"

"Know what?"

Her red-rimmed eyes filled with tears. "I've grounded Debbie for a month."

"Come in." I beckoned Marsha inside before my nosy neighbor could pull out her binoculars. Then I hauled Max away from Marsha's crotch—Marsha didn't look as if she was in the mood for one of his exploratory sniffs. "What can I get you?"

"Nothing."

"You're sure?"

She nodded, and I led her into the living room.

"Please, have a seat." I waved to the couch then settled into the club chair closest to her. Marsha didn't say a word.

She glanced down at the hands clasped in her lap.

She bit her lower lip.

She tapped her twined fingers against her forehead.

"Marsha?"

She shook her head.

She wiped beneath her eyes.

She stared up at the ceiling.

"Marsha, what's happened?"

I waited.

And waited.

She shifted her gaze to a still life hung on the far wall. "You've had a hard year."

"Yes." My husband had been killed, I'd been a suspect in his murder, then—much to Mother's horror—I'd begun finding bodies.

"How do you..." she ducked her head.

"How do I what?"

"Find the strength to face the day?" Marsha spoke to her lap.

Oh. That. "I take one day at a time."

"I never dreamed Debbie would lie to me."

"She's a teenager."

She clasped her hands together—tight enough for her knuckles to whiten. "I know my friends are whispering. How do you deal with that?"

I had no idea what she was talking about—lying or whispering. "With what?"

"How do you handle your friends talking about you behind your back?"

Oh. That. I chose not to hear them. I'd learned long ago no one was perfect and if I expected too much I was destined for disappointment. Cheating husband. Friends who were sometimes less than loyal. A mother who did her best to manage my life. If I let those things bother me, I wouldn't make it through a day.

"I know what people are saying."

I resisted the urge to close my fingers around her shoulders and shake her. "About what?"

"They're saying we're bad mothers because our girls went to that awful bar."

"What bar?"

"Dirty Sally's."

Oh dear Lord. "When?"

"Saturday night."

I exhaled. "Grace didn't go to a bar on Saturday night."

"Yes, she did."

"Grace was with me."

"That can't be right."

It most certainly could. "Grace and I had dinner with my parents (a command performance) then we came home, made popcorn, and watched the late movie."

"But Debbie said Grace was with her."

"Debbie stretched the truth." Debbie had lied through her just-out-of-braces teeth. "What happened at this bar?"

"You're sure Grace was with you?"

"Positive."

Marsha's cheeks paled, and she stood so abruptly she nearly knocked over the couch.

"Marsha, what happened?"

"Debbie—" she pressed her hand against her mouth "—came home drunk."

"Making mistakes is how teenagers learn."

A half-gasp half-sob rose from deep in Marsha's lungs. "I'm deeply disappointed in her. She swore to me that Dirty Sally's was Grace's idea."

"Grace was with me."

"Don't worry about what people say. Ignore everything. It's one weekend. It'll be forgotten as soon as a major scandal hits." Like Marigold Applebottom swinging from Winnie and Lark Flournoy's banister.

A tear ran down Marsha's cheek. "I'm not like you. I'm not strong. I care when people say I'm a bad wife or mother."

Much of my sympathy for Marsha dried up. "What do other people's opinions matter? Debbie matters."

She sniffed. A wet sniff. "I could kill them both. Debbie and the—" she held a fist against her mouth "—Debbie and whoever convinced her to go to that bar." Marsha lifted her gaze and stared into my eyes. "I really could kill them."

"I understand." I didn't. Not unless there was something—something major—Marsha had neglected to tell me.

"And Bill." Again her teeth gnawed at her lower lip. A fresh veil of tears dampened her cheeks.

Bill was Marsha's husband. "What about him?"

"He's just destroyed. It's as if something inside him has collapsed."

Something very major.

"Marsha, what happened?"

She waved me off. "I'm sorry to have disturbed you with this. I'll see myself out."

When Marsha left, I leaned against the front door. What in the world had that been about? Grace would know.

With a sigh, I tiptoed into my late husband's study and closed the door. Tiptoed because I didn't want anyone—not even me—to realize what I was about to do.

My late husband had done things I didn't like to think about.

True, he'd been an upstanding member of the community. True, he'd been a good provider. True, he'd adored our daughter. But Henry's faults as a husband outweighed the good.

He'd cheated on me with friends. He'd cheated on me with strangers. He'd cheated on me with women who carried handcuffs and whips.

To say our marriage wasn't in the greatest shape before I did the unforgivable was an understatement.

My unforgivable sin?

I earned more money than he did.

The first year was a fluke.

The second year was a problem. A big problem.

Money was the yardstick by which Henry measured his manhood. And all of a sudden, his wife's stick was longer than his. Proving he was still in charge, in control, the master of the universe, became his number one priority. Proof could be found dominating me in the bedroom. When I declined to play with his toys (handcuffs and whips), he'd turned first to other women then to ferreting out our friends' secrets.

He extorted money from a surprisingly long list of people.

It wasn't about the money (we had plenty). For Henry, it was about control. When he had someone's secret, he controlled them. He had the power. He was the master of the universe (at least in his own mind).

I didn't know about Henry's blackmail hobby until he died, until I found his files.

That discovery had been a shock.

Unsure of what to do, I'd left the files where I found them, locked in the safe in his study. The extortion had stopped.

I spent sleepless nights wondering what to do. Return the files? But how? Burn them? Did his victims think their blackmailer had just disappeared? Died? Run away to Bali? Ended up in prison?

One thing was certain. I could never reveal what Henry had done. Our daughter didn't need to carry the weight of her father's sins.

I should have fed the files into the living room fire over the winter, but I'd put them out of my mind. I'd shoved them into a tiny closet in my brain and thrown away the key. I'd forgotten about them on purpose. Until today.

Until a murder happened in one of Henry's victim's houses.

I sat on the edge of my late husband's desk and stared at the safe (Pandora's box). I racked my brain but failed to recall Lark Flournoy's secret. I couldn't remember a single detail—I just remembered he possessed a secret he'd paid to keep quiet.

I pushed off the desk, wiped my damp palms against my tights, and spun the safe's dial.

The door swung open, and I gazed into the safe's depths. Henry's files were alphabetized. Flournoy rested near the middle.

With the file in my shaking hand, I settled into a chair and spread the papers across the massive expanse of Henry's desk. My husband had made meticulous notes—as if neatness counted in blackmail. My stomach twisted—there was something wrong about peeking at my friends' deepest secrets. The act felt dirty.

Despicable. No wonder Henry had enjoyed it so.

With the tips of my fingers, I moved the pages and read.

Ten years ago, Lark had colluded with an attorney named John Wilson. Together they'd thrown a case. Henry was thin on the facts of the case but eloquent on the repercussions. If Henry went public, Lark would be disbarred. Problematic for a district judge.

At least now I knew Lark wasn't cheating on Winnie (or he hadn't been when Henry was gathering information).

Tap, tap.

I jumped as if I'd been doing something wrong. "Yes?"

"It's me," said Aggie. "I just wanted to let you know I'm back."

"Thank you." I leaned my head against the back of the chair and rested my hands on my knees until they stopped shaking. "I'll be out in a minute."

"Do you want anything?" Aggie sounded worried—me spending time in Henry's study was a reason for concern. I avoided the room for multiple reasons: the contents of the safe, the lingering memory of the body I'd found sprawled across the carpet, my inability to find a decent decorator. "How about coffee?" she asked.

I wanted wine. And a bath. "Not right now."

Aggie's worry (I never turned down coffee) seeped through the door's eight panels. "I picked up a chicken for dinner tonight. I thought I'd roast it."

"Sounds delicious."

"What time is she coming?"

"What time is who coming?"

"Your new neighbor."

I sagged in the chair. "Is that tonight?"

"Yes."

Ugh. Jennifer and Marshall Howe had relocated from California, knew no one, and Marshall traveled. I couldn't imagine living in a city where I didn't know a soul, couldn't imagine spending night after night alone in a big house with no one for company. I'd invited Jennifer to dinner. When I'd asked her, I hadn't anticipated a murder. But it wasn't as if I could call and uninvite her. "I told her five thirty for drinks. We can eat at half-past six."

"You're sure you're all right?"

"Positive." I pictured Aggie leaning her forehead against the door and added, "I'll be done in here in a minute."

I jammed the papers back in the file, put the file in the safe, and locked Henry's collection of horrible secrets away. Then I went to the guest bathroom and scrubbed my hands with French-milled soap. The suds did nothing to wash away the filthy things my husband had done, but at least my skin smelled like hyacinths.

Max poked his head into the powder room. A run? Please?

It didn't make much sense to shower before a run. "Fine."

He wagged his stub of a tail.

I trudged up the stairs—no way was I wearing tights and a leotard out of the house again.

Max followed me with an enormous grin on his face.

At least one of us was happy.

THREE

"Ellison?"

"Good evening, Mother." I glanced at my watch. Uh-oh. Mother never called during cocktail hour. I braced myself against the kitchen counter.

"I just hung up the phone with Claudia Dillaire."

"Who?"

"Claudia Dillaire. She was Claudia Valmont."

Claudia's maiden name wasn't helping. "Who?"

"We went to college together then she married Charles Dillaire and moved to San Francisco." Mother's tone said I should know this.

"You've never mentioned her."

"Of course I have."

She hadn't. I wrapped the phone cord around my finger and waited for whatever was coming next.

"Claudia says the San Francisco gala for the Chinese exhibit netted a million dollars."

I might not know Claudia Dillaire, but she'd landed me smack in the middle of a bowl of egg-drop soup. The Kansas City gala wouldn't make anywhere near a million dollars.

"She says New York and Washington will make similar amounts."

I tightened my grip on the edge of the counter; I knew what was coming.

"Why aren't you raising that much?"

"Kansas City isn't San Francisco or New York or Washington." The museum had set a goal, and I'd exceeded it.

"And it never will be with that kind of thinking."

San Francisco had stoned hippies sleeping on the streets, New York had sanitation strikes, and Washington had politicians. Kansas City was fine the way it was. "We're a smaller city."

"Ellison—" here it came, the pronouncement from on high that would upend my life "—you need to raise more money."

"Mother, the gala is only a few weeks away. All the major sponsorships are sold."

"How much money will you raise?"

"Three-hundred-sixty-thousand dollars." It was a princely sum.

"That's nowhere near a million. We have to get to work."

"The museum is happy with the number."

"Laurence would be happier with a million." Undoubtedly true.

"I am not raising a million dollars. It cannot be done." Uh-oh. I should have kept my mouth shut. *It cannot be done* was as good as waving a red cape in front of a raging bull.

"Of course it can."

"Mother, I don't have any more tables available."

"We'll squeeze them in."

"Mother—"

"What time does the museum open? I'll call Laurence first thing in the morning."

I hoped for Laurence's sake that he had a morning full of appointments that kept him far from the telephone "The museum opens at ten but—"

"But nothing. I refuse to be outdone by people who already think Kansas City is a cow town."

She would not be outdone?

"If they thought so little of Kansas City, the exhibit wouldn't be coming here." It was a reasonable argument. But reasonable arguments didn't always work with Mother.

"This exhibit is Kansas City's opportunity to shine."

The city owed the exhibit to Laurence Sickman. The museum director was a world-renowned expert on Chinese art. It was his reputation and influence that had secured the exhibition. That a limited-time, world-class collection of art was coming to Kansas City was a coup, a feather in the city's cap, and, as my daughter Grace would say, *totally awesome.* But none of that mattered to Mother, not unless I matched San Francisco's fundraising. "Mother, those other cities are much bigger than we are. There's a larger pool of potential donors."

"Pffft."

"You've chaired countless events. You know the realities."

"I know this: we will not be shown up by the coasts."

Oh dear Lord. "Where do you propose we find six-hundred-fifty-thousand dollars?"

"I have a few ideas." The sudden silkiness in her voice had me worried.

I scrunched my eyes closed and waited.

"Call Gregory."

"Greg? You want me to call Greg for money?"

"I'm not calling him." Of course she wasn't. Mother didn't approve of my sister's husband. But that was partially Marjorie's fault. Greg was from Ohio. When Marjorie told Mother her fiancé was in the rubber business, Mother assumed tires. It was an assumption Marjorie did not correct.

It was too bad Mother found out about the King Cobra and the rest of Greg's product line the weekend of the wedding.

"Why would Greg support an event three states away from where he lives?"

"Because you're family, and because you saved his marriage."

True. But Marjorie might (would) have opinions about her husband writing an enormous check. "I'll call him, but you have to deal with Marjorie when she finds out."

"Done. Ask him for a hundred thousand."

I gasped. Six figures?

"Let me know how much he gives you." The tap of Mother's nails against the surface of her desk came through the phone line.

"You want me to ask Greg for a hundred thousand dollars?" Had she lost her mind?

"He won't give you that much, but if you start high, you might get fifty. This is your gala, Ellison."

"Meeting the museum's goal is good enough for me."

"There is no way I'm letting you lose."

"It's not a contest."

"Of course it is."

"Mother—" maybe I could reason with her (and maybe Gloria Steinem and Hugh Hefner would run away together) "—this is ridiculous."

"Ellison, you will raise more money than anyone else."

I glanced at the clock on the kitchen wall. Our new neighbor was due any minute.

"I have another question for you."

Another one? I sank onto the nearest stool. "What?"

"Who's escorting you?"

The question rendered me mute.

"Did you hear me?"

"Yes."

"He's taking you, isn't he?"

He. Anarchy Jones.

"I haven't asked him yet."

Mother breathed a relieved sigh. "Ask Hunter to take you. I'm sure he'd be delighted."

"I'm asking Anarchy." Just as soon as I screwed up my nerve. This gala was—well, he'd have to deal with Mother and her friends, subtle and not-so-subtle snubs, and a date who had responsibilities. Would he take off running? If he did, could I blame him?

"Taking that man is a mistake. He won't know anyone, and you won't have time to entertain him." Mother had put serious thought into her argument. Which meant she'd anticipated my answer.

"Anarchy can take care of himself." If only Mother's argument didn't mirror my worries.

"Would you enjoy a policeman's ball?"

Probably not. But if I went with Anarchy, I wouldn't care. Hopefully he felt the same way about the gala. "Mother, this is really none of your business."

"My child is not my business?"

"I'm not a child."

"Semantics."

"I'm grown with a daughter of my own. I'll date who I want."

"There's no reasoning with you." Pot. Kettle. Black.

Max scratched at the back door. He wanted out. He cast me a hurry-up-and-do-as-I-demand look.

I rose from the stool and opened the door, stretching the phone cord.

Max sauntered onto the patio and surveyed his domain. No rabbits or squirrels challenged his supremacy. But they might. He had to be ready. Constant vigilance—that was his motto.

"I just think you'd have a better time with Hunter." Mother wasn't giving up.

"And you're welcome to think that."

The put-upon sigh that traveled the phone line let me know what a huge disappointment I was.

Ding, dong.

"Mother, our new neighbor is here for dinner. I have to go."

"Think about what I said."

"I'll talk to you later."

"And call Greg."

"Hanging up now." I returned the receiver to its cradle and hurried down the hall.

The woman on the front stoop was tall. Five-foot-eight-in-her-stocking-feet tall. And thin. Women-lived-on-grapefruit-and-Dextrin-to-be-that-thin thin. And young. How-could-they-possibly-afford-a-house-in-this-neighborhood young. She wore a peasant skirt, platform boots, and a loose sweater belted with a braided leather sash. She had shaggy hair, blue eyes, and a smattering of freckles on her nose. The tan she'd brought to Kansas City was fading, but she still looked like a sun-kissed gypsy. She held a covered cake plate.

"Jennifer—" I opened the door wider "—please, come in."

My new next-door neighbor stepped into my foyer, gazed at me from underneath a forehead full of bangs, and handed me the plate in her arms. "I brought a salad."

A salad? Whatever was hiding beneath the cake plate weighed ten pounds. "How thoughtful. Grace—" Grace had appeared out of nowhere "—would you please run this to the kitchen?"

Grace smiled at our new neighbor then took the weight of the salad from my arms.

Max shoved his nose into Jennifer's crotch.

"Max!"

The dog ignored me.

I grabbed his collar and hauled him away from our guest. "Bad dog! Sorry about that."

"No problem. I grew up with dogs. He was just saying hello."

Max dropped his jaw into an I-knew-it-would-be-fine grin.

"He sure is handsome."

Max preened and wagged his tail.

I wagged a finger in his face and released his collar. He'd greeted our guest, and she'd passed his doggy sniff test. Now he strutted to the kitchen, where the chance of treats was better.

"How about a drink?" I led Jennifer to the living room.

She paused in the doorway and took in the velvet couches, French antiques, and art-covered walls. "I love your house."

"Thank you. What may I fix you?"

"Wine?" A question rather than a statement.

"Red or white?"

"Red."

I poured her a glass of cabernet and fixed myself a scotch and water (after the day I'd had I needed something stronger than wine).

"Please, have a seat." I handed her the glass and waved her toward a couch.

She smiled at me, sat, and sipped. "Gosh! This is really good. What is it?"

I glanced at the bar cart and squinted at the bottle. "Cabernet."

She nodded. "It's yummy. Is it a favorite of yours?"

It was whatever Aggie had grabbed at the liquor store when I realized we didn't have any red wine in the house. "My housekeeper picked it up."

"I'll have to write down the name."

Grace appeared in the door holding a can of Tab and a plate of limes. "Aggie says dinner will be ready at six thirty." Then she smiled at our guest. "How are you this evening, Mrs. Howe?"

"Oh my gosh—" our neighbor's smile was movie-star bright "—please call me Jennifer. Mrs. Howe is my mother-in-law. And I'm fine. Thanks for asking. Just thrilled to be here tonight."

Grace crossed to the bar cart, poured the Tab over ice, and added two lime wedges. Then she settled in a club chair.

I was dying to ask her if she knew what happened at Dirty Sally's—of course she knew. Debbie was one of her best friends. Instead, I took a healthy slug of scotch. "How are you settling in, Jennifer?"

Our guest wrinkled her nose. "Kansas City is nothing like California."

"Where in California are you from?" asked Grace.

"I'm from San Diego but I went to school near San Francisco."

Grace sipped her Tab. "Stanford?"

"Yes."

"That's where Mom's—" her gaze slid my way before she picked a word "—boyfriend went."

Jennifer manufactured another brilliant smile. "I met my husband there."

"What did you study?" I asked.

"I have a degree in mathematics."

"Really?" Grace and I spoke at the same time—both of us

endlessly impressed with anyone who studied math on purpose.

"Yes."

"The math gene skipped our family," Grace explained. "I blame Mom." Of course she did. "We can handle arithmetic and that's about it."

"Let me know if you ever need any help with your homework or studying for a test."

My other next-door neighbor, Margaret Hamilton, flew her broomstick at midnight. Marian Dixon, from across the street, seemed to think the happenings at my house were more interesting than her soaps. It would be nice to have a neighbor who didn't hex me or spy on me—one who understood a quadratic equation, even if she was a Bohemian gypsy who'd give Mother heart palpitations as soon as they met (*really, Ellison, what is happening in your neighborhood?*). "Be careful," I warned. "We may take you up on that."

"I'd love to help. Aside from having a few rooms painted and installing some new carpet, the house doesn't need much. I have too much time on my hands."

It was my turn to smile. "You're kind to offer."

Grace stood, walked to the bar, and squeezed a third lime into her Tab. "What brought you and your husband to Kansas City?"

"My husband's job. Although—" Jennifer took a sip of her wine and turned the wattage of her smile to blinding "—he travels more than we thought he would." In other words, if she'd known she'd be stuck by herself in a big house in a city where she didn't know anyone, she might have stayed in California. That toothy grin wasn't fooling anyone.

"I have rumaki." Aggie stood in the doorway with a silver tray in one hand and a stack of cocktail napkins in the other. "Shoo, you." She directed that last bit to Max who was all about bacon.

He followed her into the living room and watched closely as she presented the hors d'oeuvre tray to Jennifer, then me, then Grace.

"Mmmmm," said Jennifer. "These are great. I'll have to get the recipe."

"Do you enjoy cooking?" I asked.

"I do. It's such an opportunity for creativity. What about you?"

Grace choked on her rumaki.

"Aggie is the cook in this house," I said.

Aggie donned a gratified smile, put the tray down on the coffee table, and hauled Max back to the kitchen.

"Mom can't cook."

"Grace—"

"Oh, don't deny it. You could burn water."

That was an exaggeration. A teensy exaggeration.

We chatted about cooking—Grace delighted in telling Jennifer about the time I incinerated a roast (the fire engine Henry called was overkill). We told her about Kansas City—the best grocery store (McGonigle's for meat, Milgram's for everything else), best bakery (McClain's), best hair stylist (Rick McHugh at Salon B), and best restaurants (Grace and I debated BBQ—but debating the best BBQ was practically a professional sport in our home town).

"Dinner's ready." There was a strange expression on Aggie's face—as if she'd forcibly smoothed a curl off her lip.

We crossed the hall to the dining room. On the sideboard was a roasted chicken, beautifully browned new potatoes, fresh green beans sautéed in butter and oil, and Jennifer's salad.

My daughter stopped short. "What's that?"

"That's my latest creation." Jennifer didn't seem to hear the horror in Grace's voice. "I think it will taste great."

Jennifer had brought us a Jell-O salad that she'd poured into a Bundt pan. Aggie had removed the pan and found food (a determination up for debate) that looked as if it had passed through an alien's intestinal tract. Jennifer's "salad" glowed lime green in the chandelier's soft light. Unidentifiable bits of food lurked in its verdant depths.

"What's in it?" Grace's voice was painfully polite.

"Diced apples, nuts, raisins—"

Oh dear Lord. Raisins were the food equivalent of Satan.

"—olives—"

Raisins and olives? Together? Jennifer was my guest. Being a good hostess required me to eat her salad. How? My stomach was already objecting.

"—iceberg lettuce, green onion, mandarin oranges—"

"Wow." Grace looked ready to make a run for it.

But Jennifer wasn't done "—radishes and prunes."

Prunes? Did Jennifer need psychotropic drugs? Was she off her meds? I forced a smile. "It sounds delicious. We can't wait to try it."

"It's just an experiment. I hope you don't mind being guinea pigs."

We minded. "Of course not."

Jennifer smiled brightly. "If you like it, I'll have to make it for Marshall."

Not if she wanted to stay married.

We served ourselves succulent chicken, roasted potatoes with crisp edges, perfectly cooked green beans, and Jennifer's salad. The dinner plates cringed at contact with Jennifer's Jell-O (they didn't—not really—but they wanted to).

Grace spooned the smallest portion she could politely get away with onto her plate.

I did too.

Then we sat. That salad—green slime and garbage—waited on our plates. The olives looked like eyeballs. The raisins looked like—I couldn't think about that. Not when I had to take a bite.

Grace lifted her fork and managed a morsel of salad that seemed to contain nothing but Jell-O and apple.

Apparently looks were deceiving. Jell-O and apple didn't warrant the disgusted expression that flashed across her face.

I paused with my fork poised above the quivering green.

Jennifer didn't pause. She took an enormous bite. She chewed. She tilted her head to the side. "Not bad. What do you think, Ellison?"

There was no escape—Jennifer was watching me with an

expectant expression on her pretty young face.

I lifted a bite to my mouth, forced my lips apart, and ate the single most appalling thing I'd ever tasted. Somehow, I swallowed. "Wow." I reached for my water goblet.

"I know! Yummy, huh?"

Did the woman have no taste buds?

"It certainly is unique. Where did you find the recipe?"

"No recipe." She confirmed what I already knew. "It's just something I threw together."

I tightened my hold on the fork and forced another bite (please, God, let the fork's tines find no prunes—or raisins).

Grace gave me a Mom-do-I-have-to look.

I cut a bite of chicken and gave her a you-are-grounded-till-May-if-you-don't-eat-another-four-bites-of-our-guest's-horrific-side-dish look.

"This chicken is delicious," said Jennifer.

"Where did you learn to cook?" asked Grace.

"I'm self-taught."

Jennifer ate another bite of salad. A little furrow appeared between her brows. "I think I may have put in too many olives."

I smiled weakly and choked down another bite. "It certainly is unique." My roast-reduced-to-carbon sounded pretty good by comparison.

"It is, isn't it?" Jennifer's smile was genuine.

How could a woman who graduated from Stanford not recognize she'd created the single worst side dish in the history of side dishes?

"Jennifer," Grace drew Jennifer's attention, and I hid some Jell-O under my potatoes. Poor, unfortunate spuds. "What's your favorite food?"

"When I grew up, my mom was a super strict vegan. We didn't eat any sugar or meat or dairy. So, when I went to college, everything was a revelation. There's nothing I don't like."

Her story explained so much.

"Surely, you must have an absolute favorite." I drew her

attention. Grace camouflaged some Jell-O.

"Nope." She shook her head and shared another sunny smile. "Everything tastes good to me."

Jennifer Howe and her Jell-O salad from hell were the best argument I'd ever seen for letting kids eat whatever they wanted.

With a hand that barely shook, I fed myself another bite.

Ding, dong.

We heard Aggie and Max hurry down the hallway (this Jell-O salad dinner was the first time in his lifetime that Max hadn't sat next to the dinner table waiting for a morsel to fall).

A moment later, Anarchy filled the doorway. "I didn't mean to interrupt."

"I told him there was plenty of food." There was a devilish glint in Aggie's eyes. Aggie held out hope I'd get over my infatuation with Anarchy and settle down with Hunter Tafft. She might even have blamed Anarchy for turning my head away from the silver-haired lawyer. In those opinions, she and Mother were in complete accord. Setting a place for Anarchy at a table where he'd feel obligated to try Jennifer's Jell-O salad amused her.

There was no way I could warn him.

"Thanks, Aggie." Poor man, he should have run when he had the chance.

"Jennifer, this is my friend, Anarchy Jones. Anarchy, please meet my new next-door neighbor, Jennifer Howe. Jennifer went to Stanford, too."

Anarchy smiled and pulled out a chair. "Nice to meet you."

Jennifer looked a bit stunned. Anarchy had that effect on women. "Hi."

"Thanks for letting me join you." He glanced at the sideboard and his expression froze.

"Jennifer brought the salad for tonight's dinner."

He nodded. Once. And sat. Slowly.

An instant later, Aggie had a place mat and silverware in front of him. "Don't get up." There was that devilish twinkle again. "I'll fix you a plate."

She heaped his plate with Jennifer's salad.

"Anarchy's a homicide detective," said Grace.

Jennifer's eyes grew large.

"Which is handy," Grace continued.

I gave her a cut-it-out-this-minute-young-lady look.

Jennifer gave her a what-on-earth look. "Why is it handy?"

"Because Mom finds bodies."

"Grace!"

My daughter rolled her eyes. "It's not as if she won't find out. I'm surprised Mrs. Dixon hasn't been over to warn her." She smiled at Jennifer. "Mrs. Dixon is nosy."

"Grace!"

Jennifer, whose eyes were as big as the drop biscuits Aggie was passing, snapped her sprung jaw closed. "How many bodies?"

"Good question." Grace ticked off a finger. "There's—"

"One body is too many." We needed a new topic. I gave Grace a do-you-want-to-be-grounded-till-July look.

"It's not as if you've killed anyone."

I narrowed my eyes and scrunched my face at her. Yet. I hadn't killed anyone yet.

"Do you really find bodies?" Jennifer asked.

"Not on purpose."

"Ellison is—" Anarchy searched for a word "—unlucky."

"Who would care for seconds?" asked Aggie, her eyes twinkling like a mirrored ball. "I'm happy to serve."

"No, thank you." Grace and I spoke in unison.

"Detective Jones, what about you?"

Anarchy glanced at the industrial waste on his plate and grinned. "I haven't finished what I have."

"I'll take a little more of the salad," said Jennifer. "Things I make don't always turn out this well."

We stared at her in horror.

Aggie picked up Jennifer's plate and spooned more of the Jell-O mold onto it.

We all watched her do it—a reaction akin to slowing down to

gawk at an accident on the highway.

Grace was the first to look away. "Any interesting murders today?"

She was probably asking Anarchy, but I was the one who choked on a prune.

She tilted her head. "Mom, did you find a body?"

Jennifer put down her fork and stared at me. "A body?"

"My yoga instructor was murdered."

"Murdered?" Jennifer's drop-biscuit eyes were back, and she reached for her wine.

"Since when do you take yoga?" Grace demanded.

"Libba." A one-word answer that described much of what went wrong in my life.

"Libba was your yoga instructor's name?" asked Jennifer.

"No Libba's my friend who dragged me to yoga. She thought it would help with stress. It didn't."

Bzzzzzz.

"What's that?" Grace asked.

"My pager." Anarchy pushed away from the table. "Ellison, may I use your phone?"

"Of course. The line in the study."

"Thanks." He disappeared into the hallway.

"He seems nice." Jennifer's eyes were still huge. "How did you two meet?"

Grace answered with a malicious grin. "Mom found a body floating in the pool at the country club and the police thought she did it."

"Seriously?" she looked at me for confirmation.

It was too hard to explain. "What Grace said."

She leaned back in her chair. "And I thought Kansas City would be boring."

"Not on this block," Grace replied.

Anarchy appeared in the doorway. "I'm sorry to skip out on dinner, but I have to go."

Grace looked at his plate then grinned up at him. "So soon?"

"I caught another murder."

"We can have Aggie make you a plate to take with you," she offered.

Anarchy's brown eyes glinted with humor. "No, thanks. I won't have time to eat."

He'd skillfully escaped the green menace.

"Ellison, I'll call you later."

I stood and dropped my napkin onto my chair. "I'll walk you to the door."

We walked to the front door.

"Did you really get called in to work another murder?"

"Yeah. Why do you ask?" His brown eyes danced.

"I thought it might be Jell-O salad avoidance."

He shook his head. "If I was ever to lie about going to a murder scene, I can't think of a better reason."

I glanced back toward the dining room and lowered my voice. "She thinks it's good."

"She does not."

I nodded. Emphatically. "She does."

Anarchy leaned down and brushed a kiss across my lips. "I'll call you later."

"Anarchy—" I fixed my gaze on his chest and swallowed. Hard.

"What?"

I'd been meaning to ask him for weeks and couldn't put it off another day. "Do you own a tux?"

"I do."

I ignored the flutter of nerves in my stomach and raised my gaze to his face. "Would you please escort me to the gala?"

An expression I didn't recognize settled on his features. "The one at the museum?"

"Yes."

"You're sure you want to take me?"

"Yes." Who else would I take?

"I'd be honored." He kissed me again—more than just a brush across my lips. This kiss curled my toes.

He broke away too soon. "I have to go."

"Anarchy—" my voice stopped him from walking out the door "—you're already investigating a murder. Why'd you get a second one?"

He grimaced. "I'm now the go-to guy for society murders."

"Society murders? Who died?"

He brushed a last kiss across my already tingling lips. "A lawyer named John Wilson."

FOUR

I poked at the doorbell and steadied the covered cake plate I held in my arms. The cake plate held a Bundt cake—chocolate drizzled with ganache. Winnie Flournoy had a well-known weakness for chocolate.

A chilly wind whistled past my ankles. I shivered and forced a smile.

I did not think about my promise to Mother—*stay out of trouble.* Trouble found me without my looking for it.

I did not think about how angry Anarchy would be if he caught me fiddling in his investigation. I wasn't fiddling. Not really.

I did think about Henry's file on Lark Flournoy, Lark's collusion with a lawyer named John Wilson, and Anarchy's latest case. Those thoughts had kept me up half the night. They'd driven me from my bed early in the morning. And they'd placed me on Winnie's doorstep at the earliest decent hour.

Winnie opened the door and her brows lifted all the way to the mussed helmet of salt and pepper hair on her head. "Ellison."

I held out the cake. "I thought you might need a pick-me-up."

She winced and glanced over her shoulder to where Marigold's body had dangled. "How kind. Please, come in."

I stepped into the foyer and looked at the Kazak rug on the floor, the Picasso on the wall, and the treads on the stairs. I did not so much as glance at the bannister. Did not. Did not. Did. The body was gone. The rope was gone. Their memory hung in the air.

Winnie took the cake plate from me. "Let's take this to the kitchen. I'll make us some coffee to go with it."

"I never say no to coffee."

Winnie's kitchen floor was covered in linoleum that looked like sandstone pavers. The cabinets were painted harvest gold and matched the appliances. A small glass-topped wrought-iron table surrounded by matching chairs sat in the breakfast nook.

Winnie put the cake on the table. "I'll grab some plates and coffee. Make yourself at home.

I perched on one of Winnie's wrought-iron chairs (the seats were upholstered in a harvest gold and avocado green plaid that matched the curtains) and looked out the window into the backyard.

Early daffodils in the raised beds along the back fence-line ignored the nip in the spring air and reached toward the weak sunlight. A Bradford pear near the brick patio looked as if it might bloom. In the kitchen, Mr. Coffee made familiar, comforting sounds.

"I wonder if spring will ever arrive." Winnie put two plates, two dessert forks, and two plaid napkins on the table then crossed her arms over her chest as if she were cold.

"I hope it warms up soon." I glanced again at the chilly back yard then shifted my gaze to my hostess. "How are you holding up?"

"I'll be fine." Her voice was suddenly thick, and she turned her back on me. "We need coffee."

"I know how distressing something like this can be."

Winnie stiffened. "I suppose you do."

"If there's anything I can do..."

She put two mugs, a creamer, and a bowl of sugar on the table then sat down across from me. The smile she gave me was too bright. "It's kind of you to offer."

"Of course." I reached across the table and squeezed her hand.

She stood, pulling away from my touch. "I forgot a cake knife. We need a cake knife."

A moment later she resumed her seat and cut us enormous slices of Bundt cake.

I sipped my coffee and watched as she took her first bite.

"Mmmmm. Delicious."

"Aggie gets all the credit." I picked up my fork. "How's Lark handling all this?"

"Lark?" Her chin trembled.

I nodded and lifted the coffee mug to my lips.

"He blames me." Her eyes filled with tears.

"Blames you?"

"I'm the one who invited Marigold into our home. I'm the one who was locked in the yoga studio while—" her voice broke and she held up a single finger and shook her head.

Taken in the right light, Lark had a tiny point. Winnie had invited Marigold in. But blaming Winnie wasn't fair. Marigold had seemed like a nice young woman—right up until she locked us in the attic. "It's not your fault she was murdered."

"Lark doesn't care about the murder—aside from the police and the gossip and the inconvenience of it all." She shifted her gaze to her lap. "But someone ransacked his office."

"Really?" I took a bite of Aggie's cake and moaned softly—she had a way with chocolate. "What was taken?"

"Files of some sort. But Lark is beside himself that someone rifled through his papers."

"I suppose he feels violated."

"He does. But they're just papers. He's missing the bigger picture. Someone died. Violently. In our house. I *liked* Marigold. And then she—" Winnie crammed a large bite of chocolate cake into her mouth, chewed, and swallowed "—and then she betrayed me and got herself killed. Would you like some milk?"

For an instant, I was too surprised by the shift in her conversation to answer. "No. Coffee is great."

"I want milk. I'll be right back."

Winnie poured milk into a glass and returned to the table.

"Marigold let someone into the house to search Lark's office?"

Winnie took a giant gulp of milk and used her plaid napkin to wipe away the mustache on her upper lip. "What do you mean?"

"We were locked in the attic. Marigold and the person who killed her could have taken anything—your jewelry, your silver, the Picasso in the front hall—but they took papers from Lark's office. It's as if the killer planned to search his office, to take those papers."

"You know—" Winnie tilted her head "—you're right. My pearls weren't in the safe. They were on my dressing table. Untouched. This robbery is Lark's fault, not mine."

I wasn't walking down the blame pathway. Not today.

"What papers did they take?"

"Lark won't tell me." She ate the last bite of her cake then looked down at her plate as if all that chocolate had magically disappeared.

Sometimes I looked at my coffee cup the same way. "Any guesses?"

"Not one. I have no idea."

I did. "Do you know a lawyer named John Wilson?"

"I shouldn't but—" Winnie picked up the knife and cut herself another slice of cake "—it's the best cake I've had in ages. Would you like some more?"

"No, thank you. John Wilson?"

Her eyes seemed to stare into the past. "What about him?"

He'd been murdered the same day as Marigold and had done something shady enough with Lark for Lark to be willing to pay—and pay—to keep it quiet. "His name came up last night. I can't place him."

"I can't imagine you've ever met him. He's a lawyer, he's older than you by twenty years, and he and his family belong to Brookhaven." Brookhaven was a country club considerably south of my normal haunts. I went there only when our club's swim team swam against theirs.

"What kind of lawyer?" There were all sorts of lawyers—patent lawyers, estate lawyers, tax lawyers, plaintiff's lawyers, defense lawyers, corporate lawyers, and criminal lawyers.

Winnie glanced at my coffee cup—magically empty. "Would you like more coffee?"

"Please."

She rose from the table, taking our coffee mugs with her. "I'm not sure what kind of law John practices. Although—" her brow creased and the stream of coffee flowing from the pot to my cup stopped "—he might be a plaintiff's attorney."

A plaintiff's attorney represented a suing party in a lawsuit. Big-deal plaintiff's lawyers wore bespoke suits and Rolex watches. Not-big-deal plaintiff's lawyers chased ambulances. If Max did any further damage to my neighbor Margaret Hamilton's property, I was fairly certain she'd engage a plaintiff's attorney (one with an expensive watch)—not for the damage to her lawn (minimal) but for emotional distress and punitive damages (potentially huge).

"Has Lark had any cases with him?"

She resumed pouring. "He must have, or I wouldn't recognize the name. But it's been ages since I even thought of him."

"You're sure you don't remember anything?"

She brought me my coffee. "I'm sure. Why?"

"No reason." It wasn't as if I could tell her about Henry's blackmail. That her husband and John Wilson had done something, so long ago she couldn't remember when, that might have got Wilson killed, wasn't a tidbit for morning coffee. Especially not when I wasn't sure.

When I arrived home, I painted. Mixing color and texture on canvas was a far better stress-reducer than yoga—at least for me.

My third-floor ballroom served as my studio—a room filled with shabby, comfortable chairs, a huge table covered with art books, and walls papered with sketches. Large dormers and skylights allowed plenty of natural light.

As my paintbrush, loaded with a cadmium yellow, touched the canvas, the tension fell from my shoulders.

I painted from memory—the brave little daffodils at the back of Winnie's yard.

And, I pondered. And, I pondered. Should I tell Anarchy about the connection between Lark Flournoy and John Wilson? How could I explain their connection without mentioning Henry's files?

I couldn't.

Mentioning those files, revealing the depths of Henry's vileness...I would never do that. Not to Grace. Not to myself.

My paintbrush slowed, and I stared at the flowers dancing in a chilly wind.

I might have stared for hours but Aggie called up the stairs. "Jennifer Howe's cake pan and platter are clean."

"Please tell me you tossed the rest of that salad."

"Of course."

"What can we put in the Bundt pan?" I couldn't return an empty pan.

"How about some of my chocolate chip cookies?"

"Perfect. Thank you."

"I'll put it together right now."

I cleaned my brushes and descended the stairs.

Jennifer's pan sat next to the backdoor.

"You want that Bundt pan out of your kitchen?"

Aggie's lips drew back in culinary disdain. "More than you can ever imagine."

I picked up the pan and the cookies and scratched behind Max's ears. "No. You can't come."

He huffed. I never let him do anything fun.

"I'll be back soon." I cut across my front yard with Jennifer's Bundt pan and knocked.

Jennifer pulled open the door wearing a long, flowing, peasant print dress. She blinked when she saw me. "Ellison, what a lovely surprise!"

"I'm just bringing back your pan." I held the Bundt pan out to her. Aggie had found a burlap gift sack for the cookies and tied it with a red ribbon.

"What is this?" Jennifer held up the sack.

"You'll have to open it and see."

"Please," she said, "come in. Do you have time for coffee?"

"I always have time for coffee." I stepped into her foyer.

"This way." She led me to her kitchen where a Mr. Coffee identical to my own sat on the counter.

I watched as she went through the familiar steps of filling his reservoir, scooping coffee grounds into a filter, and pushing his button. Then came the heavenly sound and smell of Mr. Coffee at work.

I sighed.

"We have a percolator, but Marshall is convinced this machine makes better coffee."

Marshall was right—except for the machine part. Mr. Coffee was more than that. "There's a Mr. Coffee on my counter, too."

"Would you care for cream or sugar?"

"Cream."

We doctored our coffees then Jennifer asked, "Shall we sit in the sunroom?"

I followed her through her house—the Bohemian furniture at odds with the home's Tudor bones—and into the room closest to my house. The room was positively bathed in sunshine.

Jennifer, with both hands wrapped around her coffee mug as if her fingers were cold, sank onto a settee draped with a sari. "I miss the sun."

"You moved here in the winter. Spring will be better. And this summer you'll get plenty of sun. Promise." I settled into a wicker chair loaded with colorful pillows and took a sip of coffee.

"I'll hold you to that." Now she sipped. "Thank you for dinner last night."

"You're welcome to come anytime."

"That's kind of you." She stared down into her coffee cup. "I meant what I said, I'd be happy to help Grace with math."

"And we'd be grateful."

Jennifer shifted her gaze to the tile floor. "I'd also be happy to help her friend."

"Her friend?"

"When you were saying goodnight to Anarchy, Grace told me what happened to her friend, Debbie."

Grace hadn't told me. Not yet. What had happened?

Jennifer's gaze remained fixed on the contents of her mug. "It happened to me when I was fifteen. My parents didn't understand...anything. But they did understand I needed help. They arranged regular therapy for me. Talking helped."

What happened to Debbie? "Um...I'm at a disadvantage. I don't know what happened."

"You don't?"

"No."

Jennifer's face shuttered. "Grace didn't tell you?"

"No."

"I thought you were open and honest with each other."

I blinked. "We are. We're also busy. We haven't had time to talk about Debbie."

Jennifer's face cleared.

"What happened to Debbie?" I asked.

"She was assaulted."

Well, that explained why Marsha showed up at my house looking worse that Jennifer's Jell-O salad. "That happened to you?"

She nodded. "It's important for Grace's friend to know she's not alone. There are people she can talk to, people who will listen, people who won't judge."

"You've helped other girls?"

"When I lived in California, I volunteered with an agency that helped victims. Grace's friend should know she isn't to blame; the man who hurt her is."

I didn't reply. Not for one minute did I believe Debbie was to blame.

"Do you disagree?" There was an edge to Jennifer's voice.

"I agree." And my heart bled for Debbie and her family. "We teach our children to look both ways before crossing the street, to wash their hands before eating, not to talk to strangers. All to keep them safe. And then something like this happens." I shook my head.

"It's heartbreaking and the scars on her psyche will take years to fade."

"Are you sure you don't have a degree in psychology?"

Jennifer laughed. "I'm sure. I did one stupid thing as a teenager." She held up a single finger. "One. After that, I changed schools. My family struggled. To this day, my father blames me—not for the assault—but for the decision that put me at risk."

"What happened to the boy?"

"He went to college then found a job with a movie studio in Hollywood."

"So, nothing?"

"Nothing." A tiny smile flitted across her lips. "Not until a car flattened him like a pancake. It makes me an awful person, but I can't help thinking his death is karmic justice."

"Hopefully, the man who hurt Debbie will go to jail."

"Will the family press charges? Is she the type of girl to testify?"

It seemed unlikely. "I don't know."

"Because I can tell you what the man's lawyer will say—that she wanted it. She went to that bar, she drank too much, and she led him on."

"Did you testify?"

"I did not." She clasped her hands in her lap. "My parents' lawyer told me the kinds of questions I'd be asked." She glanced down at her hands. "At fifteen, testifying sounded like a second assault. I couldn't do it." She looked up. "The decision was the right one for me. The same thing happened to my husband's sister. But she testified. What happened in the courtroom damaged her as much as the rape."

"What happened?"

"The defense attorney put her on trial."

"How awful."

She nodded and a single tear balanced at the corner of her eye. “The man who raped her was acquitted. Katherine, that was her name, never fully recovered from that. She killed herself.”

FIVE

Six o'clock found me on the couch in the family room, reading about John Wilson's death in the evening paper. The police were investigating all leads and urged citizens with information to come forward.

I reached for the glass of wine on the coffee table in front of me and lowered the newspaper to my lap.

I didn't have information. Not really. I had guesses and suppositions and a creepy-crawly-make-my-spine-tingle feeling.

I sipped my wine and considered turning on the evening news.

Max, who'd stretched out in front of what might be the last fire of the season, chased a rabbit or squirrel in his sleep.

Above me, the barely discernible thump of bass from Grace's tape deck beat a steady rhythm.

Mouth-watering smells wafted in from the kitchen. Whatever Aggie was fixing for dinner smelled amazing.

I leaned my head back against the cushion and closed my eyes.

Brnng, brnng.

I stood, crossed from the couch to my desk, and answered the phone. "Hello."

"Ellison, it's me." Anarchy's voice had a cop-like ring.

Guilt tightened my throat. I should tell him about the file. But explaining exactly how vile Henry had been didn't appeal to me. Nor did revealing my friends' secrets to the police. Thankfully, the wine had made the trip from the couch with me. I drank. Deeply. "Hi."

"I need your help."

"Oh?"

"Someone tried to kill Lark Flournoy—"

"No!" I braced myself against the desk.

"Yes. I'm at the hospital and his wife is distraught. Would you come and sit with her? Please?"

"Of course. What happened?"

"Someone ran him down as he walked to his car after work."

"Ran him down in a car?"

"Yes."

"A blue car?"

Long seconds passed. "How did you know?"

"Lucky guess."

"Right." He didn't believe me.

"There was a blue car parked in front of the Flournoys' when Marigold was killed. I told you about it." I took another sip of wine. "It makes sense that Marigold's murder and the attempt on Lark's life are related."

Anarchy said something I couldn't understand.

"What?"

"Nothing. I was talking to someone else. Hold on—" I heard him say something about interviewing witnesses "—can you come?"

"I'll be there as soon as possible."

"Thanks, Ellison. I appreciate it."

I hung up the receiver, looked at the near-empty level in my wine glass, and called a taxi.

"Aggie—" I walked into the kitchen with Max at my heels "—I have to go to the hospital and sit with Winnie Flournoy. Would you mind staying with Grace?"

She looked up from the pot she was stirring, concern cutting stark lines across her face. "I'd be happy to. Is everything all right?"

"Her husband was hit by a car."

"How awful."

"On purpose."

"Even worse."

"I don't know how late I'll be."

"Don't give it a second thought."

Thank heavens for Aggie. "Thank you."

I arrived at the hospital twenty minutes later and entered through the Emergency Room doors.

There were plenty of people in the waiting room. None of them were Winnie.

I approached the check-in desk.

"Good evening, Mrs. Russell." The woman behind the desk made it sound as if I was a regular visitor.

I was.

"How may I help you this evening?" she asked.

"I'm looking for Winnie Flournoy. I believe her husband was in a car accident."

"Mrs. Flournoy is in the surgical waiting room. I'd be happy to have someone take you there."

I held up a hand. "No need. I know the way." I spent entirely too much time at the hospital.

My heels clicked against the tile in the otherwise quiet corridors—rounds were over, patients were fed, and day-shifts were winding down.

I found a red-nosed Winnie huddled in a chair next to a uniformed policeman who looked as if he'd graduated from the police academy last week.

Winnie stood when she saw me and launched herself into my arms.

I hugged her and patted her on the back and listened as she sobbed against my shoulder. "What's happened?" I mouthed over Winnie's shoulder to the boyish police officer.

He shook his head. "Still in surgery."

I let Winnie cry for several minutes then asked, "How long will he be in surgery?"

"They don't—" hiccup "—they don't know."

"Have you eaten?" I asked her.

"I couldn't."

Fair enough. "Let's go to the powder room. We'll wet some towels with cool water and put them on your eyes." Winnie's poor eyes were practically swollen shut from crying.

"I can't leave. What if they come?"

"Officer—" I read his name tag "—Officer Long, would you please stay here while I take Mrs. Flournoy to the ladies' room?"

He nodded, looking relieved that someone was taking the near-hysterical woman off his hands. "Of course."

"Hear that, Winnie? If anyone needs you, Officer Long will knock on the door. Now, come with me. You'll feel better after you've cleaned yourself up a bit."

Winnie didn't need a bit of a clean-up; she needed a major overhaul. We did what we could. We pressed cool towels against her eyes. We combed her hair. We applied fresh powder and lipstick. "You want to look your best when you see Lark," I told her.

"What if he doesn't make it?" Winnie's chin wobbled.

"Of course he'll make it, and you don't want the first thing he sees to be you looking a mess."

Her chin firmed. "You're right."

"Give me just a minute—" I opened the door to the toilet stall and wrinkled my nose "—never mind." If Mother, who sat on the hospital board, ever saw a bathroom in such need of a good cleaning, heads would roll.

We exited the powder room with Winnie looked marginally better. She'd even quit crying.

"Are you sure you don't want something to eat?" I asked.

"Positive."

We settled into green Naugahyde chairs and waited.

And waited.

After about thirty minutes, Winnie had twisted her handkerchief into a rope, then twisted the rope around her fingers, and I'd decided a search for a clean ladies' room was essential.

I stood and looked at Officer Long. "Where is Detective Jones?"

The young man glanced at his watch. "He should be back any

minute now."

"Where did he go?"

"He went to talk to the witnesses."

"Witnesses?"

"Lark's law clerks." Winnie's voice was faint. "They saw it happen."

"What did they see?"

She shook her head, pressed her palm against her mouth, and fresh tears welled in her eyes.

"Winnie, the doctors are taking excellent care of Lark."

"I know. It's just—" her head bent, and her neck didn't look strong enough to raise it again "—how did this happen?"

"Anarchy will do everything he can to catch whoever did this."

Winnie's head moved in a barely discernable nod. "I know that." Her shoulders straightened. "I need to think about something else."

I sighed and sat next to her. My trip to the ladies' room could wait a few more minutes. "I have new next-door neighbors," I told her.

"Who?"

"Jennifer and Marshall Howe. They moved from California."

"They won't last."

"Oh?"

"Haven't you noticed? The people who move here from the east or north stick like glue. Sometimes, the Southerners stay. People from the west coast never last."

I had not noticed that.

"They can't handle the winters." She crossed her arms as if she could feel January breezing down her neck.

The young police officer nodded his agreement.

A man in scrubs stepped into the waiting room and approached us. "Mrs. Flournoy?"

Winnie stood and clutched my hand. The lines in her face looked like cracks in a plaster wall—a wall crumbling to dust. "Yes."

"Your husband is out of surgery and everything went well."

Winnie exhaled. Loudly. Her eyes refilled with tears. "Thank, God."

The man looked at her with concern. "He'll be in recovery for at least an hour. Why don't you take a break? Eat a sandwich?"

Winnie just stood there.

"What are Lark's injuries?" I asked.

The man shifted his gaze to me. "And you are?"

"Ellison Russell." I spotted the flicker in his gaze. "A friend of the family."

The man nodded. Once. "He has a broken leg, a broken pelvis, and there was some damage to one of his kidneys, but we're cautiously optimistic."

Winnie sagged, and her breath caught.

"A nurse will fetch you in an hour or so. You can see him then." He waited as if he expected one of us to say something.

Winnie was beyond talking.

"Thank you, Dr.—" I didn't know his name.

"Dr. Goodman."

Winnie let go of my hand and pumped his. "Thank you for everything, doctor."

Dr. Goodman extricated his hand and disappeared.

Winnie collapsed into her chair. "Oh, Ellison, thank God. I'm not ready to be part of the widows' club just yet." Winnie's eyes widened and clapped her free hand to her mouth. "I didn't mean—"

"Don't give it another thought. I'm not ready for the widows' club either."

"But you're—"

"Too young to join the widows' club." Just ask Mother. She was determined to see me married again—but not to Anarchy. "Come on, Winnie." I tugged at her elbow, pulling her away from the row of uncomfortable chairs.

"Where?"

"You heard the doctor. We're getting you something to eat."

"But—"

"He said you have an hour before they'll let you see Lark. A sandwich in the coffee shop won't take thirty minutes."

She allowed herself to be led to the coffee shop where she sank onto a chair at a table next to the window and buried her head in her hands. "These last few days have been a nightmare."

I made a sympathetic sound.

"What will I do if—" her voice hitched.

"The doctor said Lark will be fine."

A waitress with an impressive beehive approached our table and put down two glasses of water. "What'll it be?"

"You go ahead, Ellison."

I didn't need a menu. And I didn't need water. My teeth were ready to float out of my head. The only thing keeping me at the table was the forlorn arch of Winnie's neck. "A club sandwich."

The waitress made a note on her pad. "Coffee?"

I couldn't say no to coffee. "Yes."

"We're running low on lemon meringue. Would you like me to put a slice back for you?"

I spent almost as much time in the coffee shop as I did in the emergency room. They knew me. "Please."

The waitress turned her attention to Winnie.

"I'd like a cup of your soup and a ham and swiss on rye, please."

"Would you like your soup with your sandwich or before?"

"Before." Winnie raised her head and rubbed a palm up and down her arm. "I can't seem to warm up."

"Anything else?" asked the waitress.

"Do you have hot tea?"

The waitress nodded and made a note. "Got it." She slipped the pad into the pocket of her ruffled apron and headed toward the kitchen.

Winnie leaned back in her chair. Her face was still far too pale and new creases ran from the edges of her nose to the corners of her mouth. She sighed. "Thank you for being here, Ellison."

"It's my pleasure." It would be more of a pleasure if I didn't need to run to the bathroom.

A wry smile twisted her lips. "I seriously doubt that."

I shifted in my chair. "I've had a rough year. I wouldn't have survived without my friends."

Winnie nodded and took a small sip of water. "It's funny..."

"What's funny?"

"I saw in the morning paper that John Wilson had died."

I waited.

"It's not funny that he's dead. It's funny that we were just talking about him."

I said nothing.

"Odd funny," she continued.

Where had that waitress got to? I ignored the water, ignored the ice melting in the glasses, and crossed my legs.

"I can't help but wonder if John's murder and what happened to Lark are related."

There were no flies on Winnie.

I squeezed my legs together. Finding a bathroom was becoming essential. "You said it yourself, you haven't thought of John Wilson in years. How could John's death and Lark being run down be related?"

Now her face looked positively bloodless. "One of the law clerks who saw it happen sat with me for a while. He said the car sped up to hit Lark."

"Oh, Winnie." I reached across the table and squeezed her hand.

"I know it sounds crazy, but I've been sitting in that waiting room making deals with God and wondering why this happened."

"That doesn't sound crazy." I'd done the same thing more than once.

"All I can come up with is a case John and Lark had together."

"What kind of case?"

She glanced down at her hands. "I don't know. I'm sure they've had more than one." She rubbed her wan cheeks. "And I got it wrong. John Wilson wasn't a plaintiff's attorney, he represented criminals."

"Why would an old case come up now?"

"I don't know, but a case is the key to all this. I'm sure of it."

"All this?"

"Marigold's death, too."

"Did you tell Detective Jones?"

Her gaze slid away from me. "No. Not yet. Do you think I should?"

I nodded with enthusiasm until I remembered part of her story involved my pulling John Wilson's name from a hat right before he was murdered. Anarchy would be especially curious about that part. "He might have already put two and two together."

"How?"

"It's not every day one lawyer is murdered, and another is almost murdered. It stands to reason the two are related." I was going to have to leave her—if only for a few minutes.

"What I don't understand is how poor Marigold was mixed up in all this."

"You're sure that's her real name?"

Something flashed across Winnie's face—an expression there and gone before I had a chance to read it. She pursed her lips. "Who could make up a name like Marigold Applebottom?"

She hadn't answered, but I ceded her point with a nod then pushed my chair away from the table. "Would you excuse me for a moment, please?" I'd ask her more about Marigold (Winnie was hiding something, I was sure of it) when I returned from the powder room.

"Of course."

I marched through the crowded coffee shop and passed through the door to the hospital lobby, pausing for an instant and looking back at Winnie. The waitress was serving her a cup of soup. Winnie would be fine for the short amount of time I'd be in the ladies' room. I zipped across the lobby and opened the door (much cleaner than the facilities near the surgical waiting room).

I took less than five minutes—the necessities, then washing my hands, running a comb through my hair, patting powder on my shiny nose, and swiping a bit of color across my lips.

I hurried back to the coffee shop where Winnie had forsaken her chin-up attitude. In fact, her chin—her whole head—was on the table.

I sat. "Are you all right?"

She didn't respond.

"Winnie." I reached out and touched her arm.

Nothing.

"Winnie!" My voice rose in both volume and pitch.

The people at the surrounding tables gaped at me.

"Winnie!"

I turned to the waitress. "Get help."

Her hands fluttered.

"Now!" I insisted. "We're in hospital, call a doctor."

"Ellison, what's wrong?" Anarchy stood next to the table.

Tension that had been spooling around me unwound. "Something has happened to Winnie."

Anarchy took charge. Barked orders. Hospital personnel rushed Winnie from the coffee shop to the emergency room.

When they disappeared into the elevator, I asked, "Where did you come from?"

"Officer Long told me where you were." He had on his cop face. "What happened?"

I paused at the entrance to the lobby. "I only left her for a few minutes. When I came back, she'd collapsed."

"Where did you go?"

What kind of question was that? "The ladies' room."

"She was fine when you left?"

"Yes. We were talking about what happened to Lark." I swallowed. "And John Wilson. And Marigold."

"And you're sure she was okay?"

I nodded. Mystified. "I wouldn't have left her."

"What exactly was she doing?"

"Nothing." I pushed a few stray strands of hair away from my face. "Eating soup."

"Soup?" Anarchy's gaze traveled back to the table where I'd sat with Winnie. The soup bowl still sat on the table, but a busboy was reaching for it. "Stop!" Anarchy's voice carried through the restaurant and every single person within its walls stopped what they were doing.

He strode across the floor to the table. "Don't touch that."

The busboy blinked and backed away.

I followed him to the table. "What's wrong?" Everything looked normal. Two sweating glasses of water, one bowl of soup, an opened pack of crackers, a few crinkled napkins. Nothing to suggest why Winnie had collapsed.

"Which water is yours?"

I pointed to the untouched glass. "That one."

Anarchy nodded as if I'd confirmed his suspicions.

"What's wrong?" I asked a second time.

"Your friend may have been poisoned."

SIX

I sat at the hospital for hours. What else could I do?

The labs ran tests as the doctors struggled to save Winnie's life.

I stared at a faded print of a bad painting of a beach and a setting sun and thought how remarkably inappropriate the art (word used loosely) was.

I wasn't looking for sunsets. I was looking for dawning hope.

I drank bad coffee.

I sipped the tar in the Styrofoam cup, shifted my weight in the uncomfortable chair, and gave up. The coffee went in the trash and I paced.

I checked my watch and marched to the nurses' desk. "Where's the nearest payphone?"

"You can use ours, Mrs. Russell," said a pretty nurse with a helpful smile.

"Isn't that against the rules?"

"No one will mind if it's a quick call."

"Thank you."

"What's the number?"

I gave her my home number.

She dialed and handed me the receiver. "It's ringing."

"Hello." Aggie's no-nonsense voice was like a gift.

I swallowed around the fist lodged in my throat. "I'm stuck at the hospital. I don't know when I'll make it home."

"I already told you—I'm here all night."

I could always count on Aggie. "Thank you." Words that failed to convey my gratitude.

"You're welcome. What happened?"

I glanced at the nurse. "It's a long story. May I tell you later?"

"Of course. You're all right? You sound tired."

"I'm fine."

"I'll let Grace know you'll be late."

I pictured them safe in our comfortable kitchen then glanced at the raw oatmeal color of the hospital walls. "Thanks again, Aggie. I'll be in touch." I handed the receiver back to the nurse. "Thank you."

She smiled at me. "Can I get you anything? Coffee?"

"No," I spoke quickly. "But thank you for offering. I'll just head back to the waiting room."

If Anarchy was right and Winnie had been poisoned, how had she ingested the poison? Was there a poison that acted faster than a quick trip to the ladies' room?

I resumed glaring at the bad print in the waiting room.

"There you are."

I turned and saw Libba. "What are you doing here?" She wasn't dressed for the hospital. Not in a saffron yellow chiffon dress with red, green, and gold thread woven into a Boho pattern. Not with a matching scarf tied around her head.

"Anarchy called and said you might need some company."

"He did?"

"He did." She regarded me with narrowed eyes and pursed lips. "He said you wouldn't leave."

"I can't." Winnie and Lark's children were in New York and London. They weren't here to sit and pray and hope. "Winnie's all alone."

"What do the doctors say?"

"Nothing, yet."

"Do you want some coffee?"

"Why does everyone keep asking me that?"

"Could be you have a slight problem with addiction, and

everyone wants to keep you happy."

"Me? Addiction? Don't be ridiculous."

"You talk to your coffee maker."

"I—" I couldn't deny it "—I do not."

Libba smirked. "If you don't want coffee, let's sit down."

She sank gracefully into one of the Naugahyde chairs and crossed her ankles.

Libba looked up at me expectantly.

With an annoyed huff, I sat.

"What happened?" she asked.

I told her everything.

"That's why you're carrying two handbags."

Winnie's Coach bucket bag was about the same size as my Gucci Jackie but three times heavier.

"She's still in ICU. She doesn't have a room yet." I eased the strap off my shoulder and rested the bag on the chair next to mine. "There was no place to put it."

"It looks heavy."

"It is."

"What does she have in there?"

"No idea."

"You haven't looked?"

I gaped at her. "Of course not."

Libba reached across me.

I slapped at her hand. "Stop that." The privacy of a woman's purse was sacrosanct. I locked my gaze on Libba's Kelly bag. "How would you like it if I dug through your handbag?"

"Pffft." Not her best comeback.

We sat in silence for all of thirty seconds. "Well—" Libba crossed her arms "—this is dull."

"It's a hospital not a Broadway show."

"Where are the good-looking doctors? Anarchy promised me handsome doctors."

"He did not."

"You don't know that. He could have."

Being contrary was Libba's way of distracting me. Sometimes it worked. Not today.

"He could have promised me—" Libba's jaw dropped.

I looked over my shoulder.

Libba was gawping at a fireman. His cheeks were blackened with soot. His tired gray t-shirt was torn at the collar. He had more muscles than I'd ever seen on a man.

Libba reached for my hand and whispered, "Yum."

"Stop it," I whispered back. "He probably has a friend in the ICU, and he's too young for you."

"Pfft."

The fireman smiled at us, his teeth a brilliant white against the darkness on his cheeks.

"Double yum." Libba sat straighter. She pulled her shoulders back. She smiled at him and whispered at me, "Do I look okay?"

My smile, not nearly as bright as Libba's, hid a whisper as well. "He's ten years younger than you."

Libba's eyes narrowed but her smile remained fixed. "That's not what I asked."

"You look gorgeous and he's still ten years younger than you."

"When did you get so conventional?"

Conventional? The smile dropped off my face—which was okay—my cheeks had begun to cramp anyway.

"Mrs. Russell?" A doctor stood in the doorway to the waiting room.

I stood. "Yes."

"A word?"

With a quelling look at Libba, I collected the two handbags and followed the doctor into the hallway. "How's Winnie?"

"Mrs. Flournoy's condition is serious."

"What can I do?" It was a stupid question.

"Mrs. Flournoy is most concerned about her cat."

I blinked. "Her cat?"

The doctor nodded. "We think if we tell her that you'll check on the cat and feed it, she might settle down."

"Of course. May I see her?"

"For just a minute. She's very weak."

I followed the doctor to Winnie's room.

She was a wisp on the hospital bed, as white as the sheets. She turned her head as I walked in.

I hurried to her side. A plethora of tubes prevented me from taking her hand. "Winnie."

Tears welled in her eyes. "Have you heard anything about Lark?"

"No." I glanced back at the doctor.

He shook his head. He had no updates.

"I'm sure he's doing okay. If he wasn't, I would have heard."

"You'll take care of Beezie?"

Beezie? "Who's Beezie?"

"My cat. He'll be worried when I don't come home."

I doubted that. My limited experience with cats had taught me they were more like stand-offish roommates than pets.

"Will you stop by the house in the morning and feed him?"

"Of course. Can I bring you anything? Your hairbrush or lipstick and powder or a fresh gown?"

She shook her head. "Just take care of Beezie. Feed him. Pet him."

I was more of a dog person and cats sensed that—they seldom were interested in letting me pet them. "What do I feed him?"

"There's 9 Lives in the kitchen. Tuna is his favorite."

"Okay."

"And Ellison—" her voice was weak "—hold him."

"You're sure you don't need anything?"

"Just take care of Beezie."

"Of course. You rest. I'll take care of the cat and come see you afterward."

"Thank you."

"You're welcome." I backed out of Winnie's room with its antiseptic smell and miles of tubes and returned to the waiting room with its brilliant smiles and miles of teeth. "Libba."

She turned her head slowly as if shifting her gaze away from the fireman required effort. "What?" Annoyance at my interruption lent a sharp edge to her voice.

"I'm going home."

"Okay." She leaned back in her chair as if she had no intention of moving. "You go ahead."

"I told Winnie I'd stop by her house in the morning. I thought you might come with me."

"Why?"

"To feed her cat."

She shook her head. "I don't like cats."

"I'm not wild about them either."

"I think cats are great," said the handsome fireman. "Except in trees."

Libba shifted her expression from stubborn mule to coquette. "Really, you like cats?"

"I do."

Libba rubbed her chin, reconsidering her anti-cat stance.

"You'll come?"

"Winnie asked you."

"She didn't know you were here."

"No one trusts me to feed their pets. I forget."

"Presumably you won't forget if you go with me."

"You can't feed a cat by yourself?"

"I don't want to go back there by myself."

Libba's expression softened. I'd won.

"I'll see you at nine."

"Nine?" Her brows lifted.

"Would eight o'clock be better?"

"I think it's nice how you're helping your friend," said the fireman.

"Nine." Libba scowled at me. She'd removed the scarf from her head while I was visiting Winnie and her dark hair framed her cheek bones in flattering waves. Oh-so casually, she pushed away a lock and shifted her gaze to the young man sitting next to her. "I'm always willing to help a friend."

He blinked. Rapidly. His Adam's apple bobbed. Oh dear Lord—the boy never stood a chance.

Libba leaned closer to him.

He leaned closer to her.

I blinked. All those muscles really were a bit overwhelming. Not to mention, he was handsome (if you liked fresh-faced youth). And he saved people for a living. If Libba wanted a young fireman in her life, who was I to judge? "I'll see you in the morning. Nine o'clock. Sharp."

The Libba who rode with me to Winnie's house looked as if she'd arrived home at five till nine. She still wore last night's dress and her hair had seen better days. "I didn't even know Winnie had a cat."

"I didn't either. It must be shy."

"How often do you feed it? And for how long? Until she's out of the hospital?"

"I'm sure she'll find someone to take care of the cat."

"She did. You."

"For today." I wasn't the best person to take care of Beezie. I knew nothing about cats—according to television commercials they were finicky. But Grace—Grace loved all animals. I could pay her to take care of Winnie's cat. "Tell me about him." No need to explain who I meant.

Libba sighed and leaned her head against the seat. She closed her eyes and a secret smile touched her lips. "His name is Jimmy."

Jimmy? Ten-year-olds were called Jimmy. Men who played tennis for a living were called Jimmy. Teamsters were called Jimmy. Responsible, dateable men—not so much.

"Don't say it," she snapped.

"Say what? I didn't say a word."

"I can hear you thinking."

How could I argue with that? We drove the rest of the way to

Winnie's in silence.

I parked in the driveway and thrust my hand into Winnie's purse, searching for keys. Pack of gum. Pack of cigarettes—those were a surprise. Pack of—it couldn't be. I pulled my hand out of the bag and stared at the item in my palm.

Why was Winnie carrying condoms? Not just condoms but King Cobra condoms manufactured by my brother-in-law in Ohio (twenty years since his marriage to my sister and Mother wasn't over the rubber shock).

Libba looked at the packet in my hand and snorted. "Winnie is more interesting than I thought."

I shuddered and returned the King Cobra to the depths of the purse. My fingers found the keys and closed around them. "Let's get this over with."

I held onto Libba's elbow as we climbed the front stairs (bricks and her high heels didn't mix).

She shook me off. "I'm fine."

"Suit yourself."

"He's really very intelligent."

That's why she liked Jimmy. His intelligence. I swallowed a sassy retort, jammed the key in the lock and turned it, pushing open the front door. I pulled on the key. It was stuck in the lock. I turned it again. Side to side. Finally the lock turned, and the door opened. "That's what attracted you? His intelligence?" Some retorts shouldn't be swallowed.

"Well, he's very smart." Libba brushed past me and marched into the house.

Yeah, right. Libba hadn't seen beyond that smile or those muscles. I was sure of it. The keys were stuck in the lock. I pulled on them. Nothing.

"*Eeeee!*" The scream was blood-curdling.

I abandoned the dangling keys and dashed into Winnie's dim foyer.

Libba was running in circles clutching her head. "*Eeeee!*"

"What's wrong?"

"*Eeeee*!" Libba ran another lap around the foyer. "*Get if off!*"

I flipped on the lights. There was a cat attached to Libba's head. And if the way its paws were sunk into her hair was any indication, the cat didn't plan on moving.

"*Yeow!*" The cat sounded every bit as unhappy as Libba.

"Stop running!"

"Get it off!" She didn't stop running.

"*Yeow!*"

"Stop! Running!"

She stopped. Dead in her tracks. The cat kept going—flying through the air like some four-legged UFO. It landed on a settee, arched its back, and hissed at us.

We were exceedingly lucky the animal was small, or we'd be dead. I'd never seen a cat so angry. There was no way—no way—I was holding or petting Beezie. Not if I wanted to live.

"*Yeow!*" Beezie wanted us out of his house.

That made two of us. I inched past him and hurried toward the kitchen.

Libba, who still clutched her head, followed me.

"Do you want some ice?" I asked.

"I want some scotch."

There were better ways to kill germs. "I bet they have a tube of antiseptic cream around here somewhere."

"To drink, Ellison."

Of course. How silly of me. I opened a cabinet and found plates. A second cabinet held glasses. I opened a louvred door and found a pantry. There I found umpteen tins of cat food. I found no scotch.

I emerged with a tin and opened a drawer, looking for a can opener.

"You're taking care of the cat first?"

"I'm hoping if I feed the cat, he'll let me sneak past him into the living room. I bet that's where they keep their liquor."

Seeing the sense in my plan, Libba opened a drawer. "That thing isn't a cat. It's the devil." She let go of the drawer handle and pointed a shaking finger at me. "The devil, I tell you. All I did was walk inside and it launched itself at my head."

"You probably scared it."

"Me? I scared the cat?" If looks could kill, the one Libba was giving me would send me to an early grave. "That demon took five years off my life."

Laughing would be bad. Maybe even unforgivable. I turned my back on my friend (my quivering lips would not be good for our friendship) and took a cereal bowl from the cabinet. Undoubtedly, Beezie had a bowl of his own—somewhere—but I wasn't in the mood to search for it. "Have you found the opener?"

Behind me, Libba slammed something onto the counter. "I could be with Jimmy right now. Instead, I'm here with you and the cat from hell."

"And I appreciate that." I opened the can and spooned Beezie's food into the bowl. I also wrinkled my nose—cat food *smelled.*

"Are you done?"

"Just a sec." I rinsed the can and threw it away. Then I put the bowl on the floor and cracked the door to the front hall. "Beezie, are you hungry?"

Beezie didn't answer.

Slowly, carefully, ready to repel any animal that leapt for my head, I tiptoed into the hall.

No Beezie. But there was an open front door.

"Hell!"

"What?" Libba dared to exit the kitchen.

"We left the front door open."

"And?"

"And the cat's not here."

"You say that as if it's a bad thing."

"I told Winnie I'd take care of that darned cat. Instead, you traumatized it. Now it might be roaming the neighborhood."

"I didn't want to come in the first place."

I closed the door. "Let's see if Beezie's inside."

"Find that beast? On purpose?"

"Get yourself a scotch first." I could be magnanimous. After all, I needed her help.

With her chin held high, Libba swanned into the living room.

I poked my head into the dining room. There was no place for a cat (or a demon) to hide.

"*Eeeee!*"

Seriously? Again?

I rushed into the hall.

Thunk!

I'd hit something solid. My arms cartwheeled, I crashed onto the floor, and all the air in my lungs escaped in one big *whoosh*.

A ski-mask wearing intruder leapt over me, threw open the front door, and ran.

I didn't move. I couldn't. My lungs needed air for me to move.

"Libba." My voice was barely a whisper. I drew a breath and choked. "Libba!"

There was no answer.

Oh dear Lord.

I rose to my hands and knees then pushed onto my feet. "Libba!" Louder now.

There was still no answer.

I stumbled into Winnie's living room. Books had been pulled off of shelves. The contents of a bow-front chest were scattered across the floor. Cushions had been ripped off the couch. And Libba? She sat in a chair cradling a bottle of Johnnie Walker Black.

She looked me dead in the eye and lifted the bottle to her lips.

Glug, glug.

"Are you hurt?"

She wiped her mouth with the back of her hand. "No."

Thank heavens.

Libba raised the bottle again.

"Don't drink it all!"

"Why not?"

"Because I need some."

My best friend in the world narrowed her eyes, tightened her hold on the bottle, and said, "Get your own."

Instead of raiding Lark's liquor cabinet, I called the police. "This is Ellison Russell calling. I stopped by my friend's house to feed her cat and there was a burglar here."

"Where are you, Mrs. Russell?"

I gave the woman the address.

"Was anything stolen?"

"I don't know."

"Was anyone hurt?"

I glanced at Libba. "No. We're fine. But the cat escaped."

The dispatcher had no response for that. "We'll have someone there in a few minutes."

"Thank you." I hung up the phone and turned to Libba. "They're on their way."

She and her bottle stood.

"Where are you going?"

"If you think I'm staying in this house for one more minute, you have another think coming."

With as much dignity as a woman clutching a bottle of scotch—one who's faced down a lunatic cat and a burglar—could muster, she staggered out of the living room, through the front door, and into the front lawn.

I looked around the shambles of the Flournoy's living room. What had the burglar been looking for?

"Ellison!" Libba's voice carried from the outside.

I gave up my perusal and hurried to the front door.

Libba pointed at the oak in the front yard. Specifically, she pointed to a branch in the oak. "I found the cat." Then she grinned. "You'd better call the fire department."

SEVEN

A marked police car parked in the driveway. A firetruck parked at the curb. The neighbors turned out for a view of the latest disaster to befall the Flournoys. Or maybe they were just watching Libba, who stood in the front lawn with her yellow dress and high heels, clutching the bottle of Johnnie (they were definitely on a first-name basis).

"You might want to leave the cat in the tree until you've gone through the house."

My suggestion to the uniformed police officer—I read his name badge—was met with a raised brow.

"I'm Ellison Russell."

"You're the homeowner?" Officer Stevens asked.

"No. I came to feed the cat."

"Have you notified the homeowner?"

"They're not available."

"Oh?"

I pointed at the tree. "The cat is not happy." An understatement. "Also—" I shifted my gaze to Libba, who was chatting with two strapping firefighters. Was that Jimmy? "—earlier this week, there was a murder at this house."

The police officer's gaze sharpened. "Here?"

He was grasping things quickly. I nodded. "The homeowner is in the hospital."

The officer tilted his head. "You just said there was a homicide."

"There was."

"Not the homeowner?" His grasp of the situation was tight. "Who died?"

"The yoga instructor."

Officer Stevens looked at the firemen with longing in his eyes, as if he regretted his choice to fight crime instead of fires. "Why is the homeowner in the hospital?"

"Someone tried to kill him."

"Here?"

"No."

"What about the lady of the house?"

"She's in the hospital as well."

"At her husband's side?"

"Not exactly."

"Another attempted murder?" His tone said he was humoring me. Kidding.

I wasn't in the mood to kid. "Maybe. They're running tests. Anarchy Jones is the lead investigator.

His shoulders—they stiffened. "I need to call this in."

"You're calling Detective Jones?"

His raised brows and thinned lips suggested mine was a stupid question.

"*Yeow!*" Beezie grabbed our attention. The cat was not pleased with the fireman at the base of his tree.

"Trust me, if anyone plans on searching the house, they don't want that cat in the house with them." On a good day, Beezie might be a pleasant cat—one who purred and curled in laps and lounged in the sun. But today was not a good day. And Beezie looked ready to flay the skin off the next human who touched him.

"*Yeow!*" Man-eating tigers sounded less vicious.

"Wait!" The police officer left me and hurried across the lawn to the fireman.

A discussion ensued, and the fireman removed the ladder. Then, the two men stared into the tree as if the force of their gazes could save the cat.

Not likely.

I left them to their gazing, slipped back inside the house, and used Winnie's guest bathroom. Metallic silver wallpaper featuring large, blue-stemmed, iridescent white flowers covered the walls. Pendant lights hung on either side of the sink (the sink, the toilet and the rug exactly matched the cerulean blue in the wallpaper). The tiny room looked like a gift box and smelled of patchouli.

When I emerged, I peeked into the upended living room. What had the burglar been looking for? Had he been in the house when we came in? Had he snuck through the front door when Libba and I were in the kitchen? Surely, we would have heard someone making this level of mess.

Was the burglar the same man who'd killed Marigold?

My blood chilled at the thought and I rubbed my hands against my arms.

If so, why had he come back? What had he missed on his first trip to Lark and Winnie's?

I took a tiny step into the living room. And then another tiny step. And then another.

"What are you doing?"

My heart leapt to my throat and when I turned my hands shook. "Just looking."

The uniformed police officer was not convinced. His arms were crossed. His brow was furrowed. His chin was low. "This is a crime scene, ma'am."

"Fine. I'll wait outside."

The man followed me out onto the front steps as if he thought I'd go wandering around the house if I wasn't supervised. The nerve! He was right.

With a sigh, I settled onto the steps and rested my elbows on my knees.

Libba was still talking to the firemen. Talking was a loose term—her eyelashes were fluttering a mile a minute, she'd fluffed her cat-ravaged hair, and her smile was set at high-noon. The entranced firemen—one of them was definitely Jimmy—had forgotten all about the animal in the tree.

Since we've been old enough to wear Mary Janes, Libba has been effortlessly fascinating the opposite sex.

With nothing better to do, I watched her weave her spell. More fluttering. More fluffing. More smiling. Lots of laughing.

She could have kept it going forever except for the arrival of Detective Peters. He had his usual quelling effect on everyone. Even Libba. Especially me. I forced my ears out of my shoulders and pushed myself to standing.

Peters cast Libba and the firemen a wet-blanket gaze then marched up to me. "One week, Mrs. Russell. I'd like to go one week without seeing you."

I eyed his hopelessly wrinkled raincoat, his funny little mustache, and the mean twist of his lips. "The feeling is mutual, Detective."

The corner of his right eye twitched. "What happened?"

I told him.

"A ski mask, you say? In April?"

"Yes."

"Why would he stay in the house when he could have snuck out when you and your—" he cast a dismissive glance at Libba "—friend were in the kitchen?"

"He hadn't found what he came for?"

"Which was?"

"How would I know?" Suspecting the break-ins and murders had something to do with a decades-old legal case and knowing were two entirely different things.

Detective Peters grunted at me.

"I came here to feed the cat."

"Sure you did."

"Winnie is in the hospital. She was worried about her cat."

Detective Peters' squinty eyes narrowed. "Right."

"If you don't believe me, you can ask."

He grunted. Again. Then he closed his fingers around the door handle. "Stay here."

It wasn't as if I wanted to go wandering around Winnie's house with a detective who was sure (always) I was guilty of something (that should land me in jail). I resumed my seat on the steps.

Libba and Jimmy resumed their flirting.

Officer Stevens seemed torn. After a few seconds, he followed Detective Peters into the house.

No doubt the officer would tell Peters I'd returned to the living room.

No doubt that revelation would stoke Peters' suspicions. He'd be outside asking me more questions soon. Prying questions. Suggestive questions. You're-guilty-as-sin questions.

If Libba was done drinking, I knew someone who wouldn't mind holding onto that bottle of Johnnie Walker. I pushed off the steps and crossed the lawn to the tree.

Beezie hissed a welcome.

Libba took one look at me and handed me the bottle. "Here."

"Thank you." Gratitude warmed my voice.

I lifted the bottle, parted my lips, and let liquid fire trickle down my throat.

That's what Mother saw when she parked her car at the curb—her youngest daughter standing in Winnie and Lark Flournoy's lawn, drinking Scotch from the bottle with a couple of firemen.

"Ellison Walford Russell, what on God's green earth are you doing?" Mother marched across the lawn with deadly intent.

I considered another sip but decided I wanted to live.

The firemen melted away.

Libba smoothed her dress and her hair.

The cat snickered.

Really.

"Mother—" I let the bottle hang loosely from my fingers and searched for the right words.

"Carol Barton just called me and told me you were sitting on Winnie's front steps with a full complement of police and firemen."

I tightened my grip on the scotch. "I have had a tough morning."

"I have too but you don't catch me in a front yard drinking scotch from a bottle."

She hadn't dealt with Detective Peters.

"What—" her steely gaze encompassed the fire truck, the police cars, their personnel, and the cat "—is going on here."

"I—" I glanced at Libba. If I was going down, she was coming with me "—*we* came over to feed Beezie." I pointed at the cat "And someone broke into Winnie and Lark's house."

"Where is Winnie?"

"The hospital."

"Surely she could leave Lark long enough to come home and feed the cat herself."

"No, Mother." I braced myself. "Winnie is in the hospital."

"Why?" The wind whipping around the north pole was warmer than Mother's voice.

"We were having a bite to eat together and—" I couldn't do it. I couldn't tell her.

"And?" Mother was waiting.

Why couldn't Beezie do something helpful—like jump on Libba's head? Why couldn't the firemen flex their muscles? Why couldn't Libba speak up?

"And?" Mother was still waiting.

Silence wasn't an option. I should have taken that extra slug of Johnnie Walker when I had the chance. "It's possible she was poisoned."

Mother looked at Libba. Libba nodded.

Mother looked at the cat. The cat swished its tail.

Mother looked at the firemen. The firemen tried to appear busy (they weren't fooling anyone reorganizing those hoses).

Mother looked at me and held out her hand.

Without a word, I gave her the scotch.

Detective Peters and the uniformed officer searched the whole house, but without Winnie or Lark present, determining if anything had been stolen was impossible.

A sour Peters (was there any other kind?) walked across the lawn, eyed the bottle of scotch, and pointed to the cat.

The firefighters stared up into the tree.

Beezie flexed his claws.

Jimmy retreated, donned a coat that looked as if it could repel a lion, and grabbed a ladder.

When the ladder was in place, Jimmy reached into his pocket and pulled out a sandwich bag.

"What's that?" asked Libba.

"I have some leftover chicken." He held up a bit of breast meat.

"How smart of you," Libba cooed.

The cat watched Jimmy climb the ladder. Libba did too.

The cat was focused on Jimmy's hands. Libba focused on an entirely different part of his anatomy.

"Here you go." Jimmy's voice was soothing, and he held out the chicken.

Beezie considered. His tail swished. His eyes darted. He darted.

The chicken disappeared.

"Just grab the damned animal." Mother was out of patience with the whole operation.

Jimmy ignored her and held out another bite. "You want some more?"

Beezie ate that too.

Jimmy held out a third bite—this time just out of Beezie's reach.

The cat crept forward, and the fireman snatched the feline off the branch.

"*Yeow!*"

Beezie clawed. Beezie scratched. Beezie hissed.

But Jimmy was made of stern stuff. He descended the ladder and hurried across the yard to the house.

A second firefighter opened the front door.

Jimmy, who was presumably coated in some non-scratch

chemical, let Beezie go.

The cat dashed into the house. They slammed the door behind him.

"Well done!" Libba clapped.

Detective Peters rolled his squinty little eyes.

Mother indicated her approval with a tiny nod of her head.

I wished I'd thought to get my handbag and keys out of the house before they put the cat in it.

"I'll tell Jones about this. If one of the Flournoys comes around, he can let them know what happened." Detective Peters lips curled into a sneer. "He'll have questions for you." He pulled up the collar of his disreputable raincoat and left us.

The uniformed officer followed.

That left me, Libba, Mother, and a couple of smitten firefighters.

"I'm sure you gentlemen have things to do." Mother didn't flick her fingers at them, but the sentiment was there.

Jimmy smiled at Libba. "I'll call you." He climbed onto his truck and drove away.

"Such nice men," said Libba.

Mother sighed—and not an I-agree-with-you sigh. No, the sound Mother made was more of a what-would-your-sainted-mother-say-if-she-could-see-you-now sigh. "He's hardly suitable."

"Suitable, shmootable." Johnnie Walker was talking. A fully sober Libba would never say anything so foolish—at least not to Mother's face.

Mother looked down her nose. "Shall we go?"

"My purse is inside." With the furious feline. "My keys."

Mother tsked. "Poor planning on your part."

Libba shook her head sadly. "That cat will rip you limb from limb."

"The cat is probably hiding." At least I hoped it was. More likely, the beast was lying in wait.

"Forget the purse," Libba insisted. "Aggie can let you in."

"I need my purse. I can't just leave my car here."

"Of course, you can.

"Libba—" my voice took on a wheedling note "—please, come with me."

"I'm not going in there." Libba crossed her arms.

Something like amusement flitted across Mother's face. "I'll be happy to take you home, Libba. Ellison can fetch a bag by herself."

Libba and I turned our heads and stared at her.

The color drained from Libba's face. "You don't need to do that, Mrs. Walford. Ellison can give me a ride."

"Not without her keys. Besides, it's no trouble." Mother took in the small handbag hanging from Libba's shoulder. "I see you were smart enough to keep your possessions with you. You can leave anytime."

"I'd hate for Ellison to face Beezie alone."

Had Mother done this on purpose? Libba had certainly changed her tune.

"Ellison has faced down killers, I'm sure she can handle a cat. Come along."

"But—"

Mother's brows lifted. Was that a *smile* tickling the very corner of her lips?

"I couldn't possibly leave Ellison." Libba sounded almost triumphant.

"You're certain?" Mother's gaze shifted to the scotch bottle in Libba's hand. "I'm happy to take you. Give the Johnnie Walker to Ellison and we'll be on our way."

"No. Ellison might need help with the cat."

"You're sure? Because I'm happy to give you a ride."

"I'm sure. Thanks for the offer." Libba hurried toward the front door, leaving me, Mother, and Johnnie on the lawn.

"She makes it almost too easy," said Mother.

I hadn't imagined that small smile. It graced Mother's face now.

"She hates being told what her mother—God rest her soul—would have to say about her behavior."

"You didn't mention her mother."

"But I would have mentioned her on the drive back. Libba knew it." Mother looked at the scotch. "No more drinking straight from the bottle, Ellison. And, if you must drink, please refrain from doing so in public."

"Of course."

"No more bodies."

"I'll do my best."

"You and Grace will join us for Sunday dinner?" It wasn't a question.

I nodded. "Okay."

Mother turned on the sensible heel of her sensible pump and returned to her car.

I followed Libba up to the house.

The front door was still unlocked, and we opened it slowly.

"Beezie?"

The cat didn't answer me.

"The coast is clear," I whispered.

We tiptoed through the foyer and into the kitchen where Beezie ate from his bowl full of smelly tuna. The cat stood between me and my purse.

He hissed at us.

We backed up.

"What now?" Libba demanded.

"We wait until he's done eating. When he leaves the kitchen, we'll grab my purse."

"What do we do in the meantime?" she whined.

"Retreat."

After Peters' passage, the living room was even more of a shamble. I returned the seriously dented bottle of Johnnie Walker to the liquor cabinet.

Libba bent, picked up a handful of papers, and put them on the writing desk in the corner. Then she collapsed on the couch. "How long does it take a cat to eat?"

"No idea. I'm a dog person. Max doesn't eat his food, he

inhales it."

Libba lifted her feet onto the coffee table and leaned her head against the sofa cushions. "What was that man looking for?"

We both considered the living room. Herend cats covered every surface. Cats arching. Cats wearing that slit-eyed expression they wear so well. Cats batting at imaginary bits of twine. A cat playing the fiddle. Cats stretching. Cats balancing on balls. Cats.

"I have no idea."

"Well—" Libba tilted her head until the tip of her chin pointed to the ceiling "—either Winnie or Lark has a deep, dark secret."

"You're probably right." Lark. It was Lark. And it probably had something to do with an old case.

"Whatever it is, it's big enough and bad enough to commit murder."

I made a noncommittal sound.

"We're stuck in here," said Libba.

"So?"

She lifted her head from the cushion. "We should look for it."

Obviously. "It?"

"The burglar was going through papers. Where would you hide papers?"

"In a safe."

We both eyed the paintings on the walls. Did their frames hide a safe?

"You look," said Libba. "I'm too tired."

"Yes, flirting with firemen is terribly draining."

She wrinkled her nose and stuck out her tongue. "It is."

I peeked behind every painting in the room and found nothing. "Any other ideas?"

Libba stretched her arms over her head and yawned. "Not a one." She swung her feet to the floor. "Let's check on that darned cat."

We tiptoed back to the kitchen where Beezie's empty bowl was the only sign of his presence.

I put Beezie's bowl in the dishwasher, grabbed my purse from the counter, and paused. Somewhere in this house there was a secret worth killing for. What was it? Could I find it?

Libba looked at me expectantly. “We’re not going to find it. Let’s go.”

“Fine.” I could always come back later.

EIGHT

I peeked into the small card room at the club—the one overlooking the golf course.

My friend Jinx, the queen of gossip, was already at the table playing solitaire. She looked up, spotted me, and an avid smile touched her lips. "Oh, good. You're here! How are you? I was going to call but—"

But she knew she'd see me at our weekly bridge game and hearing Winnie's story in person trumped hearing it sooner, but over the phone.

"—I knew your phone had to be ringing off the hook."

I took my seat at the table. The one facing the doorway.

"Were you really locked in the attic while Winnie's yoga instructor was murdered?"

"Yes."

"And did someone really run down Lark?"

"Yes. He's still hospitalized." I really ought to call and check on him.

"And someone poisoned Winnie?"

"Yes."

One-word answers would never satisfy Jinx. She'd dig and dig and dig. That I obviously didn't want to talk about Winnie made no never-mind. Where were Libba and Daisy? Late. As usual. The real question was why hadn't I had the foresight to be even later?

Jinx rested her arms on the table and leaned toward me. "Who slipped Winnie poison?"

"Why are you asking me?" How someone slipped Winnie poison remained a mystery. That a waitress who'd worked at the coffee shop for years would suddenly start poisoning her customers' soup stretched credulity. But doctors confirmed poor Winnie had definitely been poisoned. Who and how were questions I hadn't answered.

She leaned even closer. "Everyone says you find bodies, but I know the truth."

"The truth?" My voice was faint.

"You solve murders."

Not on purpose. I said as much.

"That just makes it more impressive."

"I hope you don't share that observation with anyone." Ever.

She reached across the table, caught my hand, and squeezed. "Of course not. I'll never forget what you did for me and George."

"It's not as if I investigate."

"Of course not. But if you were investigating—"

I glanced at the door. "If I were investigating—and I'm not—I'd ask you what you know about John Wilson."

"The name's not familiar."

"Brookhaven."

She wrinkled her nose. "So far away." Code for not-our-kind. Jinx and I lived in the Country Club District, where three golfing clubs and two tennis clubs ate up a healthy amount of prime real estate. Except for a downtown dining club with a breath-taking view of the river, those Country Club District clubs were where we held large committee meetings, teas, showers, annual meetings, cards, parties, and dinners. The clubs outside the district, while undoubtedly lovely, weren't *ours*. "But I'll let you know if I hear anything."

I squeezed her hand—a warning squeeze. "Jinx, be discreet."

"I always am."

That didn't deserve a response. Well, it did. Jinx was discreet like Cher was modest. But arguing with her wouldn't be helpful. Also, one of my least favorite people in the world stood in the doorway looking down the length of her exceedingly long nose. Prudence Davies' eyes glittered with malice. "I heard Grace got into trouble on Saturday night."

"You heard wrong."

"I heard she went to some bar named Skanky Sally's."

"Grace was with me on Saturday night."

"Sure she was." Prudence obviously didn't believe me.

I'd about had it with Prudence. And her long, nosy nose. And her long, horsey teeth. And her long, unspeakable history with my late husband—Prudence was one of the many women with whom Henry cheated. "As someone who claims to have loved Henry, I'd think you'd understand why Grace wanted to be with her family on her father's birthday."

Prudence's cheeks flushed—a deep scarlet and her lower jaw dropped. "Henry's birthday?"

Jinx tittered.

"Isn't this cozy?" Libba elbowed past Prudence, stopped, and stared. "What's wrong, Prudence? You're as red as a brick. Did Ellison one-up you? Again?"

Prudence snapped her mouth closed and glared at Libba with raw hatred in her eyes.

I searched for something to say—something to diffuse the situation—something to dissuade Prudence from ripping our eyes out with the tips of her manicured nails.

"Am I late?" Now Daisy slipped past Prudence. "What am I saying? Of course I'm late. I'm always late." She glanced back at the doorway. "That's a pretty skirt, Prudence."

Prudence wore a green wrap skirt embroidered with blue and yellow umbrellas.

"Perfect for April," Daisy continued.

With one last, hate-filled glare, Prudence turned on her heel and left.

"What?" Daisy, whose character included actual kindness, looked distressed. "What did I say?"

"It wasn't you," Libba assured her.

Daisy sat. "It must be awful to go through life feeling bitter and miserable."

"Not everyone can be Pollyanna," Jinx replied.

Daisy, who was more Pollyanna than Pollyanna, smiled as if she'd missed Jinx's barb, and spread the deck. "Shall we draw for the deal?"

Jinx drew the ace of spades.

"I guess we know who's dealing." Daisy picked up the second deck and shuffled.

Libba cut the cards for Jinx.

Jinx dealt. "Ellison, what was Prudence talking about? What's Skanky Sal's?"

"The name of the bar is Dirty Sally's—"

"Tomato. Tomahto," Jinx replied.

I wasn't about to quibble. "A couple of Grace's friends went there on Saturday night and listened to a band."

"Why was Prudence so—" Jinx searched for a word.

"So Prudence?" Which was to say bitter, miserable, and mean. "She's stirring up trouble because the girls aren't old enough to go to a bar." There was no way I was mentioning a single word about what happened to Debbie.

Libba yawned—her interest in teenage drama being nonexistent. "Are you recovered from this morning?"

"Are you?" I replied.

Libba touched her scalp.

"What happened this morning?" Jinx picked up her cards.

"Ellison is feeding Winnie's cat while she's in the hospital."

"That's kind of you." Daisy arranged her hand.

"This cat—" Libba touched her hair "—it's possessed by the devil."

"Well then it's doubly nice of you, Ellison." Daisy's smile was warm.

"I thought you didn't like cats." Jinx squinted at the cards fanned in her hand. "One club."

"I prefer dogs. Pass."

"One heart," said Daisy.

"I went with her. That cat is a menace." Libba ran the tip of her finger over the top edge of her cards. "One spade."

"Two hearts," said Jinx.

I held four spades and nine points. "Two spades."

"Beezie," said Libba. "That's the cat's name. I bet that's short for Beelzebub."

Daisy passed.

"Four spades." Libba snapped her cards closed and glanced across the table at me. "What kind of band plays at a place called Salty Sally's?"

"Dirty Sally's," I corrected.

"Pfft."

Jinx leaned back in her chair. "Pass." She played the ace of hearts.

"I have no idea about the band." I laid down the dummy hand. "I don't even know where Dirty Sally's is."

"Just be glad Grace wasn't there," said Jinx. "I wonder what kind of trouble the girls got into."

That I knew.

"What are you all talking about?" Daisy had missed Prudence's opening salvo. She pitched the two of hearts.

"Grace's friends snuck into a bar." Libba played the nine of hearts.

Daisy swept the trick. "And that's news? I figured you'd be talking about what happened to Winnie."

"Which part?" asked Libba. "The yoga instructor who was killed in her foyer, Lark being hit by a car, or the poisoning?"

Poor Winnie—she'd had a bad few days by any standards.

"I can't imagine Winnie's too upset about the yoga teacher," said Daisy.

We all stared at her.

"She was hanged off Winnie's banister." Libba's voice was unexpectedly gentle.

"I heard. So sad." A frown flitted across Daisy's pretty face.

"But she was sleeping with Lark."

Libba and Jinx gaped above the fan of cards in their hands.

I merely gaped. "What?"

Daisy nodded. "Lark was having an affair with that woman."

"How do you know?" Jinx demanded.

Daisy, who was looking less like Pollyanna with each passing second, glanced at the empty doorway then leaned forward. "Remember last month when Charlie sheared the hair off Annie's Barbies?" Daisy's many children were constantly at each other's throats.

"What does that have to do with Winnie?" asked Jinx.

"Annie was absolutely furious. She flushed about a hundred of Charlie's Hot Wheels down the toilet—one after the other."

"Sounds reasonable," said Libba.

"It was awful. Those cars backed up our plumbing all the way to the street. We had to spend two days in a hotel while the plumbers snaked all the pipes. We found a hotel with an indoor pool."

Jinx's nose twitched. She scented juicy gossip. "And while you were there, you saw Lark with Marigold?"

"How do you know it was Marigold?" I asked. To my knowledge, Daisy had never met Marigold.

"How many women named Marigold do you meet sitting poolside at a Holidome?"

None of us had an answer.

"She checked in early and came down to the pool." Daisy shook her head. "You should have seen the look on Lark's face when he recognized me."

"You never mentioned this before." Jinx sounded put out.

"I didn't think of it."

"You're kidding?" Jinx's tone said we should have heard this story weeks ago.

"I'm sorry. I didn't remember till now. The kids have been sick, and Ellison found a body—"

"Ellison is always finding bodies." Libba dispensed with that excuse.

"Well, she found a sister, too. We've had lots to talk about. Stuff far more interesting than Lark cheating on Winnie. And—" her chin rose and her slightly defiant gaze traveled the table "—I didn't realize she was Winnie's yoga instructor till I heard about her being found dead. If I'd known that part, I would have said something sooner."

Her disapproval of Daisy's failure to pass on gossip evident in the purse of her lips, Jinx slapped the three of hearts on the table.

A silent Libba played the high heart from the board—the ten.

With a quick, apologetic glance at her partner, Daisy played her king.

Libba trumped from her hand.

Daisy sighed. "I should have known."

"We all should have known," replied Jinx. She was not talking about Libba's singleton heart.

"Do you think Winnie knew?" I asked.

"She couldn't have." Libba sounded positive. "There's no way Winnie would continue to have Marigold teach yoga if she knew." She played the ace of spades.

I wasn't so sure. I'd known about Henry's other women, but I'd looked the other way. Confrontations and tears and divorce attorneys had held no appeal—not while Grace lived under our roof.

Jinx played the four of spades. "If you ask me, Winnie's lucky she was locked in the attic."

"Lucky?" Libba pulled the three of spades from the board. "Why would you say that?"

"Because she has the perfect alibi," Jinx replied.

Daisy played the six of spades. "It's all so sordid."

Murder often was.

Back at home, I glanced at the clock on the kitchen wall. Three o'clock. I shouldn't put off calling any longer—except, Max needed exercise.

"Want to go for a walk?" I asked him.

He lifted his head off his paws, stared out the window at the afternoon rain, huffed his displeasure, then returned his face to the cradle of his paws.

"Some help you are."

He opened one eye—and judged me harshly.

"Fine." I gathered my courage and a fresh cup of coffee, went to my desk in the family room, and dialed. "May I please speak to Mr. Blake?"

"May I say who's calling?"

"This is Ellison Russell. I'm his sister-in-law."

"Please hold, Mrs. Russell."

I listened to Marvin Gaye sing, "Let's Get It On." All in all, the perfect song for a condom manufacturer.

"Ellison!" Greg sounded happy to hear from me. "How are you? Found any bodies lately?" He was joking. Sort of.

"Yes."

"Who? Lawyer? Doctor? Crooked politician?" He thought I was joking.

"Yoga instructor."

He chuckled. "Seriously?"

"Seriously." I actually sounded serious. This call was not going as planned.

"You found your yoga instructor dead?"

"I didn't find her, but I did identify her."

"You're serious." Now he sounded contrite. "I'm sorry."

Everyone—especially me—would love it if I could go for a while (a long while) without tripping over dead people. "Thanks."

"What can I do for you?"

My mouth went dry and my heart beat too fast. "I'm calling about the gala."

"We have it on our calendar."

"I'm glad you're coming." I took a deep breath. "I'm calling about sponsorships."

"Oh?" He drew the word out.

"I know it's last minute, but I'm hoping you and Marjorie will consider—"

"Yes."

"Yes? You don't know what I'm asking for."

"It doesn't matter."

"I—" I couldn't do it. I couldn't take advantage of my brother-in-law. "Greg that's very nice of you, but—"

"How about twenty-five?"

"Twenty-five?" I squeaked.

"Fifty."

"Greg!"

"I have the money, Ellison. The sexual revolution has been good for business. Besides, I like the museum, and it will get Frances off your back."

"How did you know about that?"

"She's always riding you about something. The gala. The length of Grace's skirts. Bodies. Marjorie and I are aware you take the brunt of her focus. Let us do this."

"I'm overwhelmed."

"We're happy to do it.

"I can't thank you enough."

"I'll put a check in the mail this afternoon. Payable to the museum?"

"Yes, please. Thank you."

"Like I said, my pleasure. There is one thing—" here it came, a fifty-thousand-dollar favor "—I don't want to sit with your parents."

"That I can do."

"Great! I wish I could catch up—hear more about the yoga instructor—but I'm late for a meeting. We'll talk soon." He hung up.

I propped myself up on the edge of the desk and stared at the receiver in my hand. Fifty thousand dollars. I swallowed. It was an incredibly generous donation.

"Mom!" Grace's voice carried from the kitchen.

"In the family room."

She appeared in the doorway and stared at me. "What? What

happened?"

"Your uncle just made a generous donation to the gala."

She shrugged. "Cool."

Very cool. "How was your day?"

She slung her backpack onto the couch then sat down next to it. "Debbie's still not at school and her mom won't put our calls through. I was wondering if you'd call Mrs. Clayton and check on her."

"Of course. I've been meaning to talk to you about Debbie."

Her expression grew guarded.

"Did you know Debbie's plan to go to that bar?"

Grace glanced down at her feet. "Yes. She asked me to go—" she lifted her gaze "—but I said no. I knew you'd kill me. And Dad's birthday. But I keep thinking if I'd been there, I might have saved her."

Oh. Wow.

"I know you love your friends, but you can't watch out for them all the time."

"I know." Grace unzipped her bulging backpack and dug for something. "But I still feel guilty." Her shoulders stiffened. "A strange man raped her."

Where was the parenting handbook when I needed it? "Do you want to talk about it?"

"No." She dropped her backpack onto the floor. "I think she'd feel better if she could talk to her friends."

"Why can't she?"

"Her Mom screens her calls."

"I'll phone Marsha."

Grace grinned at me. "Maybe you could tell Mrs. Clayton about Jennifer? It might help if Debbie could talk to someone who understands what she's going through."

"I'll mention the offer." If Marsha didn't want Debbie talking to friends, talking to a stranger was probably not an option.

Grace bent over and pulled a denim-covered three-ring binder and a textbook out of her bag. "I'm going next door."

"Next door?"

She held up the book. "Jennifer said she'd help me study for my algebra test."

I nodded. "I think Aggie made some brownies. Take some with you."

"Okay." Grace and her incomprehensible algebra textbook disappeared into the kitchen.

Brnng, brnng.

I picked up the phone. "Hello."

"You forgot to mention John Wilson was murdered." Jinx sounded amused rather than annoyed.

"You're right. Sorry." I settled into my desk chair. "What did you find out?"

"He was a successful criminal defense attorney."

"And?"

"And, nothing. No one has a single harsh word to say about him."

"Well, someone didn't like him."

"The consensus is that someone he represented—a convicted criminal—got out of jail and got even."

"You'd think anyone getting out of jail would be angry with the prosecuting attorney."

"Exactly what I said. But, according to my sources, criminals think the prosecutor is doing his job. The defense attorney's job is to get them acquitted or, failing that, the best deal possible."

I was tempted to ask about John Wilson's cases—cases he'd had in Lark Flournoy's courtroom. My thoughts turned to the file in Henry's safe and I kept my lips sealed. Besides, I had someone else I could ask—someone who'd worked as an investigator for a law firm. "Thanks for asking around, Jinx. I appreciate it."

"You'll keep me posted?"

"Of course." Not on a bet.

"I'll talk to you later."

I hung up the phone and walked into the kitchen. "Aggie, I need your help."

Aggie looked up from a skillet on the stove. "Can it wait? I'm browning chicken." She cut her gaze to Max, who'd be only too happy to clean off the stove for her.

Max gazed back with wide, innocent eyes. He wasn't fooling anyone.

"This is more like a project."

Her gaze turned wary. "Oh?"

My projects had, on occasion, landed us in trouble.

But this project was different. This project involved nothing more dangerous than reading. "You know how to look up old law cases?"

She nodded. Slowly.

"I was hoping you could look up cases where Lark Flournoy was the judge and John Wilson was the attorney."

She frowned. "What year?"

"I don't know."

Her frown deepened. "Why?"

"John Wilson's death and the attack on Lark Flournoy might be related to a case."

She flipped the chicken breasts—the tops were a lovely golden brown. "Have you told Detective Jones?"

"No."

"Why not?"

"He might wonder why I think that."

"Why do you think that?"

I offered her an apologetic smile. "I can't tell you."

She glanced at the ceiling—not quite an eye roll. But close.

"Will you look? Please?"

"What should I look for?"

"I'm not sure." I leaned against the counter. "Look for any of Wilson's clients who received particularly harsh sentences."

"Revenge? Should I look for someone who was released from prison? Someone who'd go after the people responsible for locking him up."

"That's a good place to start."

NINE

I curled up on the couch in the family room and watched *Happy Days*. Sort of. The Cunninghams weren't holding my attention. My mind wandered. Who wanted Lark dead? Who had tried to kill Winnie?

Brnng, brnng.

I glared at the phone as if it were responsible for ringing.

"I'll get it!" Grace's voice carried from the second floor. It was probably just as well—most calls in the evening were for her. You'd think spending all day together would give teenage girls ample opportunity to talk. But, no. They spent hours on the phone at night.

"Mom!" Grace hollered. "It's for you."

With a sigh, I hauled myself off the couch and picked up the extension. "Hello."

"Tell your daughter not to yell when someone is on the line."

"Good evening, Mother."

"Did you talk to Gregory?"

"Yes."

"Well? Is he making a donation?"

"He is."

"How much?"

"Fifty thousand dollars."

There was no response.

I allowed myself a small smile. It wasn't often I struck Mother speechless over something positive. I glanced at my reflection in the window and gave myself a thumb up.

"You should have asked for seventy-five." There was the mother I knew.

"Too late now."

"I'm calling because I ran into Penny Hawkins on the Plaza today. She's Penny Sylvester now."

I hadn't seen Penny in years. She'd grown up on acreage in the southern reaches of the city, surrounded by horses and dogs and the sweet scent of fresh-cut hay. Her parents and mine were friends and I'd been a frequent weekend guest at the Hawkins' enormous stone farmhouse. "How is she?"

"Getting divorced." Mother tsked her disapproval. "I told her you'd call her tonight."

I hadn't seen Penny in years. The basis of our friendship had been our near identical ages and a love of horses. "Mother—"

"She's going through a rough time. Her husband wasn't faithful and since you have some experience with—"

"I'll call her."

"I have her number right here." Mother rattled off digits while I scrambled for a pen.

I located a pencil. "Would you repeat that, please?"

With a sigh—in a properly run house, there were pens and notepads positioned next to the phones—Mother gave me the number a second time.

I jotted it on an empty envelope.

"You might ask her about the gala."

"The gala?"

"She's getting a hefty divorce settlement."

"Are you kidding? I'm happy to call her, but I'm not asking her for money."

"We'll never get to a million dollars with that attitude."

"Then we won't get to a million dollars." I glanced at the TV. Richie and Potsie sat in a booth at Arnold's. "Mother, I don't want to argue. Not tonight. I'll call Penny and I'll talk to you soon. Good night." Gently, I hung up the phone.

Penny Hawkins—she'd been a quiet girl, more comfortable with horses than with people. Together we'd ridden horseback over much of southern Johnson County—an activity our older sisters deemed a colossal waste of time.

It hadn't been. We'd talked. And laughed. And had picnics.

Penny had been sweet and kind and funny.

I picked up the receiver and dialed.

"Hello."

"May I please speak with Penny?"

"This is she."

"Penny, this is Ellison Russell—Ellison Walford—calling."

"Ellison! How nice to hear from you. I saw your mother on the Plaza today."

"She told me."

"She's as formidable as ever."

No argument there. "How are you?"

"Fine." Her voice was bright. "I'm fine."

"I'd love to see you. Maybe we could get together for lunch or coffee or even dinner."

"I'd like that. I don't suppose you're free tomorrow?"

"Tomorrow?"

"I have a ten o'clock appointment with my lawyer—I'm sure your mother told you I'm getting divorced. Maybe we could grab a bite of lunch afterwards?"

"Where would you like to go?"

"Nabil's? At noon?"

"I'll see you there."

We hung up, and I returned to the couch and my program—Richie and Potsie were still in the booth.

"Mom?" Grace stood in the doorway. "Can we talk?"

"Of course." I stood, crossed to the television, and turned the dial to off. "What's up?"

"It's about Debbie."

I returned to the couch and patted the cushion next to mine. "What about her?"

Grace sat (flopped), crossed her arms, and stared at the blank television screen. “What happened to her is bothering me. Things like this aren’t supposed to happen to people we know.”

“It can happen to anyone.”

“I know. But—” she shook her head hard enough for her ponytail to whip from side to side. “Everyone’s saying she shouldn’t have gone to that bar.”

“She shouldn’t have. She’s not twenty-one. But what happened to Debbie isn’t her fault.”

“I know. In my mind—” Grace tapped her temple “—I know. But if she hadn’t gone to that bar, the rest of this wouldn’t have happened.”

“That doesn’t mean what happened to Debbie is her fault.”

Grace looked down at her hands.

“Blaming the victim isn’t fair, Grace. Being a woman—even a woman who makes a poor choice—isn’t an invitation for rape. The man who did this to Debbie is to blame.”

“You’re always telling me to be careful.”

“I am. There are bad people out there. People who commit murder. And rape. Bad things happen. I don’t want them to happen to you. Asking you to be mindful, to be safe, is just my way of protecting you as best I can. If something happened to you, I’d—” I didn’t know what I’d do, but it wouldn’t be good.

“I wish there was something I could do for Debbie.”

“Be there for her. And be her voice. Tell anyone who says anything ugly that what happened to Debbie wasn’t her fault.”

“Is that it?”

“Debbie needs support from her friends and family right now. Your being there for her will make a huge difference.”

“Thanks, Mom.” She leaned over and kissed me on the cheek. “I love you.”

“Love you too, honey.” I gathered her into my arms and held her close.

* * *

I paused just inside the entrance to Nabil's and closed my umbrella.

The maître d' stepped forward. "May I take your coat, Mrs. Russell?"

"Thank you." I handed over my damp raincoat and umbrella. "I'm meeting a friend."

"She's already seated." He handed my belongings off to a passing waiter and led me to our table.

The years had been kind to Penny. She looked young—too young for such sad eyes.

She stood as I approached the table, and we hugged.

"Ellison, you haven't changed a bit."

"I was thinking the same thing about you."

She resumed her seat. "Your mother told me you lost your husband."

I took the chair across from her. "Last summer."

"I'm sorry for your loss."

"Thank you. It's been especially hard on my daughter."

"How old is she?"

"Sixteen."

"Mine are twelve and nine."

"Girls?"

She nodded. "The divorce has been rough on them."

My favorite waiter appeared next to our table. "Good afternoon, Mrs. Russell. I'll be taking care of you today. What may I get you ladies to drink?"

I glanced out the window at the steady rain. "Hot tea with lemon, please."

"Oooh! That sounds good. I'll have the same."

"Have we decided on lunch?"

"Why don't you give us a few minutes?" I picked up the menu and glanced down. No reason why—I always had the grilled chicken breast in lemon-caper sauce, but maybe today would be the day I'd try something different.

"Of course." The waiter—Todd—left us.

I smiled at Penny. "Aside from the divorce, what's happening in your life?"

"The usual. I'm busy with the kids' school."

"Where are they?"

"Barton." Barton was the smaller, out-south equivalent to Suncrest, where Grace attended.

"How do they like it?"

"They love it but they're already looking forward to summer. After swim team is over, I promised them a month at a dude ranch in Wyoming."

"Where do they swim?"

"Brookhaven."

"Really?"

"It's close." She sounded slightly defensive.

"Did you know John Wilson?"

She nodded and touched her throat. "What a horrible way to die."

"What happened?"

She leaned forward and whispered, "He was murdered."

That I knew. "How?"

She leaned even closer. Her pearls brushed the tablecloth. "He was garroted."

"Oh dear Lord."

Penny nodded. "In his car."

"His car?"

"Apparently, he got into the driver's seat and someone was hiding in the back. They draped a piano wire around his neck and pulled until he was dead."

My hand rose to my neck and my stomach completed a somersault. "How awful."

Todd appeared with our tea. "Are we ready to order?"

"The shrimp creole." Apparently garroting wasn't affecting Penny's appetite.

"The usual, please."

"Of course." Todd made a note on his pad and shimmied off.

Penny watched him go. "Over the years, John represented some unsavory people. Everyone thinks one of his former clients killed him."

"Did he have a family?"

Penny's nose wrinkled as if she'd just smelled something rotten. "His current wife's name is Arlene. His children, from his first marriage, are grown."

"You don't like her?"

"She's a bit—" Penny stared at the white linen spread across our table "—brassy. I'm not sure how they got into Brookhaven."

"Oh?"

"Well, I am, but—" she squeezed lemon into her tea.

"But?"

"It's gossip."

"You can tell me."

"John represented one of the board member's sons. Got him cleared of all charges. This was years ago—I think anyone who's dealt with Arlene wishes the kid had ended up in jail. Enough about the Wilsons. Your mother tells me you're a famous artist. She's very proud of you."

I blinked. Mother, proud, and artist did not compute.

"I still have a drawer full of the sketches you did of our horses. Should I have them appraised?"

"Ellison—"

I looked up into Hunter Tafft's handsome face. "Hunter! What a surprise!" Why did I feel as if he'd caught me doing something wrong? I shifted my gaze back to the woman across from me. "Do you know my friend, Penny Sylvester?"

"Penny Hawkins." Penny, obviously taken with Hunter's perfect suit, silver hair, and successful aura, extended her hand and smiled. "I'm taking my name back."

"A pleasure." Hunter shook Penny's hand, and his eyes twinkled. "Have you known Ellison long?"

"All our lives."

"Penny's parents and mine are close. We spent a lot of time together as children but somehow lost touch. We're having a catch-up lunch."

"I'm sorry to interrupt." He returned his gaze to me. "I saw Aggie in my law library. Is there anything we need to discuss?" Besides me, Hunter was the only person in the world who knew about Henry's cache of files.

My stomach bypassed somersaults and plummeted. "I'll call you."

His eyes narrowed. If I hadn't been looking closely, I would have missed it. "I'll look forward to hearing from you. Soon. Nice meeting you, Penny."

Penny watched him walk away. "He seems nice."

"He is. Divorced three times, but very nice."

"Are the two of you—"

"I'm seeing someone else."

She rested her forearms on the table and leaned in. "Do tell."

Whap!

Max's paw hitting the mattress practically bounced me off the bed.

I opened one eye—one—and looked at the clock.

2:13.

"Go back to bed," I mumbled.

Whap!

"Max, go back to bed."

Max whined softly.

"Seriously?"

He whined louder.

"What did you eat?"

No answer. Whatever was responsible for this need to take a middle-of-the-night trip outside, Max wasn't telling.

I opened the other eye.

Experience told me Max wouldn't give up. There'd be more

whaps and whines and maybe a groan or two until I relented.

"Fine." I threw off the blanket and swung my feet to the floor. "You owe me."

Together we padded the length of the hallway.

I paused at the top of the stairs.

He nudged me. A hurry-up nudge.

"I'm going." I descended the stairs with Max at my heels. When we reached the bottom step, he surged past me and sat on his haunches next to the front door.

"Not on your life, buddy." Max would be off like a shot if I let him out front.

He huffed his displeasure and followed me to the backdoor, which opened onto a fenced yard.

I opened the door, and Max stepped outside, sniffed the air, and raced toward the fence that separated my property from Marshall and Jennifer's. He sailed over said fence like a hunter/jumper clearing a low-set crossrod.

Dammit.

I jammed my feet into the nearest footwear—Grace's rain boots—and followed Max into the night.

At least he hadn't jumped the fence into my other next-door neighbor's yard. Margaret Hamilton had shifted from active dislike of Max to ambivalence. Given that she rode a broom when the moon was full, I didn't want to move back to dislike.

"Max!" I whisper-yelled.

Wherever he was, he ignored me.

Double dammit.

I picked up the hem of my nightgown and trudged through the damp grass to the gate hidden by a blue spruce. Above me, the tattered remains of clouds played hide-and-seek with the stars. The air was damp and cool, and I wished I'd grabbed a coat.

"Max!"

No response.

I paused. Did I really want to wander my neighbor's backyard clad in a silk nightgown and yellow rain boots?

I did not.

With a sigh, I lifted the latch and trespassed. "Max!"

In May, when the weather warmed up, this backyard would be filled with peonies and flag irises and lilacs. Now, in the dark of an April morning, the yard looked barren and vaguely threatening.

Where was that dog?

A breeze rustled through the trees, drowning out the possibility of hearing Max's tags jangle.

I smelled smoke.

Smoke? A fire?

I clutched my nightgown, lifted my hem still higher, stepped over a boxwood hedge, and tiptoed into the yard.

Woof!

"Max!"

Woof, woof!

I slipped and slid (rubber boots and wet grass weren't great together) toward his bark.

The smell of smoke grew stronger.

I rounded the carriage house and stopped short. My jaw dropped.

Max's silver coat gleamed in the light cast by a fire burning in a metal drum. That same fire reflected off his bared teeth. A ridge of hair stood on his back.

Marshall glanced my way. "Can you call him off?"

"Of course. I'm so sorry. Max!"

Max ignored me.

All too aware of my sheer nightgown (I lowered the hem back to my ankles) and rain boots (I'd met Marshall once—a polite how-do-you-do—nothing to prepare us for this), I stepped into the light and grabbed Max's collar.

Marshall pulled at his own collar, one attached to a Giants sweatshirt. "I bet you're wondering what I'm doing."

"Now that you mention it—" as a rule my neighbors didn't burn things in the middle of the night.

"Those are letters from an old girlfriend." He motioned toward the drum. "Jennifer found them and insisted I get rid of them."

At two in the morning? In a fiery drum? "Really?"

"We had a big fight, and I thought a grand gesture might make things better."

Did the man think I'd just fallen off a turnip truck? Obviously, the letters were recent. No woman expected her husband to burn *old* letters in the middle of the night. By burning them, Marshall had ensured Jennifer couldn't fish them out of the trash.

Not that she'd do that, but the temptation—

Sometimes it was better not to know the details. Poor, Jennifer. I empathized. I knew all too well the pain and humiliation of a cheating spouse.

"I hope it works out." My tone was chilly. "I apologize for Max." I pulled on his collar.

My dog's feet remained firmly planted.

"C'mon, Max." I pulled harder.

Woof!

"Now!" I'd had enough of this. During the day, the situation would be awkward. In the middle of the night, clad in a nightgown and rain boots, the situation was intolerable.

The fire crackled.

I hauled on Max's collar.

Max reluctantly gave ground.

With a final glance at Jennifer's cheating husband, I took another step back. "Good night, Marshall."

"Good night."

Max and I tug-of-warred our way back to the fence (two steps my way, one step his).

"Bad dog."

My opinion didn't interest him.

We skirted the boxwood and passed through the gate.

When we touched my property, Max's resistance melted away. I let him go, and he trotted to the back door and waited for me with a bored expression on his doggy face. As if I was the one who'd inconvenienced him.

We entered the kitchen, and I locked the door behind me.

"It's a good thing you're cute," I told him.

He merely stared at the cabinet where we kept the biscuits.

"If you think you're getting a treat after what you just put me through—"

Max huffed and turned his back on me.

I climbed the stairs, kicked off Grace's boots, and climbed into bed.

But I couldn't sleep.

Was being faithful a thing of the past?

Then I thought of Anarchy. Would he ever cheat? Never.

TEN

Wearing last night's gown, an actual robe, and slippers on my feet, I stumbled into the kitchen and smiled at Mr. Coffee.

Ever-faithful, he greeted me with a sunny smile and a full pot of coffee. He could tell I'd had a rough night, and he didn't judge. Nor did he ask questions—not until I'd had at least one cup.

Grace didn't share his restraint. "Mom, have you seen my boots?" She crammed half a slice of toast in her mouth and pulled on her jacket. With the barely contained energy unique to teenagers leaving for school in the morning—a strange mix of what-will-happen-today excitement and what-if-there's-a-pop-quiz dread—she bounced on her toes.

"Your boots?"

"My rain boots." She pointed to the empty floor mat. "I left them right there."

"Your boots! They're in my room." I lifted Mr. Coffee's pot and poured heaven into a mug. "I wore them when I chased Max last night."

Aggie entered the kitchen carrying a basketful of laundry and cast a baleful look at the dog. "Where did he go?"

Max sighed in his sleep.

"Next door."

Grace, who'd been a whirlwind of movement—eating her breakfast, making her lunch, stuffing books into her backpack—froze. "Not Mrs. Hamilton's?" Her tone conveyed the direneness of that situation.

"Thankfully, no. He went to Marshall and Jennifer's." I refrained from telling her about Marshall's late-night bonfire. "Which reminds me, how did your math test go?"

Grace shoved a final book into her backpack and looked down at her feet. She wore rainbow socks. "I think I did really well." She glanced out the window at the dripping sky. "I need my boots."

"They're upstairs. We'll have to take Jennifer a thank you gift." My coffee cup was empty. How had that happened?

"More coffee?" asked Aggie.

I held out my mug.

"I need my boots," Grace repeated.

"Could you get them, honey?"

Grace rolled her eyes, muttered something about borrowing things without putting them back, and dashed up the backstairs.

In the silence of her absence, I took another large sip of coffee. "I ran into Hunter yesterday."

"That's what he told me. I saw him when he returned from lunch."

"Did you find anything?"

"When I told him what I was looking for, he assigned a paralegal to help me. We found eight cases. If the paralegal finds more, she'll let me know."

Grace exploded back into the kitchen, her outfit now complete with rain boots, and grabbed her backpack off the counter. "Gotta go. See you later." She flew out the backdoor and disappeared before I could say goodbye.

Max opened a single eye.

I leaned against the counter and drained my second cup of coffee.

"I brought my notes if you'd like to look at them."

"I would, but I'm going to grab a quick shower first." Maybe hot water would jump-start my brain—coffee wasn't getting the job done this morning.

Max, the cause of the fog in my brain, lifted his head off his paws and yawned.

Thirty minutes later, clean, slightly more awake, and clad in jeans and a sweater, I went searching for more coffee.

I pushed into the kitchen and stopped dead in my tracks.

Aggie and Hunter sat on stools at the paper covered kitchen island.

Hunter? What was he doing here? I reached for Mr. Coffee's pot. "Good morning."

"Good morning. I stopped on my way to the office with notes from more cases." Hunter nodded toward a manila folder labeled Wilson-Flournoy.

"Thank you." I gripped my mug so tightly my knuckles ached. "Any defendants who received horrible deals?"

"I'm not a criminal lawyer, but nothing stands out."

"We should go through them all." I settled onto the stool next to Hunter's and reached for a piece of paper. "Here's Carl Becker." I held up a sheet torn from a legal pad.

"What did he do?" Hunter asked.

I scanned Aggie's notes. "Armed robbery. Sentenced to ten years." I glanced at Hunter. "Does ten years for armed robbery sound right?"

"I'm sorry. I don't know."

"But you could find out?"

He nodded. "Of course."

Ding, dong.

"I'll get it." Aggie stepped into the hallway.

Hunter watched her go. When the hem of her kaftan disappeared, he inched closer to me and whispered, "Have you looked at Henry's file on Flournoy."

I nodded. "I didn't find anything particular. Maybe you should look."

"They're in the kitchen." Aggie's voice reached us before she did.

The door swung open.

Anarchy stood on the other side. Instantly, I became aware of how close I sat to Hunter, the papers spread across the island, and the folder with Lark Flournoy and John Wilson's name on it. I jumped up, hurried to Anarchy, and kissed him on the cheek. "Good morning." My voice was too bright. "Would you like coffee?"

"Please." He smiled at me, but when his gaze traveled to Hunter, wariness shaded his eyes. He jerked his chin. Once. "Tafft."

"Jones."

Anarchy's gaze moved to the island, to Aggie's stack of notes, and the clearly labeled folder. His brows lifted and the corner of his left eye twitched. "Ellison, a word?"

"Of course." I poured him a cup of coffee and led him into the family room. My steps were slow—as if an extra few seconds could mellow his mood.

He sat on the edge of the desk and wrapped his fingers around the mug. "Want to tell me what's going on?"

"What do you want to know?"

"Why are you looking at John Wilson and Lark Flournoy's cases?" A second unspoken question hung in the air—*what's Tafft doing in your kitchen?*

"I think Wilson's murder and the attempt on Lark's life are related."

"Why?" Twitch went the corner of his eye.

"I can't tell you."

Twitch, twitch.

"I'd like to tell you everything—" my voice took on a pleading edge "—but I can't."

"Because of Tafft?"

"Because of Henry."

He winced. "Have you done anything illegal?"

"Of course not." I spoke with a certainty I didn't feel. It was my sincere hope that by concealing Henry's crime, I wasn't committing one of my own. "It's nothing like that. Henry knew them both. I wondered if there was anything in their old cases that might lead to murder."

"Their old cases?"

"Yes. Cases where John Wilson represented defendants in

Lark's courtroom. They're public record." I sounded defensive.

"What have you found?"

"Nothing. Yet."

He closed his eyes.

What was he thinking?

I put my coffee mug down and laced my fingers.

What should I say?

Life would be much easier if men came with instruction manuals.

"You're not looking at current cases?"

"No. Should I be?"

"You shouldn't be looking at any."

"Is there a current case?"

Anarchy nodded—a creaky nod—as if it pained him to confirm it. "Have you ever heard of Tony Bilardo?"

"No. Who is he?"

"John Wilson represented him, and the Feds offered him a deal."

"A deal?"

"If Bilardo informed on the mafia, the Feds would place him in witness protection. No jail time."

"Now the lawyer's dead and the judge is in the hospital. Where's Bilardo?"

"In the wind. He jumped bail."

"What about Marigold and Winnie?"

"What about them?"

"Why kill Marigold? She was just the yoga instructor."

"Our working theory is that she was paid to give the mafia access to Flournoy's house."

"But why kill her?"

"No witnesses."

"Why poison Winnie?"

"We haven't figured that out yet." He took a sip of coffee. "You don't look convinced."

Because I knew about the blackmail. Not that I could tell

Anarchy. "Do you mind if I look at the old cases?"

"Not at all." With a sigh, Anarchy reached for his belt and removed his pager. The message on its tiny screen wasn't good. A furrow appeared between his brows. "May I use your phone?"

"Of course."

He picked up the receiver and dialed. "This is Jones."

His eyes narrowed, and his jaw firmed. "Got it. I'll head to the hospital now." He hung up.

"What's happened?"

He pinched the bridge of his nose. "Lark Flournoy died."

I stumbled backward until my legs touched the couch. "Dead?" That couldn't be right. "He was stable. They were cautiously optimistic."

"Internal injuries can be tricky."

"Poor Lark." I stared at Anarchy, at the plaid of his jacket, at the worried line of his brows.

"The man was a federal judge."

"Poor Winnie."

Anarchy shook his head as if I'd missed his point. "Do you have any idea the pressure there will be to find his killer?"

"A lot?" I didn't have an exact answer.

"So much pressure it will make your mother, on her pushiest day, look like a pussycat."

Oh dear. "What can I do?"

Anarchy looked back toward the kitchen and his lips thinned. He rubbed his palm against the back of his neck. "If you find anything poking through those old cases, let me know." He brushed a kiss across my lips, strode across the room, but stopped in the doorway. "Ellison?"

"Yes?"

"The information about Bilardo stays between us." He disappeared through the door.

I lingered for a moment—being in the kitchen with both Anarchy and Hunter wasn't my idea of a fun morning—then headed back for more coffee.

Seeing me, Aggie lifted the pot and raised her eyebrows.

I nodded gratefully.

Max yawned, and his stomach grumbled.

"Oh no." How could I have forgotten?

"What?" Aggie paused with the coffeepot above my mug.

"I forgot to feed the cat."

"What cat?" asked Hunter.

"Beezie."

Max growled deep in his throat.

Aggie, God bless her, poured.

Hunter tilted his head and waited for me to elaborate.

"Winnie's cat." Dread made me sigh. Guilt made me elaborate. "The last few times I've been at the Flournoys' something awful has happened. Maybe I forgot on purpose."

"What awful things?" he asked.

"The murder, and, when Libba and I went to feed Beezie, there was an intruder." I closed my eyes. "And as if that's not bad enough, the cat is possessed by a demon."

"A burglar?" Hunter skipped right over the demon part.

I nodded. "And a demon-cat. He landed on Libba's head, dug his claws into her scalp, and wouldn't let go." The image of Libba careening around Winnie's foyer with a cat affixed to her head would stay with me forever.

"I'm going with you."

"You don't need to do that." My objection was half-hearted at best. Truth was, I didn't want to go alone. And I had to go, the demon-cat was probably hungry.

"It sounds as if I do."

"It can't hurt," said Aggie.

"I suppose. But I hate to put you out."

"I insist." Hunter nodded once. The matter was closed. "Before we go, wasn't there something you wanted to show me?"

Right. Henry's file. "It's in the study."

We topped off our coffee mugs and walked down the hallway. "I didn't see much in the file," I told him. "It's more about a payment from John Wilson to Lark."

"Was there a year?"

"Honestly, I don't remember." Looking at Henry's files made me feel dirty. I'd washed everything but the broadest details from my mind.

Hunter sat in one of the club chairs across from Henry's desk and waited while I opened the safe.

"Here." I handed him the Flournoy file.

After a few minutes, Hunter looked up. "It looks as if Henry blackmailed Lark for years. We can get rid of the recent cases."

I should have thought of that—given Aggie better parameters, assuming we weren't wasting our time. If Anarchy was right about Bilardo, we were digging in the wrong place. If Anarchy was right, there was no point in digging at all.

Hunter returned his gaze to the file. "I don't find any mention of—wait a minute." He tapped his finger on the papers in his lap. "Wilson paid Lark $20,000 in June 1965."

"For what?"

Hunter's lips narrowed. "It doesn't say."

But Lark had done something worthy of blackmail. The more I thought about it, the more certain I was it was the reason he'd been killed.

"How did Henry know about the money? Did Lark deposit it?" My late husband owned a bank. It was possible he'd monitored large deposits.

Hunter looked up. "Nothing in here addresses an actual case—just that Wilson paid Flournoy. Maybe it was for something else. Maybe they didn't fix a case."

Henry—dead nearly a year—still making my life difficult.

Hunter tapped the papers against the chair's arm until the bottom edges were perfectly aligned, returned the pages to the envelope, and pushed the file across the desk toward me.

I simply stared at the envelope. "Why? We had more than enough." I knew the answer. For Henry, blackmail had been about control not money.

"I can't pretend to understand Henry. He had you and—" Hunter shook his head and a scowl darkened his features. He stood. Abruptly. "I have an appointment downtown in an hour. Shall I follow you to the Flournoys'?"

"Sure."

Beezie (half-cat, half-demon) hid from us, which was fine by me. I rinsed the empty bowl, put it in the dishwasher, found a clean bowl, and served up another can of cat food—chicken this time. Then I made sure Beezie had plenty of water.

I found Hunter in Lark's messy office. Being a crime scene (twice) hadn't done Winnie's house any favors—and Lark's office seemed to have taken the brunt of the chaos. Leather-bound books that should have lined shelves sat in heaps on the floor. Desk drawers hung open. Cushions leaned at drunken angles. Even the oak-paneled walls looked dusty.

Hunter stood next to the front window and looked out at the street. He turned when I entered. "What happened the morning the yoga teacher was killed?"

"Winnie converted the third-floor ballroom into a yoga studio. We were there for a class. Marigold locked us in."

"Why?"

"When it happened, I assumed she was robbing Winnie blind."

"But she wasn't."

"No. She was being murdered." I shuddered.

"I assume she let her killer into the house."

It was a safe assumption. "Libba and I arrived last. And I'm pretty sure Winnie locked the door behind us. But Gertie, the neighbor who found Marigold, entered through the front door. Marigold must have opened the door after she locked us upstairs. Maybe she and the killer were in cahoots."

Hunter's lips twitched. "Cahoots?"

"Maybe they planned on robbing the house together but disagreed. Then he killed her."

"And he just happened to have a rope?" Hunter destroyed my theory with a single question.

"If the goal was to kill Marigold, why do it here? Do you think it has something to do with the reason Henry was blackmailing Lark?"

Hunter shrugged. "It's possible." His tone gave my suggestion a million-to-one odds. "What do you know about Marigold?"

"She was young. She was pretty. And word at the bridge table is she was having an affair with Lark."

That caught Hunter's attention. "What else?"

Hunter knew what I knew.

Yeoooow.

"What was that?" Hunter asked.

"The demon cat." I leaned against the doorframe as Beezie's cry lingered.

"Is it injured?"

"He probably discovered I fed him chicken instead of tuna. Thank you for coming here with me."

"My pleasure."

My gaze traveled the topsy-turvy room. "I doubt that."

"I'm here whenever you need me." A pained look flashed across Hunter's face. "And, if you ever change your mind about Jones—"

Oh dear. "Don't wait for me, Hunter."

He chuckled. "Your telling me that means you're the type of woman who's worth waiting for."

ELEVEN

I drove to the hospital on autopilot. If anyone had asked me how I traveled from the Flournoys' to just north of the Plaza, I wouldn't have been able to tell them. Luckily, the car knew the way.

I'd thought Hunter understood. I was with Anarchy. That he still held out hope was troublesome. The last thing I wanted to do was cause him pain.

I walked the hospital's corridors in a fog, paused outside Winnie's door, and gathered my thoughts. Winnie had lost her husband. She needed a friend focused on her and not the specter of an almost relationship. I drew breath deep into my lungs and stepped into her room.

A young woman clad in a wrinkled dress sat at Winnie's bedside, her head was bent as if in prayer. She looked up and I recognized her—she had her mother's bone structure. Lois Flournoy rose from the Naugahyde recliner slowly—as if the effort required was almost too much for her—and nodded toward the hallway.

Winnie didn't move. Her eyes remained closed and her lips slightly parted.

Lois and I stepped out of Winnie's room, and she sized me up with red-rimmed eyes.

"I am sorry for your loss." I held out my hand. "You probably don't remember me. I'm Ellison Russell."

Lois' ice-cold fingers surrounded my hand. "Of course I remember you, Mrs. Russell. You're the painter."

"Please, call me Ellison." I glanced back at Winnie's room. "How's your mother?"

Her shoulders slumped. "They had to give her a sedative."

Poor Winnie. "When did you get in?"

"Early this morning. I drove to Washington and caught the first flight out." Lois was enrolled in law school at the University of Virginia. "I haven't even been to the house yet." She raked her fingers through hair that had definitely seen better days. "My brother can't get here until tomorrow. He's flying in from London."

"Did you get any sleep?" I knew the answer. Dark half-moons hung beneath Lois's eyes and her skin looked wan.

"No."

"I'm happy to sit with your mother if you'd like to go home and rest."

"Thank you, but I couldn't leave her."

"At least go and get yourself something to eat."

"You mean in the coffee shop where Mom was poisoned?"

"Or the cafeteria." I kept my tone mild.

"I'm sorry. That wasn't fair of me." She rubbed her palms over her cheeks. "Maybe I should get something to eat. I might be nicer. You're sure you don't mind sitting with Mom?"

"Not at all. Take your time."

"Thank you." Lois shuffled down the hall.

I stepped into Winnie's room. An array of spring flowers filled the window ledge—two bunches of daffodils, a potted hyacinth that smelled like heaven, and a mixed bouquet that probably came from the hospital gift shop downstairs. Three books waited for someone to crack their spines. The morning paper was folded to the crossword. Winnie snored softly.

I picked up the book on the top of the stack—*Helter Skelter*—I had quite enough death in my life without reading that. Winnie did, too. Who on earth had brought her a story about the Manson killings? I stuck the book on the bottom of the stack and picked up *The Moneychangers*. The inside cover promised a riveting tale of ambition and greed. I wasn't in the mood. I let the book fall to my lap.

"Ellison." Winnie's voice was barely a croak. She regarded me with tired eyes.

I reached out for her hand. "How are you?"

"Where's Lois?"

"I sent her to get something to eat."

Worry lines creased Winnie's forehead. "How's Beezie?"

"Beezie's fine. I stopped by your house this morning. Plenty of food. Plenty of water." That I hadn't actually seen the cat wasn't worth mentioning.

"Thank you." Winnie's eyes fluttered closed.

I tightened my grip on her hand. "I'm very sorry about Lark."

Winnie opened her eyes and stared at something over my right shoulder. "I worry. Beezie's not used to being alone. I begged Lois to check on him, but she won't leave me."

"Beezie's fine," I promised. Did Winnie not understand her husband was dead? "How are you?"

"Tired. I don't know why I'm so sleepy." The fingers of her free hand plucked at the blanket covering the bed.

"What can I do to help you?"

She opened her eyes. "Take care of Beezie. The kids don't like him. LJ says he's possessed."

LJ—Lark, Jr—was right. "Lois told me he'll arrive tomorrow."

Winnie's chin moved slightly—barely a nod. "London. So far away." LJ worked for some bank in England. "Lark was proud of him." Her eyes drifted shut. "The children will have to plan the funeral. I'm too tired."

"Winnie—"

"What?" She sounded far away. The sedative might reclaim her at any second.

"The other day, when you were poisoned, did anyone come up to the table after I left you?"

Her eyes opened, and there was a sharpness in their depths that had been missing when I talked about Lark. "They must have, but I don't remember."

"Did anyone get near your soup?"

"My soup?" Now she seemed confused.

"Yes."

"I didn't touch my soup."

"You didn't?"

Her face crinkled with distaste. "I should have asked the waitress whether it was broth or cream-based. I don't like cream-based soups." She shook her head. "The waitress should have mentioned the cream before she brought it."

If Winnie hadn't touched her soup, how had she been poisoned? We'd both drank the coffee.

"I wasn't hungry anyway." She was drifting again.

"Did you put anything in your coffee?"

"My usual. Cream and Sweet'N Low."

I thought back to our table in the coffee shop. I remembered a paper napkins dispenser, salt and pepper shakers, a spouted glass jar with a metal lid for sugar, and a ramekin filled with melting ice and individual creamers. "There wasn't any Sweet'N Low on the table."

"There wasn't? Then I must have taken some from my purse. I always carry a few packets just in case." Winnie's eyes shut, and she sighed as if the effort of talking had wrung her out.

"Winnie?" I spoke softly.

She didn't respond.

"Winnie?"

She was asleep, and I couldn't exactly wake her up—no matter how badly I wanted to—the woman had lost her husband. Sleeping was probably her only escape from grief.

Except Winnie hadn't seemed remotely sad. I sat back in the chair and thought. Had someone poisoned Winnie's sweetener? Had anyone checked the other packets of Sweet'N Low in her purse? I glanced at the woman in the bed—the one more concerned with her cat than her dead husband, the dead husband who just happened to be having an affair with the woman murdered in the foyer. There was another possibility. Had Winnie made herself sick? And if so, why?

I knew exactly where to find Winnie's purse. I could have other packets of Sweet'N Low tested.

Thunk.

The sound came from outside Winnie's door.

"Lois?"

No one answered.

I rose from the recliner and crossed to the doorway.

Someone had dropped a near empty cup of coffee. I glanced down the hallway and spotted a man walking away.

He'd created a falling hazard and hadn't even tried to clean it up.

"Excuse me," I called.

He kept walking.

"Excuse me!"

He had to have heard me—the nurses manning the station turned their heads and looked at me—but he didn't stop.

Had he been lurking outside Winnie's door? Who was he?

I stepped all the way into the hallway but stopped. I'd promised to stay with Winnie.

"Is there a problem, Mrs. Russell?" One of the nurses from the station stood in front of me.

"Someone dropped their coffee."

"The man who was waiting to see you?"

"Waiting to see me?"

"He didn't want to disturb your visit with Mrs. Flournoy, so he waited in the hall."

"What did he look like?"

"Tall with brown hair and brown eyes."

That description applied to about half the men I knew. "Old or young?"

"I'm sorry, I didn't pay close enough attention to be able to tell you."

"Well, whoever he was, he's gone now."

She nodded and glanced down at the puddle of coffee. "We

called the janitor. He's on his way."

When Lois returned, she hugged me. "Thank you, I feel much better."

"I'm glad. She woke up for a few minutes."

Lois frowned. "What did she say?"

"She's worried about Beezie."

"That cat." She shook her head. "I think she cares more about that cat than she did about Dad."

Given my conversation with Winnie, Lois had a point.

"The cat is named after the devil. Beelzebub. If you ask me, the name fits."

I wasn't about to argue that. "Will you call me if I can do anything to help?"

"I will. I promise. Thank you."

I drove to the club with my mind on pink packets and one eye focused on the rearview mirror. Who was the man outside Winnie's door? Was he following me?

If he was, I didn't see him.

No surprise, Libba wasn't there yet. In the history of our friendship, she'd never been early. I sat at a table by the window and looked out at the sodden golf course. I couldn't remember such a rainy April.

"What's the latest?" Libba, who wore a new Thea Porter dress, slid into the chair across from mine.

"I called you here for a working lunch. We are not going to gossip."

Libba frowned. "A working lunch?"

"Yes. For the gala."

Libba was the gala's food and beverage chairman. A job which she'd completed in a matter of minutes. "There's no work left."

"Unfortunately, you're wrong. Mother insists we make a million dollars. I'm doing my best to raise more money, but I can only raise so much. We need to cut expenses."

"You're not serious?" She caught a waiter's eye and beckoned him over. "I need a martini. Right away."

He nodded. "Anything for you. Mrs. Russell?"

"Iced tea, please."

As soon as his back was turned, Libba leaned in. "Have you lost your mind?" A million dollars?"

"That's what the other cities are raising."

"Those cities are on the coasts."

"I pointed that out to Mother. She doesn't care."

"We can't cut corners."

"I know. I'm not suggesting you replace wine with cheap beer, but I am asking you to look at the cost of the menu and liquor and find a few less expensive options."

Libba's mulish expression didn't bode well for my plan.

"I'm talking to the ambiance committee as well." The chairman of that committee was going to have to overcome her aversion to carnations. Carnations were cheap. Carnations were colorful. And carnations made great filler for more expensive flowers. I reckoned we could save thousands.

"You could tell Frances no."

"No one has ever done that and lived to tell. If I tried that, and she didn't kill me outright, what life I had left wouldn't be worth living."

"I like the menu the way it is."

"What about serving pork dumplings instead of shrimp." It was a reasonable suggestion.

"The cost is in the labor not the fillings." How did Libba know that?

"Did you just make that up?"

She flushed. As good as an admission.

I reached across the table and grabbed her hand. "I need your help with this. Please."

"You're lucky I like you." She leaned back in her chair and sighed—a sigh that reached all the way to the tips of her Ferragamos. "And you're lucky Jimmy has left me in a very good mood."

"Jimmy? Again?"

She raised her brows. "You sound surprised."

"He's so...young."

"Young is good." She licked her lips. "Lots of stamina and enthusiasm. And—" her eyes narrowed "—it's not as if I'm old. How are things with Anarchy?"

"Fine."

"Fine?" She gave me an appraising look, laced her fingers together, and rested her chin on her hands. "I'd have thought he'd be better than fine."

Heat warmed my cheeks. She meant sex. Libba always meant sex. "We haven't."

"You're kidding!" Surprise had her sitting ramrod straight. "What are you waiting for?" She sounded absolutely scandalized.

I shifted in my chair. Where was the waiter with that iced tea? "There's no hurry."

She stared at me as if she couldn't believe the words coming out of my mouth. "You really haven't? Why not?"

"How is this any of your business?"

She ignored my question, and, with her left pointer finger, she ticked off fingers on her right hand. "April, March, February, January, December—"

"What are you doing?"

"Counting the months since Henry died."

"Why?" And why had I asked? I wasn't going to like the answer—I could tell from the gleam in her eyes.

"Because I'm going to add that number to the eighteen months you didn't let Henry near you." She screwed up her face. "It's more than two years." She gripped the edge of the table. "You haven't had sex in more than two years!"

The red-faced waiter put Libba's martini on the table. With his gaze locked on the carpet, he served my iced tea, and scurried away.

Libba was unconcerned with his embarrassment—or mine. She shook her head. "Two years. It's like you're a virgin all over again."

"Would you please lower your voice?"

Marilyn Barker and Myrtle Bridewell, who were seated at the table next to ours, were staring at us with matching expressions of horror on their faces.

Libba glanced at Myrtle's pinched face and leaned forward. "You've known him for ten months, what are you waiting for?"

"We're supposed to be talking about the menu for the gala not my sex life."

"You don't have a sex life."

Marilyn Barker choked on a bite of chicken salad.

Libba rubbed her chin. "Let's make a deal, if you tell me why you haven't been to bed with Anarchy, I'll reduce the cost per person at the gala by fifteen percent."

"Are you kidding?

"I am not. Seriously, Ellison. The man's gorgeous and he's crazy about you. What's stopping you?"

She'd hector me till I answered. "A twenty-five percent reduction in cost."

"Twenty." She held out her hand.

I shook it then leaned close and whispered my deepest fear. "Suppose he thinks I'm boring?"

She leaned back and stared at me. "Are you?"

"Henry thought so."

"Oh, please." She rolled her eyes. "Henry was into kink. The man liked whips and handcuffs, of course he grew bored with you. You're one hundred percent vanilla."

Libba wasn't making me feel any better and Myrtle Bridewell looked as if she might faint. Or have a stroke. Maybe both. And I finally understood the expression *pursed lips*—the fine lines surrounding Myrtle's lips were as puckered as the mouth of a tightly closed drawstring bag.

Libba reclaimed my attention. "You can't take Henry's tastes personally."

"I was his wife. It felt pretty personal to me." I stared down at the white linen covering the table and said nothing more. I'd already said far more than I should.

Libba dismissed my concerns with a wave of her hand. "Henry would have grown bored with me—and I can promise you, I'm not boring."

That I believed.

"Don't let your past with Henry determine your future."

"That's unexpectedly wise."

"I have my moments." She took a sip of her martini. "The writing is on the wall. Everyone can see it except for Frances."

"See what?"

"You and Anarchy were meant to be." She took another larger sip. "Although, I have to admit. It worries me sometimes."

"What worries you?"

"Have you ever wondered how a man as handsome as Anarchy is still single at forty? There has to be a story there."

I stared at her. "Really? That's what keeps you up at night?"

"I wouldn't say I lose sleep, but it's a valid question."

"I find bodies like most people find change in parking lots—" I glanced at Marilyn and Myrtle (they were both eavesdropping and wore matching appalled expressions) and lowered my voice "—and you're worried about Anarchy's past? I don't know. And I don't care."

"Wow."

I waited for her to say more.

She didn't.

"What do you mean *wow*?"

"You're in love with Anarchy Jones."

I'd never fallen from a tall building or jumped out of an airplane, so I didn't know for sure, but I bet the flash of blinding panic followed by acceptance was similar to what I felt. I reached for my tea with a shaking hand and lifted my chin. "What if I am?"

"You're not the casual-relationship type. You will never have a Jimmy."

"What are you talking about Libba?" Couldn't we go back to arguing about dumplings?

"I'm talking about Jimmy. Jimmy and I aren't going anywhere.

We don't have a future. We're in it for the here and now. You don't want Anarchy till next week or next month, you want him for the next fifty years."

She was right. Where was that waiter? I needed a martini. I reached across the table and took Libba's.

"What will Frances say?"

I looked at the glass in my hand. "If I had this conversation with Frances, she'd need three martinis."

"She'd need three pitchers." Libba wrapped her hand around my wrist. "That worry of mine—"

"Yes?"

"Anarchy's past may not worry you, but it will concern your parents and Grace. Maybe you should ask him about it."

"Ask him what?"

"Why he's single, why he's in Kansas City, and how long he intends to stay."

TWELVE

The smell of something mouth-wateringly delicious hung in the air and I followed my nose to the kitchen.

Max watched Aggie with rapt attention.

She ignored him and settled a casserole on a hot-pan holder she'd put on the counter.

"What is that?" I asked. "It smells divine."

"Chicken and broccoli casserole. I'm making two. I thought you could take this one to your new neighbor. Her husband might be hungry."

Woof! Max was hungry.

"You're always hungry," I replied. "What a lovely idea, thank you. I'll take the casserole as a thank you for helping Grace with her math.

Aggie slipped off her oven mitts. "It should cool for a while. I can write out the heating instructions for both of you."

"Is tonight the night you're going to the theater with Mac?"

She nodded, and the secret smile she reserved for thoughts of the new man in her life lightened her features. "I'm trying to decide what to wear. I have a new teal green kaftan."

"I bet that looks nice with your hair." Aggie possessed a head full of sproingy red curls.

"Or I could wear one of the outfits you picked out for me." In February, Aggie needed to pass for a lady-who-lunched. I'd taken her to Swanson's, my favorite store, and bought her all the right clothes.

"My advice is to wear what's most comfortable."

"Then I'll wear the kaftan." No surprise there. Aggie loved her kaftans, and she wore them well. The one she had on now—navy with a fringe of lime green pom-poms—was also new. The trip to Swanson's hadn't changed her signature style one bit.

"How long till that cools?" I nodded toward the casserole.

"An hour."

"I might take advantage of the break in the rain and take Max running.

Max, hearing his name and "run" in the same sentence, shifted his gaze away from the chicken-filled Pyrex.

"Do you want to go for a run?"

He grinned his answer and wagged his stubby tail.

Ten minutes later, we jogged down the sidewalk.

"Loose Park?" I asked.

His pace increased.

"Okay but behave around the pond."

He made no promises.

It didn't take long for the even rhythm of our footsteps on the pavement to clear my mind. There were three people dead. Had the same person killed all three? A hanging, a hit-and-run, and a garroting. Didn't killers choose one method and stick with it? It was beyond the realm of credulity to imagine three different killers; I was left with one killer and three methods.

Why those people?

There were obvious connections between John Wilson and Lark—their past and the Bilardo case. And Lark and Marigold had been having an affair. But was there a connection between John and Marigold?

We approached the pond, and I tightened my grip on Max's leash.

Max ignored the ducks on the water. He ignored the squirrel primed to jump into the redbud tree. He even ignored the rabbit frozen next to a forsythia bush. We jogged past the pond without incident.

I breathed easier. The park, on a wet weekday afternoon, was almost deserted. Just me, Max, and a man running about a hundred feet behind us.

Ugh. Men who wore hooded sweatshirts made me nervous. Who or what were they hiding from?

Max and I picked up the pace, rounded the northern edge of the park, and turned west.

I glanced behind us. The man had sped up, too.

Worry gave me wings. We ran faster.

One would think a near-hundred-pound dog would be a deterrent. Not the man behind us. He kept pace with us.

The first raindrop hit me square on the nose.

Despite his fascination with the pond, Max had an aversion to getting wet. He ran still faster.

I let him.

We flew.

The last I saw of the man, he was bent over with his arms clutched across his belly. He gasped for air. He hadn't been following me. He'd been setting his pace. Now he was spent.

By the time Max and I burst through the back door, we were both soaked. We shivered with cold.

Aggie waited for us with a stack of towels and a stern look for Max. "Don't you even think about shaking water all over my kitchen."

Max, who'd probably intended to do just that, donned a put-upon expression and allowed me to towel him dry.

When I was done, Aggie collected the wet towels and deposited them in the washing machine. "I'll wait to run it until you're done with your shower." A nice way of telling me I looked like a drowned rat.

Drowned rat or no, the thought of being doused with hot water was heaven. "I'll be quick. If I don't see you before you leave, have a wonderful time."

She gave me another glimpse of the secret smile.

Thirty minutes later, I was washed, dried, dressed, and ready to take the casserole to Jennifer's. The rain had even stopped.

I grabbed the Pyrex and the instructions and headed across the lawn to Jennifer and Marshall's.

Jennifer opened the door wearing a pair of faded jeans and one of Marshall's shirts. "Ellison, what a surprise." She smiled at me as if pleasant surprises were rare. "Come in."

"I can't stay." I stepped into the foyer. "But Aggie made this for you as a thank you for helping Grace."

"A thank you?"

"Grace did well on her math test."

Jennifer accepted the casserole. "She's a bright girl."

"Math trips her up."

"Sometimes it's not the material, it's how the material is presented."

"Whatever it is, we're grateful."

"Are you sure you can't stay for a few minutes? With Marshall working so much, I feel as if I spend most of my time alone."

"I don't want to bother you."

"Bother me?" She shook her head. "Are you kidding? I'd be grateful for your company."

"In that case, I'd love to stay for a few minutes."

"I'll put this in the fridge." She balanced the casserole on one arm and waved me toward the living room. "I'll be right back."

Jennifer's Bohemian living room with its squashy couches covered in deep purple velvet, Flokati rugs, silk pillows in shades of sienna and crimson, and turquoise-hued Chinese garden stools was a near overwhelming mixture of color and texture. I liked it. I wandered over to the sofa table and looked at the display of framed photographs. Jennifer and Marshall on their wedding day—she was barefoot with daisies braided in her hair. Jennifer and a woman, who looked just like her only twenty-five years older, with the Golden Gate Bridge in the background. And, in a mother-of-pearl frame, a very young Marshall and a cluster of people who had to be his family—a sister, a brother, and parents. I picked up the frame and looked at them closely. They were on the Plaza.

Jennifer entered holding a wine bottle and two glasses.

I held up the photograph. "I was looking at your pictures. Where was this one of Marshall taken?"

"The Plaza."

"I thought he was from California."

"His family lives there now, but when he was younger, his family lived here. Marshall always liked Kansas City. It's one of the reasons he agreed to a job here."

"What is it Marshall does?"

"He works for a pharmaceutical company."

"Is he a chemist?"

"A salesman. He visits with doctors and gets them to write prescriptions for his company's drugs."

A prosaic job for a man who burned love letters at three in the morning. "Really?"

Apparently, she heard the surprise in my voice because she nodded. "When we first met, I told him he didn't strike me as the salesman type. He's too quiet."

"How did you meet?"

"His sister introduced us." A shadow passed over her face.

"It must be hard to live so far from family." Or it might be heaven. Mother couldn't drop in whenever she felt like it, gossip from the club—after today's lunch there would be gossip—would never reach her ears, and there would be no command-performance Sunday dinners.

Jennifer poured the wine. "Marshall's sister passed away recently. I think he wanted a fresh start."

"She was so young."

Jennifer handed me a glass. "She struggled."

Struggled? What did that mean? "Oh?"

"Drugs." Jennifer sipped. "We all have our demons."

Did that mean Marshall's sister overdosed? On purpose? "How terrible for her family."

"Marshall may never recover from the loss." She glanced around the colorful living room. "This conversation has taken a turn for the dark." She sipped again. "How's Grace's friend?"

"This is awful, but I don't know. I have a friend who lost her husband. She's in the hospital and between visiting her, taking care of her cat, and a gala I'm planning, I haven't called Debbie's mother."

"I'm sure you'll talk to her soon. When you do, please let her know if Debbie needs anyone to talk to, I'm available."

"I'll tell her." I scanned the room, looking for another topic. "Is that a Stella?" I pointed to a painting filled with bright colors and geometric lines.

"It is."

"And is that a Warhol?" I nodded toward a pen and ink drawing of a cat with a Napoleonic hat.

"Yes."

My gaze traveled the walls and stopped on a lithograph of a bride and groom trailed by exuberant flowers. "A Chagall?"

"A wedding gift from my parents."

The art on Jennifer's walls was worth as much as her house.

"You're a collector?" Marshall and Jennifer weren't yet thirty.

"I love art."

It was official, Jennifer was the perfect next-door neighbor.

I returned home and found the house strangely quiet. Aggie had left for her date. Grace was babysitting. And, after our sprint through the pouring rain, Max slept.

Per Aggie's instructions, I preheated the oven to three-fifty.

While the oven warmed, I picked up the phone and called Marsha Clayton.

The phone rang three times. "Hello."

"Marsha, it's Ellison calling. How are you?"

"Surviving." Her voice was tired, and I pictured her slumped in a chair with the receiver pressed against her ear.

"How's Debbie?"

She offered me silence as an answer.

"My next-door neighbor went through a similar experience. She's young and pretty, and Debbie might relate to her. Jennifer asked me to tell you she'd be happy to talk to Debbie."

"I don't know."

"Is she getting any counseling?"

"We all are. I know—" Marsha was silent for long seconds "—I know this awful thing happened to Debbie, but it feels as if it happened to me, too. I'm angry. All the time."

"I would be, too."

"You'd be angry with the man, not Grace. I'm furious—furious—with Debbie for putting herself in a situation where this could happen."

I knew precisely how I'd feel if something similar happened to Grace. I'd question every parenting decision I'd ever made. "You're angry at yourself."

"You get it."

"I'd be feeling the same things."

Again, Marsha was quiet for long seconds. "Do you like your neighbor?"

"I do. A lot."

"I'll mention her to Debbie."

And I'd have Grace mention her. Debbie had been through a hellish experience—she needed all the help and support she could get.

"Ellison, the timer on my oven just dinged. I have to go. Thank you for calling. And for understanding." All things considered, Marsha was coping remarkably well.

"Please call me if you need anything."

"I will," she promised. "Thank you."

I returned the receiver to its cradle and fingered the stretched-out cord. If some man hurt Grace the way Debbie had been hurt, my anger would set the whole city ablaze.

I glanced at the oven. Three-fifty. I put the casserole in and set the timer.

Ding dong.

Max raised a single eyelid but didn't get up.

"Lazy." I walked to the front door without him.

Anarchy stood on my front stoop. "Hi."

I opened the door wider. "Hi."

He stepped into the foyer and gathered me into his arms.

I relaxed into the warmth of his chest.

"How was your day?" His breath was a whisper through my hair.

"Long." I pulled away and looked up into his lean face. "How was yours?"

"Long is as good a word as any. Where is everybody?"

"Aggie's on a date. Max is napping. And Grace should be home any minute." For a few seconds I wished Grace wasn't coming home—that Anarchy and I had the house to ourselves. "Aggie left a casserole. Why don't you stay for dinner?"

His eyes smiled at me. "I'd like that."

My heart hiccupped—just a little. "How about a drink?" I led him toward the kitchen.

"I'd better not. An arrest warrant has been issued for Nick DiGiovanni. If he's located, I have to go in."

"He's behind the murders?"

"That's the working theory."

I poured myself a glass of wine. "I have something to tell you."

"Oh?" He sounded wary.

"I visited Winnie today."

"And?" Now he sounded relieved.

"She put her own Sweet'N Low in her coffee at the coffee shop."

"She carries sweetener with her?"

He was missing the point. "Plenty of women have a few packets in their handbags. Not every restaurant keeps Sweet'N Low on the table. What if one of those packets held the poison?"

He closed his eyes. "The last time I saw Winnie Flournoy's purse, you had it."

"I took it back to her house." I took in the disappointment that flashed across his face. "I still have her house keys."

His brows rose.

"I'm taking care of her demon-cat. We could go over there after dinner."

Anarchy glanced at the oven timer.

I shook my head. "We can't go now. If we were held up, and I burned Aggie's casserole, I'd never hear the end of it."

Grace blew through the backdoor, carrying the scent of rain with her. She stopped when she saw us, and her eyes widened.

"How was babysitting?"

"Fine. Where's Aggie?"

"On a date with Mac."

Worry creased her brow. "Did you cook?"

"Aggie left us a casserole."

Grace relaxed. Visibly. Everyone's a critic.

We ate Aggie's casserole with a salad she'd left in the fridge and crusty rolls.

After dinner, Grace disappeared upstairs with a one-word explanation. "Homework."

Anarchy and I rinsed the dishes and loaded the dishwasher.

When we'd finished, I dried my hands on an embroidered tea towel. "Shall we head over to the Flournoys'?"

"In a minute." Anarchy snaked his arms around my waist and pulled me close. "Thanks for dinner."

"You're always welcome."

He lowered his head and kissed me—the type of kiss that warmed me all the way to my toenails. The kind of kiss that made me forget every single question Libba urged me to ask.

Max nudged us with his nose. If there was affection being doled out, he wanted his share.

"Go away, Max."

He nudged again. Harder.

Somehow, I separated my lips from Anarchy's. "We should go."

"Go?"

"Winnie's house. Purse. Sweet'N Low. Poison."

"That purse isn't going anywhere." He kissed me again.

My toes curled.

Nudge.

Maybe if I ignored him, Max would go away.

Woof.

"Go away, Max."

Woof!

Again I pulled away from Anarchy. I scowled down at my dog.

He wore a particularly obdurate expression.

"We might as well go." If nothing else, we could kiss in the car without a nosy audience. "Winnie's keys are in my purse." I frowned at Max. "You behave yourself."

Max cocked his ears. *Fat chance.*

The rain beat against the roof of the car with such force that talking was impossible. We drove in silence, parked in Winnie's drive, and dashed for the front door.

I fitted the key into the lock, and we stepped inside. Winnie's house felt cold and empty and dark.

"Where did you leave the purse?"

"The living room."

I stepped inside and flipped the light switch on the wall. Several table lamps came on.

"Where is it?"

"I don't know. I'm sure I left it in here."

There was no handbag.

"Maybe Lois put it in the bedroom."

"Lois?"

"Winnie's daughter," I explained.

Neither of us mentioned the other possibility—that Winnie's handbag had been stolen.

Anarchy took my hand and together we climbed the stairs.

We walked down the hallway, opening doors as we went.

I peered into a guest room. "Interesting."

"What?"

"Winnie and Lark weren't sleeping together." I waved a hand at the stack of law books on the bedside table, the slippers by the bed, and a plaid bathrobe hung over the corner of the closet door. "Looks like Daisy might be right."

"Daisy?"

I nodded. "She told me Lark was having an affair with Marigold."

"You didn't tell me before now?"

"I haven't known for very long and it's not as if Winnie could have killed Marigold. She was locked in the attic with the rest of us."

"But—"

"Daisy told me, not Jinx."

"What does that mean?"

"If Jinx passes something on, you can take it to the bank. Daisy's information can be iffy. Besides, you know who killed Lark."

"Promise me something."

"What?"

"If you hear gossip that pertains to one of my cases, you'll tell me."

"When I can."

His lips thinned.

"You can't expect me to betray my friends' confidences."

"If it means catching a killer, I can."

"Trust me, if I ever know something that might lead you to a killer, I'll tell you." Guilt nudged me—as insistent as Max. Even now, I was hiding the contents of Henry's file on John Wilson and Lark.

It was easy to ignore guilt when I knew someone named DiGiovanni was about to be arrested.

"That's your final word?" From Anarchy's tone, I assumed we were done kissing for the night.

"Yes." I opened another door. "Winnie sleeps here." The master bedroom was papered with a cheery floral print. That same print repeated in the curtains, bedding, and upholstery. The carpet was a grass green shag. Standing in Winnie's room was like standing in a bower. "I don't see her purse."

"How can you see anything in here?"

"It's just a few flowers."

"It's busier than 435 at rush hour."

"Be that as it may—" I liked all the flowers "—Winnie's purse isn't here. Someone must have taken it."

THIRTEEN

Tap, tap.

I opened one eye and snuggled deeper into the covers.

"Mrs. Russell?"

I opened the other eye and looked at the raindrop covered window. "Come in." I sounded about as sunny as the weather.

Aggie, wearing last night's kaftan and carrying a cup of Mr. Coffee's finest, slipped into my room. "I'm sorry to disturb you but—"

I held up a restraining hand. "Coffee first."

She gave me the mug.

I let the aroma tease my nose for a few seconds before I drank. Three sips and I was ready. "But?"

"Lois Flournoy called. She's taking her mother home this morning."

I took another sip.

"She's hoping you'll meet them at her parents' house."

There went my morning. "Is she still on the phone?"

"She left a message on the machine. She's hoping to see you at eight. She'd like you to call if you can't make it."

"When did she call?"

"Last night."

I'd been so exhausted, I hadn't heard the phone ring. Another sip. "How was your date?"

Aggie blushed—blushed—and smoothed the fabric of her kaftan. "It was nice."

"Nice?" Spending the night with the man who made her eyes light up like the Plaza at Christmas deserved a better adjective. "Finding Tab is on sale is nice."

The shine in Aggie's eyes dimmed, and she shifted her gaze to the carpet beneath her feet. "Sometimes it's hard. I know Al would want me to be happy, but saying last night was magical feels like a betrayal." She crossed her arms. "What about you?"

"What about me?"

"Three sets of dishes in the dishwasher."

"Last night was nice."

"Nope." She shook her head. "You didn't let me get away with nice."

"It's different, you said *nice* because being happy feels like a betrayal. I said *nice* because I was betrayed." Libba's insidious question—*why was Anarchy still single at forty?*—waved at me from the recesses of my brain. "What if Anarchy is another mistake?"

"That man adores you and he's as straight an arrow as they come."

"What if the problem wasn't Henry?" I spoke into my coffee cup. "What if it was me?"

Aggie snorted. "Please. It takes two to make a marriage work, just one to make it fail. Women, and I have no idea why, have a tendency to blame themselves for the sins visited upon them. Look at that friend of Grace's who was raped."

I looked up from my coffee. "What do you mean?"

"I bet she's telling herself that she shouldn't have gone to that bar, shouldn't have had those drinks, shouldn't have trusted a stranger."

"You're probably right."

"The man who committed the crime. Why should she feel guilty? You and the late Mr. Russell, you stayed together for Grace."

"Yes."

"You didn't run around town with a different man every night of the week. You didn't take up with your husband's friends."

"No."

"But you blame yourself." She planted her hands on her hips. "What happened in your marriage wasn't your fault."

Nice to hear, but I couldn't get past the idea that if I'd been better, *more*, Henry and I wouldn't have imploded. "I'll think about that. Now, tell me about your date."

The secret smile returned. "The show was funny and afterwards we went to Mac's for a night cap—" she blushed again "—and we lost track of time."

Aggie had a small apartment over her sister's garage and a room at my house. Sometimes she spent the night at her sister's, sometimes with Grace and me. "You didn't have to rush over here."

"I know but—" her face puckered.

"But what?"

"The other shoe hasn't dropped."

"What do you mean?"

"Something else—something bad—is going to happen. I can feel it. I want to review my notes on those cases again."

"An arrest warrant has been issued."

"For whom?" Her voice was sharp.

"Nick DiGiovanni."

Her jaw dropped. "The mobster? Why?"

"Presumably because they think he did it."

Aggie frowned. "Why would Nick DiGiovanni kill a federal judge?"

"Someone named Tony Bilardo was going to testify against him."

Aggie shook her head. "That explains why DiGiovanni would kill Bilardo." She shook her head and her curls sproinged. "But a federal judge? A mobster wouldn't bring heat like that on himself. Don't the police read the papers?"

"What do you mean?"

"The local mafia blow each other up. They shoot people in the head. They don't commit vehicular homicide."

Aggie had a point. When the strip clubs on Twelfth Street had been moved, it seemed as if there was a murder every day as rival families struggled for control of the new district. Lots of bombings. Lots of shootings. Not a hit-and-run. Not a single garroting.

"Did you notice anything when you looked at the cases?" I asked.

"No," she replied. "You should review them."

"Of course." I handed her the empty coffee mug. "I'll do it as soon as I get back from the Flournoys'."

Aggie nodded. "We'd better figure it out quick. I can't help thinking your friend, Mrs. Flournoy, is still in danger."

I grabbed a quick shower and readied myself for whatever the day might bring—I was pretty sure the day would call for navy pants, a navy blouse with green piping, and my new floral trench coat.

Dressed to face adversity, I trotted downstairs in search of more coffee.

Grace stood at the counter and jammed books into her backpack and peanut butter slathered toast into her mouth. With callous indifference to Max's pleading expression (he loved peanut butter), she ate the final bite.

Max huffed his disappointment.

"Good morning."

She waved, too busy chewing to answer.

"Are you coming home after school?"

She held a hand in front of her lips. "Nope. Jennifer offered to help me with my math homework."

I swallowed a sigh. It seemed the older Grace became, the less I saw her.

"Will you be home for dinner?" asked Aggie.

Grace nodded and hefted her backpack over her shoulder. "That casserole last night was awesome."

Aggie beamed at the compliment. "I'm glad you liked it."

"Gotta go." Grace was out the door.

Brnng, brnng.

Aggie and I shifted our gazes from the still-vibrating back door to the clock on the wall. 7:20. It was too early for anyone to be calling.

Brnng, brnng.

"It can't be Mother." Mother only called early when things were dire—when she'd heard I'd found a body or when someone with newly acquired wealth was put up for membership at the club. But who else could it be? I reached for the phone. "Hello."

"Ellison Walford Russell, tell me you did not discuss your sex life at the country club where everyone and their sister could hear you?" Righteous indignation made Mother enunciate every word with extra care.

"I did not."

That stopped her—for half a second. "Myrtle Bridewell has called me three times."

"Myrtle Bridewell should stop eavesdropping."

"Did you discuss sex?"

"Libba discussed sex. I listened."

Was that grinding sound I heard Mother's teeth?

"Libba didn't just discuss sex. Libba discussed your having sex."

"Strictly speaking, Libba discussed me *not* having sex."

"Don't play games with me."

"Look on the bright side, Mother. I made it through the whole day without finding a body."

"Don't jinx yourself. And this is not a joke. If you ever want a decent man to be interested in you, you can't discuss intimate details in public."

"I didn't." In for a penny, in for a pound. "And Anarchy is a decent man. He's escorting me to the gala."

Twenty seconds of silence ensued.

"Mother?"

"I can't talk to you when you're like this." Mother hung up on me.

"That went well."

Aggie comforted me with a fresh cup of coffee and a half-apologetic smile. Like Mother, she preferred Hunter.

With a few minutes to kill before I was due at Winnie's, I took my coffee and Aggie's notes to the family room, settled into my desk chair, and read. John Wilson had represented some horrible people—robbers, murderers, rapists, and con men who'd swindled little old ladies out of their life savings.

Because of Debbie, I read the notes on the rapist first. Despite the victim's testimony, the defendant had received a judgment of acquittal. "Aggie," I called. "What's the difference between an acquittal and a judgment of acquittal?"

She appeared in the doorway. "An acquittal comes from a jury. A judgment of acquittal is a procedural device where the judge takes the case out of the jury's hands. He decides the prosecutor hasn't made their case."

"This defendant—" I tapped my finger on Aggie's notes "—would be happy with his defense attorney and the judge?"

"Absolutely. Any other questions?"

"Not right now."

She left me with her notes.

I pushed the rape case aside and reached for the armed robber who'd been sentenced to ten years. Had Aggie heard back from Hunter? Was ten years reasonable?

I finished my coffee and pulled the notes on the murderer to the center of the desk. He'd been charged with murder in the second degree and he too had been sentenced to ten years.

Suddenly the armed robber's sentence didn't seem all that reasonable.

"More?" Aggie had returned, and (bless her) she held the coffeepot.

"Please." I held out my mug.

"Have you found anything?"

"Maybe."

"The robber and murderer were each sentenced to ten years."

"That hardly seems fair. Ten years for murder?"

"I know." I sipped my coffee and thought. Something niggled

at the edge of my brain. If I chased the thought, it would hide. I glanced at my watch. "I'd better get going or I'll be late." I left the notes on the desk and went to Winnie's.

I parked at the curb and listened to the rain on the Mercedes' roof. What I wouldn't give for a sunny, warm spring day—this relentless rain was depressing.

When Lois pulled into the driveway, I unfurled my umbrella and climbed out of the car.

I met her and Winnie at the front door where Lois fumbled with the house keys.

"Hurry," Winnie snapped. "I'm getting wet."

"We're all getting wet, Mom." Lois' voice had an about-to-break quality.

"Give me the keys." Winnie held out her hand.

"Fine." Lois dropped them into her mother's open palm.

Winnie had the door open in seconds. She hurried inside. "Beezie, Mommy's home."

Lois and I followed her into the house. "Where's Beezie?" she whispered.

"I haven't seen him since yesterday." A small lie—I hadn't actually seen Beezie, only heard his demon's cry.

"Beezie!" Winnie called.

Meow! The cat ran down the front stairs and launched itself at Winnie.

She caught him mid-leap and cradled him in her arms like a baby. "Mommy's home now."

"I need coffee," said Lois. "Mom, why don't you and Ellison sit down in the living room while I make us something warm?"

Winnie nodded and led me to the living room door. "Such a mess. It will take me days to get the house back in order." She turned on her heel, crossed the hall, and peered into Lark's study. "This room is even worse." Her eyes scanned the chaos. "It looks as if someone's been into my husband's journals." She nodded at the emptied bookshelves.

"His journals?"

"He kept notes on every case ever argued in his courtroom. He was a fine judge." She dropped a kiss on Beezie's head. "A better judge than husband."

The bitterness in Winnie's voice suggested she knew about Lark's affair, but I asked anyway. "Did you know about Marigold?"

"I suspected. That girl—" she shook her head "—I gave her a chance, and she seduced my husband."

"How did you find out?"

Winnie's answering smile held a malicious edge. "I found the condoms. It's not as if Lark needed King Cobras. Maybe Baronet Cobras, and that was when he was—"

"Mom!" A red-faced Lois stood in the foyer. "Ellison, how do you take your coffee?"

"With cream. Thank you."

Lois turned away.

"Lois."

She looked over her shoulder with a questioning look on her face.

"I brought your mother's purse back here from the hospital. But yesterday, when I was feeding Beezie, I didn't see it. Did you move it?"

She frowned. "Mom's purse?"

"Yes."

"A cognac Coach bucket bag?"

"Yes," said Winnie.

"It's sitting on the kitchen counter."

I was a hundred percent sure I hadn't taken that purse to the kitchen. I'd wanted my hands free in case Beezie attacked. "I think we should take the Sweet'N Low out of your bag, Winnie."

"Why?"

I glanced at Lois. "It's possible your coffee was poisoned with it."

Winnies forehead creased. "Are you saying I poisoned my own

coffee?"

The thought had crossed my mind. "Not on purpose."

Her eyes searched my face. "You really think it could've been the sweetener?"

"You didn't touch your soup, and we both had coffee with cream. The Sweet'N Low is the only possibility."

Lois stared at us, her eyebrows so high they kissed her hairline. "How would someone know Mom carried Sweet'N Low in her purse?"

"It's possible someone saw her take some out of her bag when she was out."

"Or put it in," said Winnie.

"What do you mean?" asked Lois.

Winnie flushed slightly. "Sometimes, when I have coffee in a place with Sweet'N Low, I take a few packets."

"You steal sugar substitute?" Daughters-judging-mothers—the tone was always the same.

"It's not stealing." Mothers-telling-daughters-they-had-no-business-judging—that tone was also always the same. "Not all restaurants have it on the table."

"So—" Lois rubbed her eyes "—if someone wasn't picky about when you took the poison, putting a packet in your purse would eventually kill you."

Winnie went pale.

"Let's get you a chair." I led Winnie to one of the seats in front of Lark's desk.

"If I hadn't been at the hospital when I used that packet..."

"I'll grab the bag." Lois dashed out of the room.

Winnie leaned back in her chair. "This whole week has been a nightmare."

Having your husband murdered was no picnic. "What can you tell me about Marigold?"

"You don't think she put the poison in my purse?"

"I think it's a possibility." Lark was another possibility. One I didn't mention.

"What do you want to know?"

"Why was she murdered in such a gruesome way?"

"You don't think I killed her?"

"You were locked in the attic when she died. I was with you. I'm positive you didn't kill her."

Winnie relaxed in her chair.

Of course, Winnie could have had an accomplice.

"Marigold wasn't her real name."

Imagine that. "Oh?"

"Her real name was Janice Young."

"And she went by Marigold Applebottom instead?"

Winnie shrugged.

"Here's the purse." Lois stood in the doorway and held up Winnie's handbag. "I checked. There's no Sweet'N Low in it." The brick red rising from her neck suggested she'd found the King Cobras.

"You went through my purse?" Winnie sounded outraged.

"Focus, Winnie. Someone tried to kill you. And they've removed the evidence."

My logic stole the remaining color from Winnie's already wan cheeks.

"We need to hire security," said Lois.

"Security?" Winnie shook her head. "No."

"Mom, someone killed Dad. They tried to kill you. We're hiring security."

"LJ can look out for us."

Lois snorted. "LJ? Security? He can't even handle connecting flights. He's stuck in Chicago."

"What do you think, Ellison?" Winnie asked.

"Given the three murders—"

"Three?" Lois's eyebrows were back up by her hairline.

"Marigold, your father, and John Wilson."

"John Wilson is dead?" Winnie's voice shook.

"Yes. The police think it's related to a case."

Winnie forgot about the cat in her lap and gripped the arms of the chair. "Which case?"

Meow. Beezie disapproved of anything that stopped Winnie from stroking his fur.

"I don't know the details, but it involves Tony Bilardo and Nick DiGiovanni."

"The mobster?" Lois's voice squeaked.

Winnie ran her hand down Beezie's back.

"Have the police made an arrest?"

"Not that I know of."

"That's it," said Lois. "We are absolutely hiring security. Right away. Who should I call?" She looked at me.

"We don't need security."

"We do. And either we hire some, or we get on a plane for Charlottesville this afternoon."

"Fine," Winnie ceded. "Hire security."

"Who do I call?"

"I have a friend who's a detective. I can ask him."

"Would you? Please?" Lois glanced at the phone. "Would you call right away?"

I picked up the receiver and dialed.

"KCPD."

"May I please speak with Detective Anarchy Jones?"

"One moment, please. I'll connect you."

I listened to dreadful canned music until Anarchy picked up. "Anarchy, it's Ellison calling."

"Hi." His tone was warm.

I caught myself smiling in response. "I'm at the Flournoys' with Winnie and her daughter. Lois thinks Winnie needs security. We were hoping you'd be able to recommend someone."

"Hold on, there's a card in my desk." The sounds of rummaging carried through the phone line. "Found it. Marvin Hancock at Tall Oaks Security. Do you have a pen?"

It was my turn to rummage. I laid hands on a pen and notepad. "Ready."

He gave me the number, and I jotted it down.

"Any luck locating Nick DiGiovanni?"

"Not yet. He's disappeared."

The niggling thought at the edge of my brain stuck out a long, bony finger and poked me. "Why?"

"Why what?"

"Never mind. Thanks for the number. I'll share it with Lois."

"Are you free for dinner tonight?"

There it was again. That smile that came from nowhere. "I am. Why don't you come by the house? We can eat there. I have something to tell you."

"About the case?"

"Yes." He needed to know Winnie's purse had mysteriously reappeared.

"I'll call you later. Be careful."

"Always."

I hung up the phone and handed Lois the information.

"Thank you." She turned to her mother. "We're going to do everything possible to keep you safe."

Winnie mumbled something in response. Something that sounded like *all the security in the world won't do any good.*

FOURTEEN

I went home, looked over Aggie's notes, and offered Max a run.

With the air of one doing me a tremendous favor, he peered out the back door. Seeing the dripping skies, he refused to set a paw outside.

"Fine," I told him. "But the weather's not getting any better."

He huffed and settled into his favorite spot in the kitchen.

"I'm going upstairs to paint."

He lifted his brows but didn't move.

I changed my clothes and climbed the stairs to the attic.

As usual, the application of color and texture to canvas calmed my mind.

The painting on my easel—an arrangement of pink peonies—represented what spring should be—sunlight and air scented with flowers in full bloom. I ignored the cold, wet reality outside my window and painted until the light, such as it was, faded.

When my brushes were clean, I headed for the kitchen. "Whatever you're cooking smells heavenly."

Aggie stood at the sink washing vegetables. "There's a roast in the oven." She dried her hands on the apron covering her kaftan. "Did you review the rest of the cases?"

"Not yet. I'll go through them tonight."

The back door swung open and Grace burst into the house. Rain streaked her face and droplets of water fell from her slicker to Aggie's spotless floor. "Mom!"

"What?"

"I have something amazing for you." She dug in her pocket and handed me a folded piece of paper. "Here."

A check.

For ten thousand dollars.

"How?"

"Jennifer helped me with my math, and I told her about the gala, and she said she loved museums and whipped out her check book."

"This is incredible, Grace. Thank you."

She grinned. "It might get Granna off your back."

"How did you know about that?"

"I heard at school."

Mother had a lot to answer for.

"Well this—" I waved the check "—is awesome. I should go thank Jennifer."

"I bet she'd like that."

Brnng, Brnng.

Aggie wiped her hands again and picked up the phone. "Russell residence." She listened. "One moment, I'll see if she's available."

"Who is it?" I whispered.

"Your mother," she whispered back.

I took a deep breath then accepted the phone. "Hello, Mother."

"Have you raised any money today?"

I smiled at Grace. "Ten thousand dollars and—" a fabulous, raise-all-the-money-and-then-some idea landed in my brain, a gift from above "—I can raise the rest."

"How?"

"I'm still working on the details."

"You're sure you can raise the rest of the money?"

"I think so."

"If you need my help, I'm here." If I raised a million dollars, she would forgive me for discussing S-E-X at the club. "I ran into Hunter today."

"Oh?"

"He doesn't have a date for the gala."

"I'm sure he won't have any trouble finding one."

"He could escort you."

"I already have an escort."

"It's not fair to him. He won't know a soul." We both knew that wasn't her real objection.

"He'll know Karma."

"Karma's coming?"

Karma was my slightly scandalous half-sister. "She made a generous donation."

Mother sighed. She liked Karma—she really did—but she didn't embrace the circumstances of Karma's birth.

"Listen, Mother, I need to thank the most recent donor. I'll let you know if I need help with the big idea."

We hung up, and I slid on my floral trench.

"You're going like that?" Grace wrinkled her nose at my painting clothes.

"Too casual?"

"Yes." Grace had the daughter-judging-mother tone down pat.

"Fine." I ran upstairs, changed back into the navy outfit, and returned to the kitchen. "Better?"

"Much."

I grabbed an umbrella and braved the dripping twilight. The grass beneath my feet was slippery, and I balanced my desire to get out of the rain with the desire not to fall on my hiney. Going slow won.

When I finally rang Jennifer's doorbell, I was more damp than dry.

Jennifer opened the door wearing a peasant skirt, loose top, and moccasins. "Oh, good gracious, you're soaked. Come in." She waved me inside.

I stood in the foyer and dripped on Jennifer's hardwood floors. "I came to thank you—" my nose twitched. What was that smell? Jennifer was cooking something awful. "I came to thank you for your donation. It was—" my eyes watered. Seriously, what was that smell? "Jennifer, is something burning?"

She sniffed the air. "Oh, golly!"

I ran after her to the kitchen where a pan on the stove held flames that reached for the ceiling.

Jennifer ran to the sink and filled a pitcher.

I turned off the burner, held up my hands, and stepped in front of her. "Wait!"

"There's a fire!" She stepped to the left.

I stepped with her. "What kind of fire?"

She stepped to the right and annoyance flashed across her face. "The kind that's going to burn down my house."

Again, I stepped with her. "What's burning?"

"I was toasting ravioli."

"In oil?"

"Yes." She took two steps. "Move, please."

I took two steps, blocking her access. "No water!"

She gaped at me. "Then how do I put it out?

"Flour. Do you have any flour?"

She hesitated then pulled an unopened five-pound bag of Gold Medal from a cabinet. "What do I do?"

"Give it to me."

She handed over the bag.

I ripped open the bag and tossed handful after handful of flour onto the flames.

Jennifer dug her hand into the bag and tossed as well.

We tossed until the bag was empty. We tossed until the flames were smothered. Fortunately, that happened at the same time.

Then we surveyed the damage.

Jennifer's toasted ravioli had singed the walls and ceiling, filled her kitchen with smoke, and reduced a perfectly good pan to a piece of carbon. Plus, flour dusted every surface.

Including me. My navy pants were now white.

She slumped against the counter's edge. "Oh, dear."

Oh, dear was right.

She pressed her hands to her cheeks. "How did you know to

use flour instead of water?"

"I've burned a few things in my day. If you throw water on a grease fire, you make things worse."

A hard-won lesson.

"That was dinner."

"Eat at my house." I crossed to the back door. "May I?" The smoke needed an escape route.

"Of course."

I reached for the handle, but the door opened, and Marshall stepped inside. He scanned the smoke-darkened walls, the flour, and the remains of the pan. "What happened?"

"A tiny fire." Jennifer measured a half-inch between her thumb and pointer finger.

Tiny? There was ample evidence to the contrary.

"But Ellison—" Jennifer offered me a brilliant smile "—put it out. We should go out to eat."

"You're coming to my house," I said. "Aggie made a roast."

Marshall shifted his gaze from the flour-covered stove to me. "Aggie who made the casserole?"

"Exactly."

"We'd love to come."

Marshall carried the remains of the pan to the patio, and we trudged across the wet lawn to my house.

"Aggie," I called from the front hall. "I brought friends for dinner."

Max appeared in the hallway, sniffed, and drew his lips back from his teeth in a doggy sneer.

Aggie followed him, a smile of welcome on her face. The smile faltered when she saw me. "What happened?"

"A kitchen mishap. If you'll get Jennifer and Marshall a drink, I'll run upstairs and change."

"Of course."

As I climbed the stairs, she led Jennifer and Marshall to the living room. "There's a roast in the oven and homemade apple pie for dessert."

"Honey, you should set the kitchen on fire more often."

Something Henry never said. Not once.

Five minutes later, wearing fresh clothes and considerably less flour, I stepped into the living room.

Jennifer had kicked off her shoes and was curled in a club chair (good thing Mother wasn't here—she'd sooner die than kick off her shoes in someone else's living room). Marshall held a drink in both hands. Grace sipped a Tab with two limes.

"I was just telling Marshall and Grace how lucky we are you came when you did."

"Maybe if I hadn't come, there wouldn't have been a fire."

None of us believed that.

I poured myself a scotch and soda. "I came over to thank you for the gift to the museum."

"Gift to the museum?" Marshall turned in his chair and stared at his wife. If there was one thing I knew about marriage, it was that husbands liked to be consulted before major expenditures.

"For the Chinese exhibit," she explained. "Ellison is chairing the gala."

"As long as it's for a good cause." His voice was bone dry.

I cast about for another topic. "Marshall, I understand you're originally from the area."

"South of here."

Ding dong.

Grace popped out of her chair. "I'll get it."

Voices carried from the hallway and Grace reappeared with Anarchy behind her.

I rose from my chair. "You made it."

"I did."

"You've met Jennifer. Marshall, this is my friend Anarchy.

The usual nice-to-meet-yous ensued.

"May I get you a drink?"

"I'd better not."

"Are you a doctor?" asked Marshall.

"No. Why?"

"My uncle is a doctor, and he never drinks when he's on call."

"Anarchy's a homicide detective," said Grace.

Marshall stared, slack-jawed.

"A detective?" Marshall croaked.

"A homicide detective," Grace corrected.

"You catch killers?"

Anarchy nodded. "I try."

"Grace, would you please ask Aggie to put on another place for dinner?" I glanced at Anarchy. "You are staying?"

"Yes." Anarchy settled into the club chair set at an angle to Jennifer's. "How are you enjoying the neighborhood?"

"Everyone's been super nice," she replied. "But I miss the sun."

"That's right. West coast." Anarchy turned his gaze to Marshall. "Are you from California, too?"

"Overland Park. But my family moved to California when I was a kid."

"What brought you back here?"

"A job. I'm in sales."

Anarchy's brows lifted slightly. A twenty-something salesman shouldn't be able to afford a house in my neighborhood.

A twenty-something salesman's wife shouldn't be penning checks for ten thousand dollars. I thought about the art on their walls—there had to be family money involved.

"Do you still have family here?" asked Anarchy.

"No." Marshall sounded almost bleak. "What about you? What brought you to Kansas City?"

"The job."

"You can be a cop anywhere."

Anarchy blinked, and his lips thinned.

But Marshall had a point. Anarchy could be a cop anywhere. Why Kansas City? Libba's question—*why was Anarchy still single at forty?*—rode my brain waves like a surfer on a board.

"We know you didn't come for the weather." There was a smudge of flour on Jennifer's forehead. She caught me staring and wiped it away with the back of her hand.

Grace stepped into the living room carrying a serving platter filled with cheese, meat, and crackers. "Aggie says dinner will be ready in twenty minutes."

She passed the hors d'oeuvres. First to Jennifer, then to Marshall, and finally to Anarchy and me.

I picked up a Ritz topped with a small slice of Swiss cheese and nibbled.

Grace set Aggie's last-minute canapés down on the coffee table. "Jennifer's been helping me with math," she told Anarchy. "And—" she turned my way "—tomorrow Debbie and I are going to hang out with her."

"That's very nice of you, Jennifer."

"I'm happy to do it."

"Who's Debbie?" asked Marshall.

"A friend of Grace's who was assaulted," said Jennifer.

Marshall's open, affable face darkened. "That's awful."

"It's kind of you to listen." Too bad all my neighbors weren't as nice as Jennifer.

Anarchy reached for his belt, glanced at his pager, and stood. "Ellison, may I use the phone?"

"Of course. The study is open."

I rose, picked up the cheese plate, and held it out to Jennifer. "Would you have another?"

"No, thank you."

"Marshall, may I tempt you?"

Marshall picked up a cracker. "Thank you." He bit. "This salami is delicious."

"Aggie gets it from her boyfriend," said Grace. "He owns a deli."

Anarchy appeared in the doorway. "I've changed my mind about that drink."

"What's wrong?"

He crossed to the bar cart. "Arlene Wilson ran an ad in the evening paper."

"She did what?"

He poured out a finger of scotch over a single ice cube. "Five thousand dollars for a tip leading to the arrest of her husband's killer. The phone lines at the station are swamped."

"But an arrest warrant's already been issued."

"Arlene isn't convinced we have the right guy."

I wasn't convinced either.

"Who's Arlene Wilson?" Jennifer asked.

"Her husband, John, was murdered," I replied.

"John Wilson?" She glanced at Marshall and her forehead wrinkled. "Why do I know that name?"

"I don't know, honey. It's a fairly common name."

Her face cleared. "There was a real estate broker in La Jolla named John Wilson."

Anarchy took a large sip of his drink. "The number of cranks who'll call the station is mind-boggling."

"You're the lead detective on Wilson's murder?" asked Marshall.

"Yes."

"You can get away for dinner?"

"Like I said, we have a suspect."

"Dinner is served." Aggie looked pleased by the addition of three people to the dinner table. Like most good cooks, she was happiest when people were enjoying her food.

The meal was, of course, delicious.

Marshall turned down a second slice of apple pie with obvious regret. "We should get home. We have a lot of cleaning up to do in the kitchen." He stood. "Thank you for having us."

"We should do this more often." If the poor man was enduring Jennifer's culinary creations, he needed a decent home-cooked meal from time to time.

"We'd like that. A lot. Honey?" He held out a hand to his wife.

She rose from her chair. "Ellison, thank you for a delicious dinner and for saving my kitchen."

"Thanks for saving Grace's math grade and for your support of the gala."

Grace and I walked them to the front door.

"Grace, I'll see you and your friend tomorrow afternoon."

"We'll be there."

Jennifer and Marshall ventured out into the rain, and I closed the door behind them.

Anarchy stood in the hallway. "How did you save Jennifer's kitchen?"

"She started a grease fire. As it happens, I know how to put those out."

Grace snorted. "I have homework." She climbed the front stairs.

I turned to Anarchy. "Coffee in the family room?"

"I should go."

"You should stay."

"Well—" a smile teased his lips "—when you put it that way."

Together we walked to the kitchen where Mr. Coffee kept half a pot warm for me.

I poured two mugs, handed one to Anarchy, and led him to the family room.

He sank onto the couch and looked at me expectantly.

I sat next to him. "How was your day?"

He groaned. "Don't ask. What about you?"

"I painted."

"That sounds nice."

"It was. I needed it."

"Needed it?"

"Painting centers me. Does that sound too woo-woo?"

"I'm from San Francisco. There's nothing you could say that would sound too woo-woo."

"You're sure?" I leaned the back of my head against the arm Anarchy had stretched across the couch.

"Positive."

"Why did you come to Kansas City?"

"What do you mean?"

"You could have gone anywhere. Why here?"

"I wanted to be someplace far from San Francisco."

"Why?"

"I have a complicated relationship with my father."

I understood about complicated relationships. I had several of my own. "I get the far away part. But why here?"

"The department had an opening. I applied. It seemed like kismet. Or is that too woo-woo for you?"

Anarchy could easily have ended up in St. Louis or Minneapolis or Chicago. The thought chilled me. "How long were you a cop in San Francisco?"

"Long enough to make detective and earn my father's implacable ire."

"Sounds as if there's a story there."

"Not a good one. How are you coming with Aggie's notes?"

"You identified a suspect."

"Until I hear a confession, I'm not convinced. So, what about those notes?"

"There are two cases that caught my eye. An armed robbery and a murder."

"What about them?"

"Both defendants were found guilty, and they received the same sentence."

"It happens."

"It doesn't seem fair."

"There are probably a lot of victims who'd agree with you."

"I bet there are criminals who are angry about their sentences."

"There are lots of them." He leaned close to me and brushed a feather-light kiss against the shell of my ear.

I tingled.

"Ellison." His voice was low and husky.

"Yes?"

"Why is there flour in your ear?"

FIFTEEN

Libba called at nine. "Did you forget?"

"Forget what?"

"We're playing bridge with Lisa and Amy today."

Oh dear Lord. "Is that today?" A shot of adrenalin brought me to my feet. "Am I late?"

"It is today and you're not late. We play at ten."

"When did you get organized?" I was the one who remembered things. Libba was the one who flitted from flower to flower (man to man) like a giddy butterfly.

"What are you talking about?"

"You. Remembering things. That's my job."

"Oh. That. You forget things when you've found a body or two."

"I've only found one."

"The week's not over."

"Don't jinx me. I'll see you at the club at ten."

I hung up, put Aggie's notes—dog-eared from handling—in a neat pile on the corner of my desk, and went to the kitchen for more coffee.

"Anything?" asked Aggie.

I blinked against the brightness of her kaftan. Wearing that shade of orange, she could stand in for a traffic cone. "Not yet. But, if I look at those pages any longer, my head may explode." I picked up the coffeepot and gave Mr. Coffee a grateful pat. "I have a bridge game at ten and I'm swinging by the Nelson this afternoon."

"Gala business?"

I nodded. "I'll be glad when it's over." I filled my mug too full and drank a sip of black coffee to make room for cream.

"I bet."

Crossing my fingers, I added, "Hopefully Laurence likes my idea."

"For what?"

"Raising the rest of the money."

"If it keeps your moth—" Aggie's eyes widened, and she pressed her hand against her mouth.

"Go ahead." I added cream to my coffee. "Say it."

Blushing a shade of pink that did not complement her orange kaftan, Aggie fixed her gaze the counter. "If it keeps your mother out of his office, I'm sure he'll love it."

Aggie had a point.

"Here's hoping." I climbed the stairs, changed into a Diane von Furstenberg wrap dress, draped a handful of gold chains around my neck, and applied my makeup with extra care.

Lisa and Amy. What had Libba been thinking?

Some might say Lisa married well. She'd grown up out south and had parleyed a pretty face and good grades into a bid at the right sorority. From there, she'd met and married Tommy Larson. The couple had two handsome sons, lived in a lovely home, and vacationed in all the right spots.

Perfect on the outside, but I'd overheard Tommy berate his wife for her posture. I'd seen him raise his brows when she took even a tiny bite of dessert. I'd smelled her fear when he reached over and plucked a strand of gray from her head. He demanded glamorous, thin, and young—the passing of years be damned.

No wonder she snuck off for plastic surgery and, if rumors were true, smoothed whale semen into her skin every night.

Amy also searched for the fountain of youth, but not because her husband was an ass. The two were poorly matched. Amy liked nothing better than a party. Paul's idea of a perfect evening was a book—a large, dry book about military history or European politics in the fifteenth century. Certain she'd be able to coax Paul out of his shell if she looked good enough, Amy spent hours at the salon, ate like a bird, and dressed to the absolute nines. Signing up for a library card would have been more effective.

Living on celery, lemon wedges in hot water, and the occasional bowl of cabbage soup could put the nicest of women on edge. Amy and Lisa weren't the nicest of women. They were hungry and unhappy. The pair of them made harpies look like Pollyanna. And Libba had agreed to bridge.

I drove through a downpour. Endless rain. Worse, the weatherman forecasted more precipitation. Floating away seemed like a real possibility.

A parking space near the clubhouse was available, and, after a brief hesitation, I pulled into it. Bad things happened in this parking lot. Very bad things. For once, parking close to the clubhouse was worth the risk. The car wouldn't blow up and no one would shoot at me. At least I hoped not. In this rain, a short dash appealed to me more than a long one.

I dashed.

"Good morning, Mrs. Russell," said the receptionist, who was warm and dry and wore shoes that didn't squish when she walked.

"Good morning." I closed my umbrella.

"May I take your coat?"

"Please." I handed over my damp trench-coat and the still dripping umbrella.

"It seems like forever since we've seen the sun."

"You're too right."

She smiled at me, a polite I-have-work-to-do-move-along-now smile. "Enjoy your cards."

"Thank you." I headed down the main hall toward the ladies' lounge.

Lisa was already at our table. She surveyed my ensemble. "What a fabulous dress."

"Thank you," I replied. "You look marvelous." Her skin was as taut as plastic surgery and whale semen could make it. Her hair was the perfect shade of ash blonde. She was one missed meal away from skeletal.

"I'm thrilled you and Libba could play with us today."

"I'm glad you thought of us." Liar, liar.

"You've had an exciting week."

"True." Was that why they'd invited us to play bridge? Because they wanted the horse's-mouth story on the latest murder?

"What happened at Winnie's?"

"You mean what happened to the yoga instructor?"

Lisa nodded.

"She was hanged."

The hand Amy lifted to her throat trembled. "How awful."

"It was. Of course, we were locked in the attic while she was being murdered."

"Still." She shook her head as if she'd never heard anything so terrible. "The instructor's name was Marigold?"

"Yes." I picked up the cards and shuffled. What was Amy after?

"Marigold Applebottom?"

"Yes."

Lisa slumped against her chair. "I knew her when she was Janice Young."

Now that was interesting.

"Her older sister and I were childhood friends."

"What was she like?"

"There was a fifteen-year age difference between Rose and Janice. I didn't know her well."

We both contemplated a fifteen-year span between children. I shuddered. "Were there other siblings?"

"No. Janice was a surprise."

"Do you still see your friend?"

"Not since I married." The corners of Lisa's mouth drooped, and her eyes misted. "She lives so far away." She sounded as if she needed convincing. She sure wasn't convincing me. Tommy Larson probably didn't approve of Rose.

"How did Janice become Marigold?"

"The last time I saw Rose, she said Janice had changed her name and run off to Oregon."

"Oregon?"

Amy shrugged. "Some Bikram."

Which explained the yoga.

"What's Rose doing now?"

"She married a plumber."

"Oh? I can always use the name of a good plumber."

"Cook." Lisa wrinkled her nose. "Her husband's name is Andy Cook."

Andy Cook advertised on television. I'd seen the ads. He dressed up as a wrench. He had a jingle. He danced a jig.

"You beat me here!" Libba stood in the doorway. "Lisa, if you get any thinner, you won't cast a shadow."

Lisa sat a little straighter. "Thank you."

Libba took the chair opposite mine. "Where's Amy?"

"She should be along any minute."

It was more like ten minutes. When Amy did arrive, she wore a pantsuit that looked as if she'd snatched it off a runway model's back. She air-kissed cheeks and apologized. "Sorry I'm late. It's the rain. The creek's out and they've closed the bridge to the main entrance. I had to use the back gate."

"Hopefully the water won't do too much damage," said Libba. "I'm not in the mood for an assessment."

When the creek left its banks, water invariably damaged the golf course. During one particularly expensive flood, a whole green washed away.

"Shall we play?" Amy's tone suggested we were the ones who'd kept her waiting.

We drew to deal. Libba won and dealt thirteen cards to each of us.

Amy picked up her hand and glanced at her cards. "So, Ellison, how's the gala coming along?"

I grouped suits together. Spades, hearts, clubs, diamonds—black, red, black, red. "Fine. It's going to be a marvelous party."

Amy shifted a few cards. "Paul and I bought benefactor's tickets."

"I'm glad you're coming."

"One club," said Libba.

Lisa frowned at her hand. "Pass"

"One heart," I replied to my partner.

"Pass," said Amy. "I heard everyone's a benefactor."

"It's true," I admitted. "The event sold out before we made general admission tickets available."

"Where will we be seated?" After *have you found another body?* my least favorite question. "We bought those tickets with the idea we'd have a decent table."

"We haven't completed the seating chart yet."

"So, you're not making any promises." Snide—Amy sounded snide.

"I'm afraid not."

"What will it cost to get a good table?"

"More money," Libba snapped. "Three hearts."

"Pass." Lisa kept her eyes on her cards.

"Four hearts."

"How much more money?"

"The twenty-five-thousand-dollar tables will be near the front of the room," I replied.

Amy rolled her eyes and groaned. "Fine. Twenty-five thousand. Lisa, do you and Tommy want to split it?"

Lisa's looked up from her cards. Her eyes widened, and her lips drew away from her teeth. "I'd need to discuss that with Tommy."

"I'll have Paul call him."

I added the additional donation to the running tally I kept in the under-used math section of my brain. We were closing in on half a million.

Libba drummed her nails on the table. "What's your bid, Amy?"

"I'm passing." She turned her gaze my way. "So, tell me what you're wearing."

After lunch (salads for Libba and me, clear broth for Lisa and Amy), I braved the rain and drove to the museum.

Laurence Sickman's office was on the second floor.

As I climbed the stairs, I reviewed the big idea. If Laurence agreed, we might actually make a million dollars.

His secretary was away from her desk, so I rapped my knuckles against his door.

"Come in."

When he saw me, Laurence rose from his chair and came out from behind his desk. "Ellison, what a pleasure. How are you?"

"Damp."

He glanced at the window and grimaced. "It does seem as if it's rained all week. May I get you some coffee?"

I considered his offer. Somewhere nearby, hidden from view, sat a percolator holding sub-par coffee. I'd learned this the hard way. "No, thank you."

His brows rose. "To what do I owe the pleasure?"

"I have an idea."

"Please—" he waved to one of the chairs in front of his desk, waited until I was seated, then took the other one "—tell me about it."

I settled into the chair, gripped its arms, and took one deep breath. "Has my mother said anything to you about how much money the gala is raising?"

"She might have mentioned it." Dry. So dry. His voice was a virtual drought. She'd definitely mentioned it.

"I think we can do it. I think we can raise a million dollars."

He leaned forward. "How?"

"I'll go back to a few key donors and ask for more money."

"They've already given."

"I know. And I am grateful for their gifts, but what if I asked them for multi-year commitments?"

"Pledges?"

"Yes. Pledges we count toward the gala and exhibition." I

swallowed. "The other host cities are raising millions. There are donors who might increase their commitments based purely on civic pride."

Laurence steepled his fingers. "There are other exhibits planned in the next few years. I hate using all our chits now."

"I understand." Now was the time for trump cards. "I'll tell Mother we discussed multi-year pledges, and you didn't think they were a good idea."

He held up his hands. "Don't be hasty. I didn't say no—I said the pledges might represent future challenges. Challenges we need to consider."

"The gala is weeks away. If I'm to have any hope of raising the extra money, I need every day."

"You want a decision?" If he thought I'd back down, he was wrong.

I looked him in the eye. "I do."

"Today?"

"Yes."

"The board may have an opinion."

The board would have lots of opinions. All of them different. "I'm guessing the board wants this event and the exhibit to be successful."

He stared at me, waiting for me to cave.

I stared back.

Long seconds passed.

"Fine, Ellison." He shrugged. "Go after the money."

What had I done? I stood. "Thank you."

He pushed out of his chair and extended his hand. "Good luck. The apple doesn't fall far from the tree."

"What do you mean?"

"You have quite a bit of your mother in you."

I chose to take that as a compliment.

When I arrived home, I ignored Aggie's stack of notes on the corner of my desk and pulled out my address book.

Five calls. I could do this. And if my plan worked, even Mother would have to admit I'd achieved something amazing.

Five calls. But my finger refused to turn the dial.

I *hated* asking for money.

People did this for a living. I could think of no worse fate than asking for money five days a week. And—this was the insane part—most of those people enjoyed their jobs. They found connecting donors with worthy causes fulfilling.

Maybe it was.

But it was still asking for money.

I gritted my teeth and dialed the first number.

"Woodson residence."

"May I please speak with Joan?"

"May I say who's calling?"

"Ellison Russell."

"One moment, please."

In a perfect world, I'd ask face to face. It was harder to turn someone down when they sat across a table from you. But there wasn't time to schedule the appointments.

My spine stiffened until my vertebrae ached.

"Ellison?" Joan sounded pleased to hear from me.

"Joan, how are you?"

"Fine. Looking forward to the gala."

"Me too. Actually, that's why I'm calling."

"Oh?"

I swallowed and gripped the edge of the desk with my free hand. "The other cities that are hosting the exhibit are raising a million dollars. I know how much you care about the museum and the city. Would you please consider pledging an additional hundred thousand dollars, payable over four years?"

She answered me with silence.

My heart slammed against my chest. "This isn't an annual ball. This is a once-in-a-lifetime event."

Asking for the money was the worst—worse than running over my husband's body, worse than listening to Mother after she discovered someone's ashes in her front closet, worse than the time

Max destroyed my witchy neighbor's everyday china.

"A hundred thousand dollars?"

"Yes."

"Over four years?"

"Yes."

"May I pay it over five?"

"Yes." Yes, yes, yes, yes!

"All right. Have the museum send over the pledge forms."

"Joan, I cannot thank you enough. You're really making a difference—to the museum and to the city."

She laughed softly. "Just wait till I chair something. I know the first person I'm calling for a sponsorship."

The next three calls went much the same.

I fetched a glass of wine before the fifth call. Four hundred thousand dollars. Spinning in jubilant circles till I collapsed in an ecstatic heap on the carpet seemed entirely reasonable.

I did the responsible thing. I returned to my desk, took a deep breath, and dialed the fifth number.

"Hello."

"Daddy, it's Ellison."

"I've been expecting your call."

"You have?"

"Your mother—" he sounded rueful "—set you a million-dollar goal."

"She did."

"I don't have it, sugar."

He thought I wanted a million dollars? "Daddy!"

"What?"

"I would never ask you for that much money. I've raised nine hundred thousand dollars. If I give another fifty, would you and Mother consider a fifty-thousand-dollar gift payable over four years?"

"You've raised nine hundred thousand dollars?" The surprise in his voice was a bit insulting.

"Yes." I took a celebratory sip of wine.

"Does your mother know?"

"Not yet. I wanted to hit a million before I told her."

"Well, sugar, you can tell her now."

"You mean it?"

"I do."

"Thank you, Daddy." My voice was thick.

"We don't always tell you, but we're very proud of you."

I wiped away a tear. "I love you, Daddy."

"Love you too, sugar." He hung up.

I sat for a moment, stunned. I'd done it. I'd raised a million dollars. This called for a second glass of wine. Or maybe coffee.

Grace stood at the kitchen counter. When she spotted me, the fork in her hand (a fork laden with chocolate cake) froze. "Are you okay?"

"Yes. Why?"

"You look sort of—I don't know—stunned."

"I am."

"Did you find another body?"

"No. I raised a million dollars."

SIXTEEN

When I told Mother about the million dollars, she whooped.

Mother.

Whooped.

Her response made me wish I'd told her in person and not over the phone.

"Ellison, that's fabulous! How did you do it?"

"Pledges, paid over the next few years."

"Pledges?" An edge snuck into her voice. "You don't actually have the money?"

I closed my eyes, counted to ten, and remembered the whoop. "Joan Woodson and the other people who committed will pay their pledges, Mother."

"I know, I know. But—"

"Call your friend Claudia and ask how much they collected this year and how much will come in paid pledges."

"Don't be so defensive."

"Don't be so critical. Enjoy this with me."

"I wasn't being critical. You're too sensitive."

Words—none of them nice ones—elbowed each other on their way to the tip of my tongue. "Mother—"

"What?"

"Stop."

"Stop?"

"Exactly. Stop. You would have done things differently, found opportunities I missed, raised more money. I get it. But right now, be pleased for me and the museum."

"I am pleased. And proud. But—"

I gave up. "Mother, I won't keep you." I walked toward the telephone's base. "I just wanted you to know we'd hit the goal."

"Should we have set the goal higher?"

"No!"

Getting off the phone before she moved the goal to two million dollars became *my* goal. "I must run. I'll talk to you later."

"But—"

"Got to go. Bye." I hung up.

Grace, who'd listened to the whole conversation, grinned at me. "I'm still blown away, Mom."

"Thanks, honey."

"You should eat a slice of cake to celebrate."

There was no reason I shouldn't indulge in a piece—except for the fit of my gala dress. The gala was still weeks away. "Fine."

"Sit down," she instructed. "I'll get you a plate."

"You went to the Howes'?" I climbed onto a kitchen stool. "Jennifer and Debbie talked?"

She nodded.

"Was Jennifer helpful?"

She blew a stray strand of hair away from her face. "I'm not sure."

"Oh?"

"They talked without me. I hung out in Jennifer's dining room and did homework."

"Did Debbie say anything afterwards?"

"Only that Jennifer was super nice and super cool."

"Sounds promising."

Grace shrugged and put an enormous piece of cake on the counter in front of me. "I'll get you a fork."

"Thanks."

She opened the cutlery drawer. "One thing Debbie said bothers me."

"Oh? What's that?" I accepted the fork she held out to me.

"I'm not sure she'd want me telling you."

I ate a bite of chocolate cake and moaned. "This is amazing."

"I know, right?"

"You don't have to tell me what Debbie said. I don't want you to betray a confidence."

"It's not exactly a confidence." Grace looked down at her nail polish—something frosty and pale pink. "She hates what this is doing to her family. She says her father can't look at her, and her mother seems angry all the time."

Oh, dear. "Their problem isn't with Debbie. Their issue is what happened to Debbie. Very different things. I bet they're ready to kill the man who did this to her, and they're furious with themselves for not keeping her safe."

"I get that." Grace picked at a chip in the frostiness on her nails. "But Debbie sees things differently. Her parents wouldn't be going through all this if she hadn't been raped. She blames herself."

Eating more cake bought me time to craft a response.

Grace looked up from destroying her manicure and watched me chew.

"If Debbie feels guilty about lying to her parents and sneaking into a bar when she's underage, more power to her. But the rape?" I shook my head. "Not her fault."

"What would you do if I was raped?"

My knee-jerk reaction was castration—I kept that to myself. "I'd get you all the counseling you needed and support any decision you made about prosecution." I lifted another bite of cake to my lips. "And we'd run away to Italy."

"Then I'd feel guilty."

"Boots, Grace. Think of the boots."

"But I'd be responsible for taking you away from Anarchy."

"Handbags, too." Like boots, they sang a siren's song.

"I'm serious."

I was too. "Grace—" I reached for and caught her hand in mine "—you're the most important person in the world to me. Never feel guilty about something someone does for you out of love."

"If I was raped, and you murdered the rapist, it would totally be my fault." She'd followed my reasoning down the wrong path.

"Nope. The decision to commit murder would be on me, not you. But death—even a violent death—would be too easy." I narrowed my eyes. "I'd rather let the guy live and make his life miserable."

"Whoa."

"What?"

"For a minute there, you looked and sounded exactly like Granna."

"Your grandmother has her good points."

"True. But she can be scary." Grace shuddered, and her gaze traveled to the clock on the wall. "Where's Aggie?"

"No idea."

"It's almost dinner time."

"Are you hungry?" The chocolate cake had taken care of my appetite.

"Nope. Not hungry at all."

"Cake for dinner. We could start a trend."

She grinned at me. "Thanks, Mom."

"For what?"

"For being you." She looked at me—really looked (as if she saw a woman and not the mom whose sole purpose on earth was embarrassing her). "I love you, and I'm super proud of you."

How to capture that moment, preserve it, and hold it close to my heart forever? I memorized the tilt of her chin, the stripes on her sweater, the way my throat swelled, and my jaw ached with the effort of holding back tears. "Thanks, honey."

Ding, dong.

"I bet that's Anarchy."

Again? The secret, crazy, romantic part of me—the part only allowed to express itself on canvas whirled in a delighted circle. The visible part of me grinned—for about a half-second, till reality intruded. "I have nothing to feed him for dinner." Well, nothing but chocolate cake.

Grace's eye roll revealed the whites of her eyes. "He doesn't come for the food, Mom."

With that thought warming me, I walked to the front door.

"Hi." I smiled up at the detective on my front stoop. "Come in out of the rain."

"Thanks." He stepped inside.

Rainwater dripped from his broad shoulders onto the Oriental rug beneath our feet.

"May I take your coat?" I held out my hand.

He shook off his jacket and gave it to me. "I can't stay long but I was wondering about your friend, Winnie."

"What about her?"

"Can we sit down for a minute?"

That didn't sound good. "Do you want a drink?"

"Working."

"Family room?"

"Sure."

He followed me through the kitchen where I draped his wet coat on a stool.

When we reached the den, he collapsed on the couch.

"You look tired. Would you like some coffee?"

"No, thank you."

I sat down next to him. "What about Winnie?"

His lips thinned. "These murders, they don't make sense."

"Isn't there an arrest warrant for Nick DiGiovanni?"

"DiGiovanni is the easy answer." He rubbed his palms against the planes of his cheeks. "The lawyer's dead. The judge is dead." He pressed his fingers together. "But not the witness?"

"Bilardo is next?"

Anarchy shook his head. "Maybe. There's the other unanswered question."

"Why kill Marigold?"

"Exactly."

"Her real name was Janice Young."

His stared at me—a how-do-you-know-that stare. "Let me

guess. You heard over the bridge table?"

"Yes."

"Did you hear anything about insurance policies?"

"No. But that could be arranged."

"How?"

"If I call Diane Blake, she might tell me. If I play cards with her, she will."

"Diane Blake's husband is in the insurance business?"

I nodded. "Yes."

"And his wife gossips?"

"That sounds harsh." Diane Blake shared interesting information with her friends.

"Will she tell you about the policies?"

"Not if I ask."

Anarchy stared at me. "I swear, sometimes we're speaking different languages."

"For the direct approach, ask her husband, Martin."

"I could do that but—" Anarchy rubbed his hand across his chin.

"Yes?"

"But sometimes you learn more than I do."

"I'll call her. She's on the seating committee for the gala and we've had a few changes."

"Changes?"

A smile teased my lips. "I raised more money."

"You'd already reached your goal."

"Mother moved my goal."

"How much did you raise?"

I grinned. Wide. I couldn't help it. "A million dollars."

"That's amazing. You're amazing!" He hugged me. Tight. "I wish there was time to celebrate, but I'm needed back at the station."

"We'll celebrate another time."

When he left, I curled up on the couch with a hideous crocheted afghan (a years-ago Christmas gift from Henry's aunt) and thought.

Had Winnie killed Lark for the insurance money? The idea seemed laughable. But the man had cheated on her. Maybe Winnie preferred being a rich widow to a divorcée—a woman set aside for someone half her age.

After all, she'd seemed more concerned about her cat than Lark's murder.

If she had done it, she'd put a terrific amount of faith in her accomplice.

I pulled the ugly blanket all the way to my chin. If Winnie was responsible for Marigold and Lark's murders, who'd killed John Wilson?

Brnng, brnng.

I glared at the phone.

Brnng, brnng.

Where was Grace? She usually grabbed the phone by the second ring. "I'm coming." I tossed off the afghan.

Brnng, brnng.

"Hello."

"May I please speak with Ellison?"

"This is she."

"Ellison, it's Penny calling. I was wondering if you could join me for lunch tomorrow. I'd like to introduce you to a friend who's interested in supporting your gala."

Exceeding the million-dollar mark might silence Mother. "I'd love to. Where?"

"Do you mind coming out south? We could have lunch at Brookhaven."

"Sounds lovely. What time?"

"Noon?"

"I'll see you there."

The swish of the Mercedes' wipers kept me company on my drive out to Brookhaven. I missed the sun, missed driving my convertible.

Unlike the golf clubs in the Country Club district, Brookhaven didn't have a long driveway—its golf course lay behind the clubhouse.

I parked in the near-empty lot and dashed for the porte-cochere.

Penny waited for me inside the clubhouse doors. "You made it. Can you believe this rain?"

We kissed the air next to each other's cheeks.

"I heard a rumor the sun might shine this afternoon."

"Those weathermen don't know a thing. I swear, all they do is call Denver, ask what the weather is there, and give us their best guess on when that weather will arrive here."

"In this case, I hope they're right. I'd love to see the sun."

"You and me both. Beth—" she nodded to the woman at the reception desk "—can take your coat and umbrella."

I handed over my damp rain gear then followed Penny to the dining room. "Who are we meeting?"

"Mark Roberts."

"Tell me more."

"Mark and his wife have been members here forever—he's the board member I told you about, the one who got Arlene and John Wilson in." She glanced around the near empty dining room. "He manufactures transformers."

"Transformers?"

"Those big barrel things the electrical lines run through. He's done well. Shall we sit?" She smiled at the hostess. "There will be three of us."

We sat at a table overlooking the golf course. The grass still wore hints of winter's brown, the sky dripped, and I wished Penny had opted for a table near the fireplace instead.

"What may I get you to drink?" asked the hostess.

"White wine," said Penny.

"Coffee, please."

Penny's forehead puckered. "Are you sure you won't have a

drink?"

"Maybe later. Right now I want to warm up."

"Do you take your coffee black, ma'am?"

"With cream, please."

The hostess left us.

"This is actually a pretty room when the course isn't dormant."

I glanced up at the vaulted ceiling and the brass chandeliers. "I'm sure it is."

We chatted about horses. About kids. About dogs.

"I can't imagine what's keeping Mark." Penny glanced at her watch. "It's nearly half-past."

"A problem at the office?"

"You'd think he'd call and ask the receptionist to let us know he'd be late."

"I'm in no hurry." My stomach rumbled. Loudly.

"I have plans this afternoon. Let's order."

Brookhaven built its reputation on the quality of its golf course, not its food. I glanced at the menu and chose something simple. Then my gaze wandered to the outdoors where a break in the clouds revealed a patch of blue sky. "Looks like the weatherman was right. The sun might actually shine this afternoon."

Penny frowned at her watch as if the timepiece was responsible for Mark's tardiness. She cared more about our missing lunch date than the weather. "I hope so."

We ordered. Tomato soup and grilled cheese for both of us.

When the waiter served our lunches, Penny winced. "Ellison, I'm sorry about this."

"Don't give it another thought. It's not your fault he's not here. And I'm glad we get to spend more time together." As for Mark Roberts, it was a good thing I didn't need his money because now, given the distress on Penny's face, I didn't want it.

"It's a long way to drive for a cup of soup." The apology in her voice was unnecessary.

I patted her hand and offered a bright smile. "I'm more interested in the company than the food."

At one fifteen, we rose from the table and walked to the reception desk.

The young woman who sat there returned my coat and umbrella (thankfully I didn't need the umbrella).

"Thank you for lunch," I told Penny.

"I really am sorry."

"We've all been stood up before." My late husband had been notorious for asking me to meet him at such-and-such restaurant then failing to show. "Let's get together again soon."

"I'd like that."

"Are you headed home?" I nodded toward the door leading to the parking lot.

"Actually, I have a bridge game at one thirty."

"Well—" I gave her a quick hug "—I hope you have marvelous cards."

Walking to the parking lot by myself, I looked up at the sky, now dotted with blue patches, and smiled. With any luck, the sun would peek out soon.

I swung my umbrella, danced around a puddle, and whistled the first few bars of "Here Comes the Sun" (in case the sun needed encouragement).

I closed my fingers around the car door's handle, noticed the man inside, and stepped back. "I'm sorry. I thought—" I thought it was my car. I glanced around the sparsely populated parking lot. It was my car.

Why was someone napping in the front seat?

An all-too-familiar sinking feeling dragged my stomach to my ankles.

The man in my car wasn't moving.

I swallowed, opened the car's door, and peered inside.

I smelled the blood before I saw it.

The man, whoever he was, was definitely dead. I didn't need to check for a pulse. Not when blood darkened the headrest. Something (I did not want a closer look) was seriously wrong with the back of his head.

I turned on my heel, ran back to the clubhouse, and burst through the front door.

"There's a dead man in my car."

The receptionist gasped (if I'd found a dead body at my club, the receptionist would have rolled her eyes—familiarity doesn't breed contempt, it breeds *ennui*).

"Please call the police."

She picked up the phone

"And ask for Anarchy Jones."

Her brows rose.

"What are you waiting for?"

"Anarchy?"

"Yes."

"That's his name?"

"Yes." Frustration sharpened my voice. "Detective Anarchy Jones."

"Detective?"

"Yes. The man in my car was murdered."

Her hand trembled. "And your name?"

"Ellison Russell."

She dialed. "This is Mary Beth Donovan calling. I'm the receptionist at Brookhaven Country Club. We have a guest here who says there's a dead body in her car."

I clenched my teeth. And my hands.

"She said to ask for Detective Anarchy Jones."

Mary Beth's eyebrows lifted, and her eyes widened. "How did you know?"

Whoever was on the other end of the telephone line was loquacious because Mary Beth remained silent for at least a minute.

"Thank you." She hung up and looked at me as if I were a particularly nasty communicable disease. "They knew your name. They asked if you'd found the body—as if they expected it." Her lips drew back from her teeth. "Patrol will arrive in a few minutes. Homicide detectives are on their way." She picked up the receiver.

"Who are you calling?"

"The club manager. He'll want to know."

I considered searching for Penny. But why ruin her afternoon? Instead, I walked out into the weak sunshine and waited for the police.

SEVENTEEN

The police identified the dead man as Mark Roberts, which meant he'd had a good excuse for standing Penny and me up.

"Have you ever seen him before?" Detective Peters' mustache twitched as if he'd caught the scent of a lie. He held a pen poised above a small notepad.

"Never."

"Why was he in your car?"

"No idea."

"Did you lock it?"

"I'm not sure," I admitted. "It was raining when I arrived, and I was in a hurry. It's possible I forgot to lock the door."

Detective Peters smoothed his trench coat's lapel. The coat was so rumpled and dirty, it hardly mattered that his fingers left a smudge of ink. "You never heard of this guy—"

"I didn't say that. I said I'd never seen him. We were scheduled to have lunch today."

Detective Peters' eyes bulged like Marty Feldman's. "You didn't know him, but you were having lunch with him?"

"He was considering making a donation to the gala."

"The gala? You don't say?" Detective Peters laced his voice with la-di-da.

"It's a worthy cause."

"I don't doubt it."

Detective Peters' out-of-control sarcasm stiffened my spine. "A friend arranged the luncheon, but Mr. Roberts didn't show up."

"No one called to find out why he was late?"

"No."

"Why not?"

"I didn't know Mr. Roberts. As for Penny, the man had already embarrassed her. Why put herself through the further embarrassment of tracking him down?"

"Penny?"

Keeping her out of the story was impossible. "Penny Sylvester."

"Where is she?" His eyes scanned the parking lot, now filled with police officers and a hand-wringing club manager.

"Playing bridge."

"There's a dead man in your car and your friend is playing bridge?"

"I hated to disturb her." I glanced at the Mercedes, which was crawling with police personnel. "It wasn't as if she could *do* anything."

Detective Peters tugged on his mustache and his bulging eyes looked as if they might pop clean out of his head. "We're impounding the car."

"I figured as much." Mother would have a conniption. She and Daddy gave me the Mercedes (mainly because she didn't approve of my TR6) and now a man had died—been murdered (he hadn't bashed in his own skull)—in the front seat.

Mother might be more upset by the dead body than the bloodied car.

Or not.

One could hope.

"Ellison!"

I turned toward the clubhouse where Penny stood beneath the porte-cochere.

She hurried toward me. "What happened?"

"Mark Roberts has a good reason for missing lunch."

She paled, and her gaze took in the police. "You don't mean—"

"Someone murdered him and stashed the body in my car."

She staggered, and I grabbed her arm.

"You don't mean it."

I never lied about corpses. "I'm afraid I do."

"This sort of thing doesn't happen out here." People who lived out south believed they were safe—far from the crime that plagued Kansas City's more urban neighborhoods. To them, the Plaza was a hotbed of criminal activity. Just running into Swanson's was an invitation to be mugged, a quick trip to Woolf's meant a purse snatching, a walk through a parking garage meant an assault.

"It can happen anywhere." I spoke from experience.

"Ellison."

Anarchy stood behind me.

Penny's eyes widened.

"Penny, this is Anarchy Jones. He's a homicide detective. Anarchy, this is Penny Sylvester, one of my oldest friends."

"Nice to meet you." Anarchy sounded distracted—as if he had murder on his mind.

Penny stared. Mute.

I turned and looked at him. Anarchy wore a charcoal gray suit, a crisp white shirt, and a striped tie. He looked like a partner in a law firm or a bank president. "Wow."

A dull red stained his cheeks. "I'm going to Marigold's funeral." His gaze traveled to the Mercedes. "Body in the car?"

"Yes."

"Isn't that the car your parents gave you?"

I nodded.

"Your mother won't like this." As understatements went, his was huge.

Penny giggled.

"Detective Peters says he's impounding it."

"Evidence." There was nothing he could do.

"Can you take me home?"

He glanced at his watch. "Do you mind going to the funeral first?"

I wore a beige Ultrasuede coat dress and black pumps. Not

perfect for a funeral but not disrespectful either. I pulled the colorful Hermès scarf off my neck, folded the silk, and stowed the square in my handbag. "Penny, I'll call you later."

Penny merely nodded, too stunned by the murder or Anarchy or the combination of the two to form words.

"Let's go." Anarchy escorted me to his car and opened the passenger door for me.

"Thank you," I murmured.

He slid behind the wheel but didn't turn on the ignition. "What happened?"

"I really don't know."

"You've never met Mark Roberts?"

"Never. Penny set up lunch because he was interested in the gala."

"Why put his body in your car?"

I guessed. "It was the closest?"

Anarchy didn't look satisfied with my answer, but he turned the key and drove out of the parking lot.

"Where's the funeral?" I asked.

He mentioned a church I'd never heard of.

"Methodist?"

"Yes. You sound surprised."

"I figured Marigold's funeral would be unorthodox."

"Marigold—Janice—didn't plan it."

Which was precisely why Mother had everything written out—from the hymns to the readings to a reminder that the dean was to wear his good shoes (she'd spotted him wearing Hush Puppies under his cassock at a graveside service and had been so appalled she skipped church for three Sundays in a row).

The church was nearby. Only a few minutes away from Brookhaven. Anarchy parked in the half-full lot, and we quietly slipped into one of the back pews.

"Do you always attend victim's funerals?" I whispered.

"You'd be surprised how often the killer shows up."

That had me studying the congregation carefully.

Was that Winnie? I blinked. The salt-and-pepper hair sure looked like hers.

The woman glanced over her shoulder as if she could feel the weight of my stare.

It was Winnie. And she didn't look pleased to see me.

I smiled and shifted my gaze.

Lisa sat a few rows closer to the altar. She'd done such a masterful job of erasing her out-south roots I was surprised to see her.

The organist played the first few notes of a hymn, the family filed into their seats in the front row, and the congregation quieted.

The service was awkward. The minister's vague remarks made it obvious he'd never met the deceased.

When the last prayer was completed, Anarchy and I watched the family follow Marigold's coffin up the aisle. The woman in the black print dress with smudged mascara had to be Lisa's friend, Rose.

"We should pay our respects," I whispered to Anarchy.

"What?"

"I have a feeling about Rose."

"Who's Rose?"

"Janice's sister."

Anarchy did not look convinced.

"It won't take long." A bald-faced lie. We'd be waiting in line forever and I knew it.

Twenty-five minutes later, I stood in front of Rose Cook. "I'm sorry for your loss."

"Thank you—" she couldn't place me.

"I took Marigold's class that day."

Her gaze sharpened. "You were there?"

"Locked in the attic." I pulled a calling card out of my handbag, one I'd prepared for Mark Roberts—it had my phone number jotted on the back. I handed the card to her. "If you'd like to talk..."

She slid the card into her pocket. "Thank you."

I moved on, offering condolences to Marigold's parents and a wizened woman who had to be a grandmother.

Duty complete, I surveyed the cookie selection on the buffet. Store-bought. Mother would not approve.

"Are we done?" Anarchy asked.

I nodded, and he took my arm and guided us through the throng.

We stepped outside and drank in a moment of sunshine.

"What did you give her?"

"My card."

"She knows nothing about the murder. She was out of town when her sister died, and she hadn't seen her in months."

How to explain the feeling that Rose knew something? Something important. "I doubt she calls." And I had zero interest in intruding on her grief by calling her.

"I'll take you home."

Home. Where the phone was probably ringing off the hook. Someone who knew someone who knew someone would have called Mother by now—and told her—her daughter had found another body.

I sighed. "Let's go."

Anarchy dropped me off at home.

Max met me at the door. A run? Now? Please?

"We might as well take advantage of the sunshine."

He wagged his tail in agreement and offered me a doggy grin.

I changed into running clothes then, with Max nudging me, I descended the front stairs. "Aggie?"

No one answered.

I stuck my head into the kitchen and spotted two notes stuck to the front of the refrigerator.

Aggie was at the law library.

Grace was next door getting math help.

I left a note of my own and picked up Max's leash. "Ready?"

Was he ever.

We ran four miles. Until cake for dinner didn't matter. Until the memory of the body in the Mercedes was pounded into the ground beneath my sneakers. Until even Max looked tired.

The house was still empty when we arrived home.

I leaned against the kitchen counter and chugged a glass of water.

Max, with his tongue lolling out of his mouth, flopped on the floor.

Brnng, brnng.

I stared at the phone.

Brnng, brnng.

Life before telephones must have been peaceful. Mothers had to be in front of their daughters to scold them.

"Hello."

"Would you care to explain what happened?" Mother's voice was icy.

"It wasn't my fault."

"It never is."

"Technically, that's true. I haven't murdered anyone."

A strange sound, almost like a growl, carried down the telephone line. "What happened?"

I gave her the condensed version.

"I can't believe you dragged Penny into this sordid mess."

"Some might argue Penny dragged me."

"Don't be smart, Ellison."

"I wouldn't dream of it." My voice was chocolate cake sweet—chocolate cake with a side of sarcasm.

Grace burst through the back door.

"Mother, Grace is home. I'll talk to you later. Bye." I hung up and smiled at my daughter. "How's Jennifer?"

"She should teach. She explains things much better than the actual teacher."

"I'm glad you're learning math."

Grace's eyes narrowed. "What's wrong?"

I told her about Mark Roberts and the car.

"Just now, you were on the phone with Granna?"

"Yes."

"Did you tell her about the Mercedes?"

"Not exactly."

"I wouldn't want to be you when she figures it out."

Brnng, brnng.

We both stared at the phone.

Neither of us made a single move to pick up the receiver.

Brnng, brnng.

"You're the adult."

She had a point.

I reached for the receiver. "Hello."

"May I please speak with Ellison?"

"This is she." I didn't recognize the voice.

"This is Rose Cook calling. I'm Janice's sister."

"Of course. How are you?"

"Shaky. Would you meet me for a drink?"

"I'd be happy to."

"Tonight? The rooftop bar at the Alameda?" The Alameda was a new hotel on the Plaza, not far from my house.

"That's fine. Eight o'clock?"

"I'll see you there." She hung up.

I stared at the dead receiver in my hand. What was so important that Rose had to see me the night she buried her sister?

"What was that all about?" Grace's eyes narrowed again.

"That was the yoga instructor's sister. We're meeting for a drink."

"The yoga instructor who locked you in an attic then got herself murdered?"

"That's the one."

"And you're meeting her sister? Why?"

"Presumably she has something she wants to tell me."

"You're not going alone."

"We're meeting at the rooftop bar at the Alameda. It's always crowded. I'll be fine.

"Fine? You haven't had the best luck at the Alameda."

I waved away the problems. "A few mishaps."

"Mishaps? I'll go with you."

"It's a bar and you have school tomorrow."

"Then take Libba with you."

That wasn't a bad idea. She and Jimmy could cocktail at a nearby table and if I needed them, help would be nearby. "Okay."

Grace reached past me and lifted the receiver off its cradle. "Call her now."

"Now?"

"Why not?"

With Grace watching, I dialed.

Libba answered. "Hello."

"It's me."

"What happened?"

"How do you know something has happened?"

"Your voice?"

"Really?" My best friend could hear disaster in my voice?

"And Jinx called me."

I clenched my hand into a fist. "What are you doing tonight?"

"Nothing special."

"I'm meeting Marigold's sister for a drink at the Alameda at eight. Grace doesn't want me going by myself."

"Grace has more sense than her mother."

"Would you and Jimmy have a drink there? To keep an eye on me?"

"Of course. That's a wonderful idea. Did Grace think of it?"

"Yes."

We hung up the phone, and I ran upstairs to shower and change.

I threw on a black dress, black stockings, and black heels, and glanced in the mirror. I looked like I was the one in mourning. I took everything off and started fresh—my favorite DVF dress (the color of persimmons), nude hose, nude heels, and a multitude of gold chains.

I grabbed a Chanel clutch and headed downstairs.

When I entered the kitchen, Aggie and Grace flushed—guilty flushes.

They were up to something. What? One thing was certain, the direct approach wouldn't work. I pretended I'd missed the incriminating pink on their cheeks. "What's for dinner?"

"There's quiche Lorraine in the oven and a salad in the fridge."

"Sounds delish." I opened the fridge and took out a bottle of wine. "Did you learn anything at the law library?"

"No." Aggie tapped the tip of her nose with her fist. "We're missing something. I'm sure of it."

"I agree. But the harder I chase, the faster it runs." I poured a glass of wine and returned the bottle to the fridge.

"Grace tells me you're going to the Alameda tonight."

"I am." Was that what she and Grace were whispering about when I walked in? "Libba and her beau will be there to keep an eye out."

Aggie did not look impressed. But, given Libba's track record with men, there was a real possibility Jimmy moonlighted as an axe murderer.

"The oven timer is set," she said. "Just take the quiche out of the oven when it dings and dress the salad."

"You're leaving?"

She glanced at Grace. "Mac and I have a date."

"Don't worry, Aggie. I won't let Mom burn dinner."

Even I could pull a quiche from an oven. "You two are lucky I don't take up Jell-O salads as a hobby."

Grace grimaced.

Aggie chuckled.

"Have fun with Mac," I told her.

"I will, and you be careful."

Why was everyone so worried?

Ding dong.

Had Mother come to scold in person? I froze.

Grace sent a put-upon look my way before trudging down the hall.

"I wasn't kidding." Aggie's gaze met mine. "Be careful."

"I will. I promise."

Grace and Max reappeared.

"Who was it?"

She held up a textbook. "I forgot this at Jennifer's. She brought it over." She dropped the book on the counter. "I told her you were going out tonight, and she invited me over to watch TV. Can I go?"

"Is your homework done?"

"Yes."

"Home by ten."

"I promise."

Hopefully I'd beat her home.

The rooftop bar at the Alameda overlooked the Country Club Plaza. Lacy towers, Spanish architecture, and dramatic lighting gave the buildings below me an enchanted aura.

I sipped my drink and enjoyed the view.

"Ellison?"

I looked up at Rose Cook. She wore unrelenting black (good thing I'd changed). The smudges beneath her eyes were darker than they'd been after the funeral and her nose was pink. On a good day, she was probably an attractive woman. Today was not a good day.

She pulled out a chair and sat across from me. "Thank you for meeting me."

"I'm very sorry for your loss."

She glanced down at her hands. "I keep thinking about how awful her last moments must have been."

"She's at peace now." That sounded infinitely better than *at least her neck broke and she didn't choke to death.* I scanned the room for a waiter and spotted Libba and Jimmy at the bar.

They had their backs to me.

Rose could lunge across the table and stab me, and they wouldn't notice.

"Let's get you a drink."

She dug a handkerchief out of her handbag and wiped her nose. "I've been drinking a lot this week."

"When my husband died, I drank more wine than I care to admit. Drinking was part of the grieving process."

"How did he die?"

"He was murdered."

Her eyes grew large. "You do understand."

I'd never, not once, given Henry's suffering a second thought, but I nodded. "You two were close?"

"No. In a way, that makes it worse. We'll never fix what was broken."

I waited.

"Something happened when Janice was in high school. No one handled it well, and she went off the rails. She graduated—barely—then took off. My parents didn't hear from her for years." She waved a waiter over to the table. "A vodka martini. Extra dry."

When he left the table, she continued. "I was furious with her for all she'd put them through, and I told her so."

"How long was she gone?"

"Ten years. Ten years without a word."

"Your poor parents." Their fear and anxiety and sorrow were easy to imagine. If Grace disappeared, I'd lose my mind.

"She came back as Marigold."

"What happened to her? Why did she run away?"

Rose didn't answer.

She watched the waiter put a martini on the table. She picked up said martini. She took an enormous (half-the-glass-gone) sip. She sighed.

I sipped my wine. And waited for the rest of the story.

"Janice asked a friend to spend the night. The two of them snuck out to meet a couple of boys. Boys Janice knew. Katie was raped. Janice blamed herself."

The bare bones of a tragic story.

But those bones were all it took to flip a light switch in my brain. We'd been looking at everything the wrong way.

EIGHTEEN

Three dry martinis in an hour meant Rose couldn't drive—she could barely walk. I poured her into a cab and waited for the valet to bring my car.

Libba and Jimmy didn't notice when I left. Aggie and Mac did—they'd hidden behind menus when I walked by their table. Somehow, I doubted the Alameda was their first choice for an evening out.

Grace had crossed her *t*s and dotted her *i*s when it came to my safety.

With Rose gone, and me on my way home, I hoped Aggie and Mac enjoyed their evening.

When I arrived, I let Max out and started a pot of coffee.

You've been busy. Mr. Coffee made an observation. He didn't point fingers (or pot handles). He never pointed fingers. One of his attributes I loved most.

"I didn't mean to neglect you."

You think better with my help.

"So true. And I have some serious thinking to do."

Mr. Coffee filled his pot and offered me his sunny grin. *I'm here whenever you need me.*

I poured a mug. "What would I do without you? Thank you."

You're welcome.

Brnng, brnng.

It was after nine o'clock. The caller almost certainly wanted to speak with Grace. "Hello."

"Ellison." Anarchy didn't sound tired, he sounded utterly exhausted.

"What's wrong? You sound beat."

The man was investigating four murders. Of course he was bushed.

"Long day."

"Has something happened?" As a rule Anarchy didn't call this late.

"Nick DiGiovanni didn't kill Lark Flournoy or John Wilson."

I'd never believed he had. "How do you know?"

"We found his body in the trunk of a car. He's been dead for more than a week.

My brain conjured up that image. Yuck. "Then who killed him?"

"We're back to square one. Have you found anything looking at those old cases?"

"Not yet. But I had an idea."

"What's that?"

"Aggie and I looked at the cases and sentencing from the defendant's point of view. Were the sentences fair? Would a defendant be furious about the length?"

"And?"

"What if we had it backwards? What if we consider the cases from the victim's perspective?" I took a sip from my mug and offered Mr. Coffee a grateful smile.

"What do you mean?"

"Here's an example: somewhere in Aggie's stack of notes is a murderer who was sentenced to only ten years."

"The victim is dead."

"He might have a family."

Seconds passed before Anarchy spoke. "You might be on to something. You're looking at the notes again? Tonight?"

"I am. I just made a pot of coffee." I blew Mr. Coffee a kiss.

"Do you want some company?"

"Sure." Yes!

"A few things on my desk need wrapping up. When I'm done, I'll come over."

"I'll be here."

I hung up the phone and carried my mug to the desk in the family room where I'd left Aggie's notes in a neat stack.

Except the stack had disappeared.

Max ambled in from the kitchen.

"Where are my papers?"

He yawned.

Nothing else was out of place.

Had Aggie reviewed the notes and left them someplace else?

I backtracked and scanned the kitchen counters. No stack of notes.

What's wrong? Mr. Coffee was concerned.

"The notes are missing." I stuck my head into the dining room in case Aggie had left the papers on the table. "Where could they be?"

Mr. Coffee had no thoughts on the matter.

Invading the privacy of Aggie's room wasn't an option.

Instead, I grabbed a notepad out of the junk drawer and made a list of the cases I remembered. A couple of the robberies. During one of them a jewelry store owner was shot. The second-degree-murder case with the light sentence—what were the details? Who'd died and when? How could my coffee cup be empty?

I refilled.

I'd forgotten cases.

The rape case with the acquittal!

I shook my head. That couldn't be the one. Why would a victim wait ten years to exact revenge?

Unless—my blood froze in my veins and I dropped the empty coffee mug on the floor.

Oh. Dear. Lord.

I raced out the backdoor.

Max followed me. Had I invented a new game? *Woof!*

My heels sank deep into the wet earth. I didn't care—not about the shoes, not about the holes in the yard. I stumbled, fell to my knees, then ran to the gate and pushed it open.

Woof! What was this game? How did he play?

I ran across the lawn and beat against Jennifer and Marshall's backdoor with the heel of my hand. "Grace!" The certainty my daughter was in danger made my voice high and reedy.

I beat harder. My hand pounding on the door was even louder than my heartbeat in my ears.

Thump, thump, thump!

Jennifer yanked open the door. "Ellison, what's wrong?" She wore a Mexican peasant dress and a startled expression.

"Where's Grace?" I peered past her.

"In the den. Has something happened?" Jennifer didn't look like a revenge-crazed killer. She looked like a woman who'd just discovered her next-door neighbor was a raving lunatic.

I'd been wrong. Blessedly, red-faced-with-embarrassment wrong. My limbs sagged with relief. I slumped against the door frame. "I apologize for disturbing you. I had the strangest feeling Grace needed me."

Jennifer's face cleared. "You're psychic! Or maybe not, because Grace is fine. I get those feelings, too. Not about Grace. About Marshall. And when I do, I must talk to him. Right away. He's always fine."

"Ellison!" Anarchy's voice carried through the night.

I considered and rejected yelling back. If the neighbors told Mother I'd been bellowing like a hot dog vendor, I'd never hear the end of it. The best course of action was to grab Grace and find Anarchy. Quickly.

"It's time for Grace to come home."

"Are you sure?" Jennifer's forehead wrinkled. "There are only a few minutes left in the program."

I spotted Grace. She'd ventured into the kitchen and stood next to the stove, staring at me as if I'd lost my mind.

"Ellison!" Anarchy's voice was louder.

"I'd feel better if she was safe at home with me. Come on,

Grace."

Jennifer shook her head. "Are you sure you're all right? You look—"

"Ellison!"

Woof!

"Hold on." I turned around.

Anarchy sprinted across the dark backyard. Toward me. Then he closed his hands around my upper arms. "Are you all right?"

"Fine." I cut my gaze toward Jennifer. "I'll tell you everything when we get home."

"Ellison had a feeling," Jennifer explained. "She gets them about Grace."

"She does?" Grace's question was the opposite of helpful.

"I do. Let's go. Now. Jennifer, thank you for having her."

"My pleasure." Jennifer smiled sweetly. "Grace, you're always welcome. I hope you'll come again soon."

"I'd like that."

The three of us—four counting Max—trudged across the Howes' backyard, slipped through the gate, and returned to the house.

When the backdoor closed behind us, Grace planted her hands on her denim clad hips. "What's up with that, Mom?"

"I thought Jennifer might be a murderer."

"Jennifer?"

"Yes."

"Girly, Jennifer?"

"Yes."

"Seriously?" she demanded.

"Yes."

"Why?" asked Anarchy.

"Because of the cases."

"Which one?"

"The rape case," I replied.

"Seriously?" Grace used her you're-so-lame voice.

"What about them?" asked Grace.

"There's a case—a rape case—where Lark acquitted the defendant—there's some fancy legal term for it. I thought Jennifer might—"

"You thought Jennifer was the victim?" Grace rolled her eyes. "She's from California. She's never lived here before."

"You're right. It wasn't rational." How to explain the absolute certainty I'd felt?

"Where are Aggie's notes?" Anarchy asked.

"I don't know. I left them on my desk, but Aggie must have moved them."

"We can look at them tomorrow." Concern darkened his eyes. "Tonight, we'd both better get some sleep." He meant me.

Maybe he was right. Maybe I'd flown into a panic because I was overtired.

"I'm going to bed." With one final eye roll, Grace left us.

The sound of her footsteps on the stairs faded, and Anarchy gathered me into his arms. "What's up?"

I leaned my forehead against his chest. "I was so sure."

He rested a finger under my chin, tilted my head, and looked into my eyes. "Your instincts are good."

I shook my head. "Jennifer's obviously not a killer."

"You were protecting Grace."

"Maybe it's the second-degree-murder case."

"But you thought it was the rape case. Why?"

"The defendant was acquitted. I know what I'd want to do to anyone who hurt Grace that way. If a judge and a lawyer colluded to let him walk, I'd want to hurt them just as bad." Were my feelings clouding my judgment?

"We'll review the notes tomorrow. In the meantime, you should rest."

All things being equal, I preferred standing in the shelter of his arms. Instead, I said, "You look as if you could use a few hours of sleep too."

He winced and loosened his hold on me. "Fortunately, the Feds are taking the DiGiovanni murder. But that still leaves me with four."

"Busy week."

"I look on the bright side."

"Oh?"

"You only found two of them."

I didn't sleep. How could I? I paced. And I thought. And I paced some more.

Marigold was the first to die. She'd locked us in an attic and opened the door for her killer.

Why would she do that?

Had she imagined only a burglary?

Had she meant to open the door before we ever realized she'd locked it?

That made sense. Marigold had left us near dozing on the floor and opened Winnie's house to someone who'd rifled through Lark's papers. They'd been in it—whatever *it* was—together.

Had something gone wrong? Or had the killer always planned to murder Marigold?

He'd brought a rope. Her murder was planned.

I paused at the window and peered into the darkness.

Whatever the killer had found in Lark's office, within a handful of hours John Wilson was dead, and Lark not long after.

Why poison Winnie? It didn't fit.

I flopped into a club chair, tucked my feet beneath me, and covered my lap with a blanket.

Those Sweet'N Low packets—how long had the poison been in Winnie's purse? A week? A month? Since yoga class?

Could the murders and the attempt on her life be unrelated? Had Lark poisoned his wife? Who else could have done it?

So many questions. I tilted my head back and stared at the ceiling.

Anyone with access to Winnie's purse might have slipped the poison inside.

I tossed off the blanket, resumed pacing, and considered when I left my handbag unattended. Not that often. Possibly at a committee meeting. If I played tennis, my bag sat on a bench next to the court. If I went to a party, my handbag might be tossed on a bed with the coats. Basically, anyone could slip something inside.

Ugh.

The people with opportunity to slip something into Winnie's purse had been friends, family, and Marigold.

Then there was Mark Roberts.

I pinched the bridge of my nose.

Why kill him? And why stash his body in my car?

A warning? For me?

His murder couldn't be random. Could it?

All I knew for sure was that country club parking lots were dangerous places.

I climbed into bed and picked up *Postern of Fate,* a book club read. I skimmed a page, registered zero words, and closed the book.

The rape case. I needed Aggie's notes on the rape case. And the murder. If someone killed a loved one and their punishment was a mere ten years in prison, I'd be furious.

I turned off the lamp and closed my eyes, certain I'd never sleep.

I slept.

Grrr. Max nudged me.

"What?" I mumbled.

Woof! Something was wrong.

I listened, straining to hear anything out of place, anything that would make Max growl. "What is it?"

Grrr.

I climbed out of bed and crossed to the window.

The street was quiet and empty.

Grrr. Max nudged me toward the door.

"Fine, but I need a robe."

Woof! We didn't have time for robes.

"What is wrong?" My heart beat faster. Max was a dedicated

sleeper and never awakened me unless something was amiss.

I opened my bedroom door and Max trotted down the hall. He waited for me at the top of the stairs.

Together we looked down into the foyer.

Together we descended the steps.

The smell didn't hit me till I reached the first floor.

Max's nose twitched.

I raced to the front door, turned the locks, and yanked it open. "Grace! Grace! Get up!"

That smell. Gas.

"Go get Grace!"

Max flew up the stairs.

I ran into the kitchen.

The odor nearly overpowered me.

So much gas. A single spark would blow the house into the next county.

I held my nightgown over my mouth and nose and ran for the back door. When I had it open, I turned and faced the stove.

The burner knobs were turned to high, but the flames had been extinguished. I turned them. "Grace! Get out of the house."

The window stuck, but I yanked until it opened.

I coughed and my eyes watered, but I grabbed a tea towel with both hands and waved it toward the open door.

"Mom! What are you doing?"

Wasn't it obvious? I waved the towel again. "There's gas. Get out! Now!"

"Not without you."

If that was her condition, we were both leaving.

We staggered (I staggered, Grace walked) into the backyard.

Grace glanced toward the Howes'. "We need to call the gas company and the fire department."

"And the police," I added.

"The police?"

"Someone turned on the burners and blew out the pilot lights."

Her eyes widened. "How did they get in?"

"No idea."

She took a step toward the Howes'.

I caught her arm. "Wait."

"Why?"

"I'm going to Margaret's."

"Hamilton's?" Was I nuts?

"We've imposed on the Howes enough for one night."

Grace's expression said it all—Jennifer was sweet and lovely, Margaret might turn me into a footstool.

Grace was not wrong. "Let's go." I trudged toward Margaret's.

We cut into the front yard and across Margaret's lawn. The grass was wet and cold on my feet and my skin pebbled in the chilly air.

I rang the bell. "Will you stay outside with Max?"

Max was not welcome in Margaret's house. He and her cat had a running feud. A feud that, if fought in Margaret's living room, guaranteed I'd spend the rest of my life as a place for her to rest her feet.

Grace nodded. She wore a flannel gown and slippers. She'd be all right outside for a few minutes.

I poked at the bell a second time and pressed my ear to the door. "She's coming."

Margaret, clad in unrelenting black (had she been stirring a cauldron?) opened her front door and gaped at me.

"I'm sorry to disturb you, Margaret." Please, don't turn me into a tasseled footstool. "May I use your phone?"

Her gaze shifted from me to our house. "What's wrong?"

"I smelled gas."

She offered me a grudging nod. "Come in. Grace, are you staying outside with the beast?"

"Yes, ma'am."

"I'll get you a coat, dear. Ellison, there's a phone in the kitchen. You know the way."

Only because I'd once followed Max's trail of destruction.

I reached Margaret's surprisingly colorful kitchen, picked up her phone, and dialed the operator. "Please connect me with the fire department."

A few seconds later the dispatcher was on the line.

"There's been a gas leak at my house. We need your help."

"Was there an explosion? Is anything on fire?"

"Not yet." I gave her our address, hung up, repeated the conversation with the gas company, then called the person I'd come to count on more than any other.

"Hello." Anarchy's voice was thick with sleep.

"It's me."

"What's happened?" He sounded a thousand percent more alert.

"Someone broke into the house and turned on the gas."

"Are you and Grace safe? Where are you?"

"We're safe. We're at Margaret Hamilton's."

"I'm on my way."

NINETEEN

The firetrucks attracted the neighbors.

The neighbors (probably Marian Dixon) called Mother and Daddy.

Mother and Daddy arrived, and Mother charged up Margaret's front walk. "What happened?"

"Gas leak." It was almost true.

"Thank God you're all right." Daddy wrapped me in an all-encompassing hug.

"We're fine. Thanks to Max."

Max heard his name and his ears perked. Surely heroes deserved treats?

"What are they doing in there?" Mother's gaze traveled from the house to the wide array of emergency vehicles. "And why so many police cars?"

Explaining the turned-on burners was beyond me. "I'm not sure."

She sniffed her disapproval. "You, Grace, and—" she rubbed a hand across her eyes "—the dog will spend the night at my house. Even if you found a plumber who'd come and fix the leak in the middle of the night, he'd charge you a small fortune."

I didn't argue. Nor did I tell her we didn't need a plumber. "I'll just say thank you to Margaret and goodnight to Anarchy."

"What's he doing here?" She made his presence at my house sound like a problem rather than a gift from heaven.

"I found a body today. He's making sure the gas leak isn't

related." It definitely was.

"Make it snappy."

Her gaze weighed on me as I thanked Margaret then approached Anarchy. "We're spending the night with my parents."

The planes of his face were taut, and his brown eyes were narrowed but his voice was gentle. "Tomorrow morning we'll figure out how someone broke into your house. I'll leave a patrol unit here for the rest of the night."

"Thank you."

We gazed into each other's eyes for long seconds, and my lips tingled with the need to kiss him. With the dense pressure of Mother's gaze still settled on my shoulders, I merely smiled. "Good night."

Grace, Max, and I climbed into the backseat of Mother and Daddy's sedan. We drove in exhausted silence.

When we reached their house, Mother pointed to the stairs. "The yellow bedroom is made up."

The yellow bedroom was the room where I'd slept as a child. My presence had been eradicated at least three decorators ago, but the ghost of twelve-year-old me perched cross-legged on the end of the bed and regarded me with a slight tilt to her head. Why hadn't I figured out who killed all those people? I was an adult. Adults were supposed to have all the answers. Mother did.

Twelve-year-old me was a pain. Surely, by now, that little girl should realize Mother didn't have all the answers.

At six, when the light outside the window brightened to dull gray, I abandoned the pretense of sleeping, and padded down to the kitchen.

Daddy had the newspaper spread across the counter. "Coffee, sugar?"

"Please." I sat and watched as he poured coffee into a mug, fetched a carton of cream from the fridge, and put them both in front of me. No pitcher. Mother would have a coronary.

He resumed his seat and tapped on an article in the paper. "You lead an exciting life."

"Is that about Mark Roberts?"

He nodded. "The paper says he was a successful businessman—" his finger traced the length of the article "—he made transformers."

"That's what Penny told me."

Daddy shook his head. "I'm more interested in how Roberts ended up in your car."

I poured cream into my mug. "For the record, I'd be perfectly happy leading a less exciting life."

"No you wouldn't."

I looked up from studying the color of my coffee—still a shade too dark. "What do you mean?"

"You picked the homicide detective over Tafft."

"Hunter Tafft has been divorced three times. I bet living with him would be plenty exciting."

"You know what I mean. You chose the cop. You're on a different path—one that's completely foreign to your mother and me." He reached across the counter, took my hand, and squeezed. "Forgive us if we worry. We don't doubt your judgment, but we worry where the path will lead."

"I just wish it didn't lead to bodies."

He squeezed harder. "You and me both. Do you want some breakfast?"

"No, thank you. Do you? I can make some eggs."

"No!" He turned me down with insulting alacrity.

We drank our coffee in companionable silence.

When my mug was empty, I asked, "Would you please give Grace and me a ride home?"

A smile touched his lips. "You don't want to wait until your Mother gets up?"

No. A thousand times, no. "I bet she sleeps till ten. Grace has school."

Daddy dropped us off at seven. We let ourselves into the house and sniffed. The scent of rain and wet grass and Aggie's perfume hung in the air. No gas.

"Aggie?" I called.

She opened the kitchen door, took one look at me, and said, "The coffee is on."

Grace yawned and stretched and feigned exhaustion. "Do I have to go to school?"

"Yes."

"Moooom. I didn't get any sleep last night and nothing important is happening—no tests or quizzes, no big assignments due—and the house almost blew up and—"

"You're going to school, Grace."

She stared at me, gauged my resolve, then rolled her eyes (I was totally unreasonable).

"Can I at least go late? My first period class is art."

"Fine." I didn't have the energy for a debate.

She climbed the stairs.

I stumbled into the kitchen.

Aggie put a mug in my hands. "What happened last night?"

I clutched the mug like a lifeline. "Someone snuck into the house and turned on the gas."

Her brows rose. "That's it?"

"That's plenty."

"It is," she agreed. "What I meant was no firebomb, no incendiary device, no—"

"Enough." My head ached from lack of sleep, and the dull pain reaching down to my shoulders pinched a few nerves. Thinking about Grace blowing up didn't help the tension. "The doors were locked, but somehow they got in. Was the gas a warning? Or maybe whoever turned on the burners heard Max and ran before he could set a device." I drank half the mug in one gulp. "Almost everyone in the neighborhood turned out for the spectacle." Men wearing plaid robes and leather slippers. Women wearing quilted robes in shades of ice blue and shell pink. Chins that needed shaving. Hair that needed combing. And identical expressions of curiosity and annoyance. Once again, a disaster at my home had roused them from their beds.

Aggie made a sympathetic sound and her brow creased.

I pushed the hair away from my face. "What happened last night is related to the murders—it must be. May I look at your notes, please?"

Aggie tilted her head. "You have them."

The world around me slowed. "I left them on the desk in the den. Didn't you take them?"

"No."

Which meant someone had been in my house twice. They'd stolen Aggie's notes and found something in them that made sneaking in a second time worth the risk. The creepy-crawlies running up and down my spine did my tense shoulders no favors.

I downed the rest of my coffee and went to Mr. Coffee for a refill.

He offered me an encouraging smile. I needed encouragement.

I turned to Aggie. "I hate to ask, but would you please go to Hunter's law library and look up those cases again?"

"Of course. I'll call Mr. Tafft and ask him to open early." Aggie reached for the leather bag with painted smiley faces that sat on the counter.

Before her fingers closed on the handle, Grace pounded down the back stairs and exploded into the kitchen. "Have either of you seen my keys? They're not in my backpack."

And just like that, I knew.

Proving it would be another matter.

I sent Aggie to the law library, where she might find answers. "Call me when you get there. I have questions about a specific case."

I sent Max to the backyard where the squirrels barely escaped the snap of his jaws. "Stay out of the shrubs."

I sent Grace upstairs. "Too much eyeliner. Wash your face."

I sat at the kitchen island and waited for Anarchy.

Are you sure? asked Mr. Coffee.

"Pretty sure." Very sure. "I'll know for certain once Aggie finds the case."

You might be wrong. Mr. Coffee's voice was gentle.

"I hope I am."

Ding dong.

I should have changed. I still wore last night's gown, Mother's trench coat, and slippers. I wouldn't be winning any fashion awards.

But Anarchy didn't care what I wore.

Ding dong.

I plodded to the front door.

Anarchy stood on the other side.

I let him in. "There's fresh coffee in the kitchen. I'll go change."

"Wait." He took me in his arms. "How are you?"

"Tired. Scared. Glad you're here."

His eyes scanned my face. "We didn't find any sign of a break-in."

I hadn't expected any.

His arms around me tightened. "You know something."

"I have a strong suspicion. Let me throw on some clothes then I'll tell you everything."

He dropped a kiss on my forehead and released me.

I ran upstairs, took a lightning-fast shower, and pulled on a pair of khakis, loafers, and a cashmere sweater the same shade as the blooms on the hydrangeas in the backyard—the ones waiting for spring to arrive, so summer could push it out of the way.

I dried my hair and slapped on some makeup before I returned to the kitchen.

Anarchy looked up from the paper. "Feel better?"

"Much." I bent and scratched Max's head.

"He wanted in."

"And he always gets his way."

"Tell me about your suspicion."

"It's the rape case."

He lifted his brows. "Not the murder?"

"I don't think so. In the rape case, there was a judgment of acquittal."

He nodded. "That means the judge didn't think the prosecution had proved its case."

"Or it means the defense attorney paid off the judge." That was the only way Lark could have been vulnerable to Henry's blackmail.

His eyes narrowed, and he rubbed his chin. "I'm listening."

Brnng, brnng.

"Hopefully this is Aggie." I picked up the receiver. "Hello."

"Ellison—"

"Mother, I'm sorry, but I can't talk now. I'm expecting a call. I'll phone you later." I hung up. I'd pay for that. Mother didn't easily forgive things like hang ups.

Brnng, brnng.

Again? Could Mother dial that fast?

I braced myself for disaster and squeaked, "Hello."

"It's me," said Aggie.

I breathed again.

"What are we searching for?" she asked.

"I have questions about the rape case."

"Let me find it."

Wrapping the phone cord around my finger, I waited.

"Who are you talking to?" asked Anarchy

"Aggie. She went to a law library." No need to mention whose. "She's finding the case."

"What makes you sure it's the rape case."

"A feeling." And a file locked in the safe.

Grace elephant-walked her way down the stairs, nodded at Anarchy, offered me a wave that somehow said her attendance at school bordered on child abuse, and disappeared out the back door.

"Problem?"

"I'm making her go to school."

He smiled. "You're very cruel."

"I know. Most likely, she'll never recover."

"I've got it." Aggie was back on the line.

I motioned to Anarchy, and he leaned his head close to mine. We both listened.

"John Wilson was the defense attorney. Matthew Farrell was the prosecutor. Lark Flournoy was the judge."

"What else does it say?" asked Anarchy. "How did a rape case end up in federal court?"

"The defendant was charged with transporting the victim across the state line and raping her."

For me, State Line was a road, one I crossed multiple times a day, not a reason for a federal case, but Anarchy nodded as if Aggie's answer made perfect sense.

"Who was the defendant?" I clenched the receiver and waited for the answer.

"Adam Roberts."

"Roberts?" Anarchy's tone was surprised. And grim. And serious. He gave me the slightest of nods. Maybe I'd been right.

I closed my eyes and loosened my death-grip on the phone. "What about the victim?"

"Katherine Howe."

Anarchy's head jerked away from the receiver and he stared at me. "Isn't your neighbor's last name Howe?"

"Yes." My voice was a sigh.

"What else?" asked Aggie.

"We need all the details," I replied.

"I'll write everything down and be home soon."

"Thanks, Aggie." I hung up the phone and stared at Anarchy.

He stared back. "You have a theory."

I nodded, a reluctant admission.

"What is it?"

"Adam Roberts raped Katherine Howe but was acquitted. After the trial, the Howes moved to California. New place. Fresh start. Katherine could move forward."

"All right." He waited for more.

"But Katherine didn't move forward. She struggled."

Anarchy nodded—still waiting.

"Jennifer told me Marshall's sister died. She killed herself. We need to find out when."

"Why?"

I swallowed. "What if her brother decided she deserved justice?"

"Marshall Howe?"

"Yes."

"Ten years later?"

"I got the impression Katherine died recently."

"Okay, but why kill Marigold? Why poison Winnie?" Anarchy immediately identified the holes in my theory.

"I don't know, but—" I stared down at the floor.

"But what?"

"Marigold had a childhood friend who was raped."

"And you think it was Katherine Howe?"

I looked up—looked at Anarchy. "I think it's possible. Marigold's sister said Marigold felt guilty for the horrible thing that happened to her friend. What if Marshall also thought she was responsible?"

Anarchy shook his head. "It's too coincidental. Marigold just happened to be working for the Flournoys?" His gaze searched my face. "Why the thefts?"

I had an answer ready. "Winnie told me Lark kept extensive case notes. Maybe Marshall wanted to prove Adam Roberts' guilt."

"It wouldn't make any difference. Roberts couldn't be tried twice for the same crime."

"Do you want more coffee? I want more coffee."

"I'm good."

I poured myself another cup.

"Also, why kill Winnie?" he asked.

"No idea."

"What can you prove?"

"Nothing."

Anarchy's gaze settled on the burners. "Howe is responsible for turning on the gas last night?"

Tossing around accusations without proof made me itch. I rubbed my palm against the back of my neck. "They were the only neighbors who didn't come outside and watch the excitement." Suspicious, but definitely not proof.

"They're heavy sleepers?"

Sleeping through last night's circus seemed impossible. "Also, Grace's keys are missing." Not proof but very suspicious.

"Oh?"

"Jennifer's been helping Grace with math. When Grace goes over there, she takes her backpack. She leaves the darned thing everywhere. If she left the bag in their kitchen, and was tutored at the dining room table, she'd never know if Marshall took her keys."

Mother burst into the kitchen. "What is going on?" She saw Anarchy and her eyes slitted.

"I'm sorry, Mother. I was waiting for a call."

She ignored me. "What are you doing here?"

"It's possible the person who turned on the gas last night—" Anarchy, who was returning Mother's slitty gaze, didn't see me draw my finger across my throat "—is related to one of my cases."

"Turned on the gas?" Mother shifted her gaze my way (still slitty) "You told me it was a gas leak."

Oh, dear Lord.

"I didn't want to worry you."

"Your house could have blown up."

"It didn't."

"You and Grace could have died."

"We didn't."

Mother's fingers closed around the edge of the counter. "How can you be so cavalier about putting Grace in danger?"

That question rendered me mute.

"It's not her fault, Mrs. Walford."

"Is it yours?"

Now Anarchy was mute, too.

"There was a corpse in her car yesterday." Righteous indignation straightened Mother's spine—made her taller. "One would think—" Mother had switched to "one," a sure sign of coming zingers "—you'd do a better job keeping her safe."

"Ellison does a fine job taking care of herself."

"She shouldn't have to. She—"

"Enough!" I stared Mother down. "What did you want, Mother?"

"To give you the plumber's number."

"Thank you, but I don't need a plumber."

"Which I would have known if you hadn't lied to me."

"I didn't lie." I had.

"You didn't tell the truth." She had me there. She shifted her gaze to the backyard and frowned at the sunshine. "I cannot believe you let Grace skip school."

"I didn't."

"Then why is her car still here?"

Anarchy and I exchanged a she-should-be-long-gone-by-now glance and raced toward the door.

"Where are you going?" Mother demanded.

"Grace left for school."

She followed us into the yard, not stopping till she reached the driveway. "Where is she?"

The question froze my fingers, narrowed my vision to a tunnel (I only saw the car), and dried my mouth.

Grace's backpack sat next to her car. Her spare keys hung from the driver's side lock.

"Where is she?" Mother asked again. She looked around as if she expected Grace to pop up from behind the shrubbery—as if this disappearance was a practical joke.

It wasn't.

I gripped Anarchy's arm and ignored the way Mother's stare caught where we touched. "It's possible—" I took a deep, steadying breath (the steadying part didn't work) "—my new next-door neighbor is a murderer."

Mother's death glare almost reduced me to cinders. "The one who's been tutoring Grace?"

"Her husband."

"And you think he has her?"

The question sent my heart plummeting from my chest to my ankles. I looked over at the Howes', bit my lip, and prayed we were wrong.

"What are we waiting for?" Without pausing to consider if the direct approach was best, Mother strode toward Jennifer and Marshall's.

"Mother, wait!"

She ignored me.

I ran after her. I grabbed her arm and pulled. "Mother, stop."

She glanced down at my hand on her arm. "I've had enough. Enough of you finding a body every other day. Enough of you consorting with policemen. Enough worry to last a lifetime. Let go." She shook off my grasp.

"You might be putting Grace in danger."

"Piffle."

"Piffle?" Anarchy stood next to me. "Mrs. Walford, please stop."

Mother kept walking.

We needed a plan. "Mother, please!"

Mother kept walking.

Anarchy's brow creased. "I could tackle her."

"You could try."

TWENTY

Deaf to our pleas, Mother marched up to the Howes' front door and rang the bell.

Anarchy and I stood just behind her.

"Are you ready?" he whispered.

"Ready?" I shifted my gaze from Mother to Anarchy. "Ready for what?"

"When he answers the door, I'll rush him."

"You can't do that."

He lifted his brows. "Why not?"

Because he might destroy his career. For me. "If I'm wrong, it's assault. If I'm right, he might have a gun. You or Mother might be shot." Not that a bullet would stop Mother. A bazooka wouldn't stop Mother. Not when she was in a mood like this one.

"Then what?"

"We go in. We reason. Mother bulldozes." Mother could flatten anyone—even a mass killer. "And, if that fails, you have a gun."

He nodded, but his thinned lips and eyes told me he didn't approve. "You're very calm."

Not remotely. But a nervous breakdown wouldn't locate Grace. When this was over, a full-blown meltdown was mine. But I wouldn't panic until Grace was safely home. "Wait till later."

Mother, who was ignoring us with every fiber of her highly starched being, jabbed the bell a second time.

Anarchy leaned close to my ear. "She's scary."

"You ain't seen nothing yet."

That earned me a death-glare. Did Mother take issue with the sentiment or the grammar? Probably both.

Mother gave up on the doorbell and rapped her knuckles against the door.

Anarchy stared at her back. "If I were Howe, I wouldn't answer."

A rookie mistake. "When she's like this, it's best to face her right away. She gets angrier when she stews."

A second death-glare reduced the damp grass behind me to ash.

She rapped again. "Open this door."

"What if they don't answer?" Anarchy whispered.

"She won't give up." Marshall Howe had never met a force like Mother. Few men had.

Rap, rap, rap!

Mother's knuckles against the paneled oak sounded like gunshots.

The door swung open.

Anarchy's fingers flexed above his gun.

Mother glared.

And Jennifer Howe, dressed in an enormous, ugly, green and brown plaid bathrobe (it had to be Marshall's) and a sheer shortie nightgown, blinked in the morning sunlight.

"Where is my granddaughter?"

With her left hand, Jennifer rubbed her eyes and pushed her hair away from her face. "What?"

"My granddaughter. Where is she?"

"Not here."

"You won't mind my looking." Mother breezed past her.

Jennifer's mouth dropped open. "You can't just barge into my house!"

Mother wasn't listening. "Grace!"

Jennifer, whose gaze initially followed Mother, now looked at me with a question in her eyes.

"Grace is missing."

"Missing?"

"Grace!" Mother used her answer-me-this-minute-or-else tone.

Jennifer followed her toward the back of the house. "She's not here."

Mother ignored her. "Grace!"

Anarchy and I stepped inside.

Where was Marshall?

"Grace!" Mother's voice bounced off the walls.

There was no answer.

"Jennifer." Compared to Mother, I was quiet.

She turned and looked at me.

"Where's Marshall?"

"At work." Her left hand fluttered. "I should call him."

Sounds—clanks and knocks and crinkles—came from the kitchen. It sounded as if Mother was rummaging. In the pantry.

Jennifer hurried toward her kitchen

Anarchy and I exchanged a look.

"Could Marshall have taken her somewhere?" My hands shook just thinking about it.

"He didn't have much time. And Grace wouldn't leave with him. Not without telling you. She would struggle, and we didn't hear a struggle."

That was true. We hadn't heard a thing.

I ignored my galloping heart and made myself *think*. "Grace wouldn't go anywhere with Marshall." She wouldn't. But she had. Under what circumstances would Grace leave her keys and her backpack to go off with a man she didn't know well? None. Well, almost none. "If he told Grace that Jennifer needed her, she might go with him."

"Would she get in his car?"

"No." My answer was definitive and immediate. And I doubted myself the second I said it. "If you'll stay with Mother, I'll look in the garage."

He nodded. "Good idea. Be careful."

I hurried out the front door and circled the house. Like my home, a converted carriage house served as the garage. The Howes' held space for three cars and a mud room. I opened the door and peered into the dim interior.

One car was parked. One.

That meant Marshall was gone.

Had Grace been in the garage?

I stepped inside. The Howes' garage smelled of damp and dripped oil and last year's grass clippings. Rakes and hoes and a snow shovel hung neatly on the wall. A lawn mower crouched in the corner.

"Grace?"

I walked to the front of the car, stopped, and stared.

An enormous dent dimpled the front fender. What had Jennifer hit?

The light filtering through the in-need-of-a-wash windows told me the car was blue.

Blue.

The sunbeam also revealed a rusty stain.

Not what had Jennifer hit, but who had Jennifer hit? Lark?

Had I been wrong? Marshall wasn't a killer? Jennifer was?

Every suspicion I'd harbored about Marshall still fit. Was Jennifer strong enough to drag Mark Roberts to my car? Strong enough to hang Marigold? Angry enough to kill four people?

Maybe.

With my heart relocated to my throat, I raced into the backyard.

Mother and the man I lo—the man I cared about—were alone with a killer. And neither of them suspected a thing.

I ran to the backdoor.

Locked.

Doing my best to avoid being seen from the windows, I circled the house.

I glanced at my home. Should I call for help?

There wasn't time.

I closed my fingers around the unlocked front door's handle and crept inside.

The house was quiet.

No sounds of Mother pillaging.

No sounds of Anarchy talking sense into a distraught woman—or an angry one.

Quiet.

Or maybe the blood rushing to my ears drowned out everything else.

I tiptoed toward the kitchen.

Empty.

I stopped at the stove and picked up Jennifer's cast-iron skillet. The remains of scrambled eggs stuck to the bottom and sides. The darned thing weighed more than it should, and I gripped hard to hold it. A bit of egg fell to the floor.

Which way?

I peeked through the space between the door and its frame. The dining room was empty.

Where were they?

Jennifer's sun porch?

I slipped through the empty living room, glad of the flokati rugs that muffled my steps.

"She'll be back." Jennifer's voice was clear and steady.

"You don't want to do this," said Anarchy.

I peeked around the door jamb. I couldn't see Jennifer, but Mother and Anarchy stood in front of the window facing me.

"She went home to call for help," said Anarchy. "Backup will be here any minute."

"No!"

Mother was pale, but her back was ramrod straight. She stared at Jennifer with a slight lift in the corner of her upper lip—almost a sneer. "You won't get away with this, young woman."

Well, that was the opposite of helpful.

"Adam Roberts is still alive." Jennifer's voice was low and determined.

Adam Roberts, the boy who'd raped Marshall's sister. Jennifer had killed everyone associated with the case and left Adam for last.

"Mrs. Walford and I didn't hurt you or your sister-in-law." Anarchy's was the voice of reason. "I've put countless rapists in jail."

"Liar," Jennifer shrieked. The difference between that shriek and the voice she'd used only seconds before chilled my blood.

"I'm not lying, Jennifer." Anarchy sounded calm and comforting. "Men who hurt women deserve their time in jail."

"When the courts are on their side? What then?" Jennifer no longer sounded like the sweet girl from California who made atrocious Jell-O salads and tutored my daughter in math. She sounded certifiable.

I lifted the heavy pan.

"I can't let you stop me, not until he's paid."

"Jennifer, don't do this. We can work something out." Anarchy still sounded reasonable. "I'll arrest him."

"Double jeopardy. He can't be retried." She was going to shoot Mother and Anarchy. All because she wanted to kill Adam Roberts.

I stood there—just outside the door—and my heart pounded harder than ever. Sweat slicked my hands, making it difficult to hold the skillet. I tightened my grip. What should I do?

I inched forward.

From the sound of Jennifer's voice, she stood on the other side of the wall. If I leapt into the sunroom, could I hit her before she shot me?

I wrapped my other hand around the handle, lifted the skillet to shoulder level, took one very deep breath, and jumped.

I swung the pan before my feet hit the ground. The sickening sensation of metal meeting skull reverberated up my arms.

Jennifer collapsed to the floor, and I kicked the gun she'd held in her hands out of her reach.

Anarchy and Mother wore matching shocked expressions.

I dropped the skillet onto the tiles and leaned against the wall. "Are you two all right?"

"Fine." Anarchy bent and picked up Jennifer's gun.

Mother stared at the skillet. "That's what you came up with? A skillet? You own a gun."

No, *thank you for saving me.* No, *good job, Ellison.* "I don't have the gun with me."

Jennifer groaned.

Anarchy unplugged the phone cord, wrapped the length of rubber-wrapped wire around Jennifer's wrists, and tied a knot.

Mother pursed her lips as if she'd just bit into a sour pickle. "Where's Grace?"

"I don't know."

"You haven't found her?"

"I've been busy." Busy saving one Frances Walford, thank you very little.

Anarchy handed me the gun. "I'm calling for back-up, can you watch her?"

I nodded and pointed the gun at Jennifer.

"I'll be back."

Jennifer groaned again.

"Where is my daughter?" I demanded. "Where's Grace?"

Jennifer's gaze flickered. "I haven't seen her."

A few minutes later, half the Kansas City police force was at Jennifer and Marshall's house (a slight exaggeration). Anarchy, Detective Peters, countless uniformed officers, and medics from the ambulance performed a chaotic dance.

Forgotten in the hubbub, Mother and I walked back to my house.

"Thank you," she said as we passed through the gate.

"For?"

"For saving us." That was unexpected.

"You're welcome."

"Then again, we wouldn't have needed saving if you didn't involve yourself in that man's investigations."

Mother being held at gunpoint was my fault? "Mother, I don't have the energy for this. I'm worried about—" I stumbled.

And stared.

Grace's car and backpack were gone.

I left Mother, raced to the house, threw open the backdoor, and called, "Grace!"

She didn't answer.

"Aggie!"

No answer.

Max lifted his head off his paws and yawned.

"Some help you are."

He blinked.

A note lay on the counter. I snatched it up. *Mom, where are you? Mrs. Hamilton invited me over and gave me this. I figured you wouldn't mind about me being a few minutes late to school...Congratulations.*

A check floated to the floor.

I bent, picked up the scrap of paper, and read the amount. Ten thousand dollars made out to the museum.

Dropping the note and the check on the counter, I picked up the receiver and dialed Grace's school. "This is Ellison Russell calling. Did Grace Russell arrive safely?"

"She was tardy."

"But she's there?"

"Yes, Mrs. Russell, I checked her in myself."

"Thank you." The two words didn't come close to expressing my gratitude or relief.

I hung up the phone and propped myself against the counter.

"She's at school?" Mother stood in the doorway.

"Yes."

"Thank heavens."

"Do you want some coffee?"

"You're kidding."

"I never kid about coffee."

"Do you have anything stronger?"

"Of course." I poured myself a mug and led Mother to the living room and the liquor. "What will you have?"

"Scotch. Neat."

I poured the scotch into an old-fashioned glass and held it out to her.

Mother wrapped her fingers around the glass. "You were terrified something happened to Grace. Your blood crystalized. Your heart beat in your ears. Your lungs couldn't fully inflate."

"Yes."

"That's how I feel whenever you get yourself mixed up in an investigation."

Her revelation froze the coffee cup halfway to my lips. "I didn't know. I'm sorry."

Mother eyed me over the rim of her glass. "Sorry means you won't do it again."

"I'll try not to." I meant what I said. I did. But my best intentions had a way of crumbling to dust.

She sighed as if she'd followed my thoughts' trail. Then she drank. Deeply. "Drinking in the morning. You and Libba are a bad influence."

"I offered coffee."

"I was held at gunpoint. I deserve a scotch."

"I'm not arguing that."

Mother sipped again. Her glass was almost empty. "You were—" she searched for a word "—resourceful. That frying pan was a good idea."

"It was heavy. I should have found a candlestick." I glanced down at my mug. The level of coffee was alarmingly low. "I was in the garage for five minutes, Mother. What happened?"

"I found one of Lark Flournoy's journals shoved in a kitchen drawer. Someone had tried to burn it."

"How did you know it was Lark's?"

"He wrote his name, the month, and the year on the first page."

"And you asked her about it?"

"Of course I did. It obviously wasn't hers. But—" Mother pointed at me "—you said the husband was responsible."

Mother blamed me. Her being held at gunpoint was my fault. I should have known. "And then?"

"She held a gun to my head. She said she'd shoot me if that detective didn't give her his gun."

"Anarchy gave up his gun?"

"Yes." Mother finished off her scotch in one gulp. "There was madness shining in that woman's eyes. She would have shot me." Mother sounded positively outraged. How dare a murderer threaten Frances Walford?

Aggie stepped into the living room. "I'm back."

Mother, who'd just downed a healthy scotch in less than five minutes, stared at Aggie's kaftan—an orange, yellow, and lime green print—with her mouth hanging open.

Before she could utter anything forthright and unforgivably rude, I said, "You missed the excitement."

"I noticed something happening next door." Aggie's voice was dry. "They arrested Marshall?"

"Jennifer."

Mother stood and crossed to the liquor. "That woman nearly killed me."

"Jennifer?" Aggie's voice said she didn't believe her.

Mother poured herself a second scotch (healthier than the first). "Exactly."

Aggie shifted her gaze to me and her brows lifted.

I nodded.

"Why?" asked Aggie.

Mother lifted her freshened drink to her lips. "She said she owed it to Katherine."

Aggie looked confused. "Katherine?"

"Marshall's sister," I explained. "Adam Roberts raped her. Adam's father convinced the defense attorney to bribe the judge and Adam was acquitted."

"So, you were right. It was the rape case." Aggie glanced at my empty mug. "More coffee?"

"Please."

She took the mug from me. "I'll be right back."

Mother watched her go. "You should get that woman a uniform."

"Not your house, Mother."

She snorted softly as if she disapproved of the way I ran things.

But she also worried. About me.

I sat next to her on the couch and took her free hand in mine. "I'm so glad you weren't hurt."

She drank. "I'm glad none of us were."

We sat like that for a long minute—silent and holding hands.

Until Aggie reappeared. "Here's your coffee." She held out my mug. "I put on a fresh pot."

TWENTY-ONE

Anarchy appeared at the back door a few hours later.

"Come in," I said. "Aggie's fixing lunch. BLTs."

"Thanks." He opened the door and stepped into the kitchen. "Good afternoon, Aggie."

"Extra bacon?" Aggie stood at the stove with a package of bacon and an enraptured dog at her feet.

"Please."

Anarchy sat next to me at the island and we passed a few seconds watching Aggie cook.

"Was Marshall part of this?" I asked.

"As far as we can tell, he didn't know what Jennifer had done until he found Lark Flournoy's journal and papers. He tried to burn them."

"He told me they were love letters."

Anarchy nodded. Once. "He wasn't sure if you believed him so he started following you."

The man in the park. The man at the hospital.

Using tongs, Aggie positioned the bacon. "I still can't believe it. Why did she do it?"

"Have you ever seen *Strangers on a Train*?" asked Anarchy.

"The Hitchcock film?" I nodded. "Yes."

Aggie shook her head. "Al and I didn't go to many movies."

"Two strangers meet on a train. They each have someone they want dead. They agree to commit each other's murders." I glanced at the man next to me. "What does a movie have to do with

Jennifer's killing spree?"

The scent of frying bacon filled the kitchen, and Max licked his chops.

"Apparently, Katherine killed the man who raped Jennifer. Jennifer was returning the favor."

"Jennifer gets bonus points." She didn't just go after Adam Roberts, she killed everyone associated with his acquittal. "Why kill Marigold?"

"Two reasons," Anarchy replied.

The toaster popped, and Aggie removed two perfectly browned pieces of bread. Why was it when I used the same toaster, I reduced the bread to carbon?

Aggie flipped the bacon. "What are the reasons?"

"Katherine held Janice partially to blame for what happened to her."

"And?" Aggie poked at a piece of bacon that wasn't browning as fast as she liked.

"Marigold, Janice, developed feelings for Lark."

"I don't understand." Aggie's brow creased. "Jennifer and Marigold were working together?"

Anarchy nodded. "Initially, Marigold was to gain Winnie's trust and find out if there was any evidence of collusion. Apparently, Marigold snuck into Lark's office and discovered the case notes. They made the plan to steal the notes incriminating Lark, John Wilson, and Roberts."

"But after Marigold let Jennifer into the house, Jennifer hit her over the head and dropped her body over the bannister. Why?" The memory of Marigold's body swinging in Winnie's foyer almost killed my appetite. "And what about Winnie? Why poison her?"

"Jennifer insists Lark did that."

"Lark?" That couldn't be right. "Lark was dead when it happened."

"There's no telling how long that poisoned packet was in Winnie's purse. Lark and Marigold fell in love. He wanted to be with Marigold, and he didn't want the embarrassment of a public divorce."

"The morning you were locked in the yoga studio, Marigold told Jennifer she wanted to leave Lark out of their revenge."

"So Jennifer killed her?" Aggie placed toast on two plates, topped the toast with lettuce and tomato, then added bacon strips. She slathered the remaining toast with mayonnaise and finished the sandwiches.

We all watched her—me, Anarchy, and Max.

Max was the only one who openly drooled.

"Yes," Anarchy replied. "She says the decision to kill Marigold was made that morning, but—"

"But she brought a rope," I finished. Jennifer had killed Marigold. Just like she'd killed John Wilson, Lark, and Mark Roberts.

"She hit Roberts over the head."

"Yes."

"Why did she put him in my car?"

"She claims she didn't know the car belonged to you."

"Hmph." Aggie added potato chips and carrot sticks to the plates and pushed them toward us.

Max whined in frustration.

She tore one of the remaining strips of bacon in half. "Sit."

Max sat.

She tossed the bacon in the air, and Max snapped it mid-air.

Anarchy and I bit into our sandwiches.

"She seemed like such a nice girl." Aggie shook her head sadly.

She'd seemed like the perfect neighbor.

"Mhmm." I chewed. "This is delicious. Napkin?"

"Sorry." Aggie opened a drawer, took out two ironed napkins, and handed them to us. "I have the laundry to do. Would you please leave your plates in the sink?"

Without waiting for a reply, she disappeared up the back stairs.

We spent the next minute concentrating on our sandwiches.

"I understand a little bit," I said.

"Understand what?"

"Why they did it."

"Jennifer and Katherine?"

I nodded. "The system let them down, the men who hurt them walked away. I understand the rage. I'd feel that rage if someone hurt Grace."

"But—"

"I'm not saying it justifies murder. It doesn't. But when someone you love is victimized, it's tempting to react."

He took my hand in his. "I get what you're saying but we can't have vigilante justice. Just look how it can go wrong. Speaking of which, is your mother okay?"

I grinned. "Drunk."

"Drunk?" His brows lifted. "Your mother?"

"Three scotches before breakfast will do that. I drove her home and put her to bed."

"Wow."

"I know." I took another bite of BLT and moaned.

Anarchy shifted on his stool. "I have a question for you."

"Mmmm." My mouth was full.

"When the gala is over, would you—" he glanced down at his plate "—would you go away with me? For the weekend?"

I finished chewing before I gave him my answer.

JULIE MULHERN

Julie Mulhern is the *USA Today* bestselling author of The Country Club Murders. She is a Kansas City native who grew up on a steady diet of Agatha Christie. She spends her spare time whipping up gourmet meals for her family, working out at the gym and finding new ways to keep her house spotlessly clean—and she's got an active imagination. Truth is—she's an expert at calling for take-out, she grumbles about walking the dog and the dust bunnies under the bed have grown into dust lions.

The Country Club Murders
by Julie Mulhern

Novels

THE DEEP END (#1)

GUARANTEED TO BLEED (#2)

CLOUDS IN MY COFFEE (#3)

SEND IN THE CLOWNS (#4)

WATCHING THE DETECTIVES (#5)

COLD AS ICE (#6)

SHADOW DANCING (#7)

BACK STABBERS (#8)

TELEPHONE LINE (#9)

Short Stories

DIAMOND GIRL
A Country Club Murder Short

Henery Press Mystery Books

And finally, before you go...
Here are a few other mysteries
you might enjoy:

MURDER AT THE PALACE

Margaret Dumas

A Movie Palace Mystery (#1)

Welcome to the Palace movie theater! Now Showing: Philandering husbands, ghostly sidekicks, and a murder or two.

When Nora Paige's movie-star husband leaves her for his latest co-star, she flees Hollywood to take refuge in San Francisco at the Palace, a historic movie theater that shows the classic films she loves. There she finds a band of misfit film buffs who care about movies (almost) as much as she does.

She also finds some shady financial dealings and the body of a murdered stranger. Oh, and then there's Trixie, the lively ghost of a 1930's usherette who appears only to Nora and has a lot to catch up on. With the help of her new ghostly friend, can Nora catch the killer before there's another murder at the Palace?

LIVING THE VIDA LOLA

Melissa Bourbon

A Lola Cruz Mystery (#1)

Meet Lola Cruz, a fiery full-fledged PI at Camacho and Associates. Her first big case? A missing mother who may not want to be found. And to make her already busy life even more complicated, Lola's helping plan her cousin's quinceañera and battling her family and their old-fashioned views on women and careers. She's also reunited with the gorgeous Jack Callaghan, her high school crush whom she shamelessly tailed years ago and photographed doing the horizontal salsa with some other lucky girl.

Lola takes it all in stride, but when the subject of her search ends up dead, she has a lot more to worry about. Soon she finds herself wrapped up in the possibly shady practices of a tattoo parlor, local politics, and someone with serious—maybe deadly—road rage. But Lola is well-equipped to handle these challenges. She's a black-belt in kung fu, and her body isn't her only weapon. She's got smarts, sass, and more tenacity than her Mexican mafioso-wannabe grandfather. A few of her famous margaritas don't hurt, either.

I SCREAM, YOU SCREAM

Wendy Lyn Watson

A Mystery A-la-mode (#1)

Tallulah Jones's whole world is melting. Her ice cream parlor, Remember the A-la-mode, is struggling, and she's stooped to catering a party for her sleezeball ex-husband Wayne and his arm candy girlfriend Brittany. Worst of all? Her dreamy high school sweetheart shows up on her front porch, swirling up feelings Tally doesn't have time to deal with.

Things go from ugly to plain old awful when Brittany turns up dead and all eyes turn to Tally as the murderer. With the help of her hell-raising cousin Bree, her precocious niece Alice, and her long-lost-super-confusing love Finn, Tally has to dip into the heart of Dalliance, Texas's most scandalous secrets to catch a murderer before someone puts Tally and her dreams on ice for good.

BOARD STIFF

Kendel Lynn

An Elliott Lisbon Mystery (#1)

As director of the Ballantyne Foundation on Sea Pine Island, SC, Elliott Lisbon scratches her detective itch by performing discreet inquiries for Foundation donors. Usually nothing more serious than retrieving a pilfered Pomeranian. Until Jane Hatting, Ballantyne board chair, is accused of murder. The Ballantyne's reputation tanks, Jane's headed to a jail cell, and Elliott's sexy ex is the new lieutenant in town.

Armed with moxie and her Mini Coop, Elliott uncovers a trail of blackmail schemes, gambling debts, illicit affairs, and investment scams. But the deeper she digs to clear Jane's name, the guiltier Jane looks. The closer she gets to the truth, the more treacherous her investigation becomes. With victims piling up faster than shells at a clambake, Elliott realizes she's next on the killer's list.

CPSIA information can be obtained
at www.ICGtesting.com
Printed in the USA
LVHW081657090719
623573LV00010B/164/P

9 781635 115505